"The only person I trust to protect you is me. Don't ever forget that, Dani."

I held his gaze. "Why is that?" Taking a chance, I placed my hands on Sam's face, wanting to connect with this warrior. I wanted to know what went on inside him, what made him so fierce.

"Why only you?"

Terror filled him. I felt it throb into my hands, and I almost pulled away, the feelings were so intense. Something had happened to him. He'd never forgotten it and never forgiven himself.

"Listen to me, Dani. I'm the only one who can protect you. We're connected like never before."

He couldn't put it into words any better than I could, but I knew what he meant.

"The Resurrectionist is a wildly sexy thriller that breathes new life into the paranormal genre. Literally."
—*New York Times* bestselling author Darynda Jones

91 D1589643

THE
RESURRECTIONIST

SIERRA WOODS

MILLS & BOON

All rights reserved including the right of reproduction in whole or in part in any form. This edition is published by arrangement with Harlequin Books S.A.

This is a work of fiction. Names, characters, places, locations and incidents are purely fictional and bear no relationship to any real life individuals, living or dead, or to any actual places, business establishments, locations, events or incidents. Any resemblance is entirely coincidental.

This book is sold subject to the condition that it shall not, by way of trade or otherwise, be lent, resold, hired out or otherwise circulated without the prior consent of the publisher in any form of binding or cover other than that in which it is published and without a similar condition including this condition being imposed on the subsequent purchaser.

® and ™ are trademarks owned and used by the trademark owner and/or its licensee. Trademarks marked with ® are registered with the United Kingdom Patent Office and/or the Office for Harmonisation in the Internal Market and in other countries.

Published in Great Britain 2014
by Mills & Boon, an imprint of Harlequin (UK) Limited,
Eton House, 18-24 Paradise Road, Richmond, Surrey, TW9 1SR

© 2014 Brenda Schetnan

ISBN: 978-0-263-91399-6

89-0714

Harlequin (UK) Limited's policy is to use papers that are natural, renewable and recyclable products and made from wood grown in sustainable forests. The logging and manufacturing processes conform to the legal environmental regulations of the country of origin.

Printed and bound in Spain
by Blackprint CPI, Barcelona

BRENT LIBRARIES	
91120000190736	
Askews & Holts	11-Jun-2014
AF	£4.99

Sierra Woods grew up in the heart of the Appalachian Mountains where folklore, mysteries and superstition surrounded everyday life. Sierra's interest in the paranormal began in her childhood and hasn't stopped yet. Today she works in health care, where interesting and unusual situations may be taken and used in her fiction writing.

She lives in New Mexico, in the foothills of the Sandia Mountains. If you'd like to drop Sierra a line, she'd love to hear from you at sierrawoodswriter@gmail.com.

This book is dedicated to the victims of crime who can no longer speak for themselves.

The inspiration for this book was yet another news story about a murder for which the motivation was pitiful. I so wanted there to be justice for this victim whose killer was caught in just a few days.

My wish is that all victims find justice for crimes committed against them.

Resurrectionists are a breed all their own. Some are born into it, some are called into it and some are murdered into it. Resurrectionists have been a constant presence on the earth plane since humanity learned right from wrong. During ancient times, superstitions forced resurrectionists to remain hidden, secretive and fiercely protective of their rituals. Over the centuries, superstition battled religious fervor, and resurrectionists remained underground.

Teachings passed from one generation to another, then the information was destroyed for the safety of all. Zombies and witches took much of the blame for the good deeds of resurrectionists, who only sought to right the wrongs humans committed against one another. With no support for their efforts, resurrectionists stayed hidden.

In this century, technology, the Age of Aquarius and an opening in global consciousness have enabled a few gifted resurrectionists to forge new trails, bringing their fight for justice into the light.

Albuquerque, NM
September
Office of Dani Wright, Resurrectionist

Chapter 1

"I'm not going to have to walk around with a bullet wound in my forehead forever, am I?" Betsy Capella looked at me, her eyes not quite focused. After being deceased and in cold storage for nearly a year, it was understandable. The senses take a little while to warm up and remember what they're supposed to do.

"I don't think so. It should fade as you recover more fully. These things take a little time." Not exactly a lie, not exactly the truth, and I hope I interjected enough sympathy into my voice. I don't know the answer to her question, as I've been performing resurrections for only a year or so. Not long enough to come up with a stat sheet. Each resurrection is different, just as each death is different. The state and success of recovery depends on how long the deceased has been gone, and on whether we've stored the body or it was buried in a traditional manner. Embalming is not a good thing if you intend to return to a living state. Yeah. Cremation is a bad idea, too. Way bad.

Betsy sat more upright and smiled, the corners of her mouth a little tight and dry. "I'll bet some makeup will help."

Yeah, and a spackling trowel to slap it on with. "Give it a go. I hear there are sales on this week." Looking down at the contract she signed, I added the date. Having been dead and on ice, she wasn't up on current events. "Do you want to go with us to the 'yard? You don't have to, but if you'd like to, someone can drive you and follow us to the site."

"The yard? What's that?" A frown of confusion made the bullet wound between her eyes pucker. *S-o-o* not attractive.

"Graveyard." Where the life-swap rituals are completed, sending killers where they belong. A one-way ticket to the nebula. Looking away, I tried not to focus on her wound, like a deadly zit on her forehead.

Before answering, Betsy put away the compact someone had given her. Most newly resurrected have a difficult transition at first, which is why I don't keep mirrors around the office. Let 'em get used to the idea of being awake and alive again before they wonder what they look like. Sometimes it ain't pretty.

"No. I just want to go home, see the kids and take a shower." Rubbing her hands on her arms, she shivered. You go a year without a shower and see how you feel. I'd recommend a good exfoliant, like steel wool. Maybe I could come up with a gift bag for the newly resurrected. Steel wool and a mild bleach solution. That would be good PR, wouldn't it? I should write that down.

Betsy looked at her ex-husband across the room and dismissed him as if he meant nothing to her. I suppose that's the best attitude. He's the one who put her in the ground, so she obviously meant nothing to him. In my book, turnaround is simply justice, served neat.

She rose from the chair and wobbled a little, then got her land legs again. I don't know quite what to call it when they've been in containment. Grave legs? Jeez. This job just gets freakier all the time. Every day is Halloween around here. We just need some candy; we've already got the nuts.

Betsy's family was weepy and gathered around her, then pulled away. A few wiped their hands on their pants, grateful for, but at the same time repulsed by, her condition. If her body hadn't been found and put in containment quickly, none of this would have been possible.

Without my death and the death of my child, it wouldn't have been possible either. The cramp in my chest that I refuse to acknowledge surfaced, but I shoved it back as I always had. This was not the time to renew the grief of my past. This was the time to kick the ass of the guy responsible for putting my client in the grave.

Some newly resurrected have a hard time remembering what happened to them, and that's probably for the best.

I, however, will never forget.

Three years ago my husband's lover stuck a butcher knife in my belly and cut my child out of me, leaving me to die in the desert. Fortunately for me, there were forces at work in the universe that took exception to that act of atrocity and rescued me. It's made me what I am now, and I can never go back to my previous life as a nurse, a wife and almost a mother.

That debt of honor can never be repaid.

Returning from the dead definitely has had some unforeseen consequences. Like the other-siders wanting something in return. Like learning how to raise the dead and performing life-swaps. Simple stuff like that.

Many of my resurrections involve women who, like me, married the wrong man and didn't live to tell about it. Other life-swap cases I handle include cops killed in the line of duty, and kids murdered by their mothers' new boyfriend, who just happens to be a pedophile. Fortunately, I was sent back to right the wrongs done to others just like me. It's a living as well as a mission. There are other resurrectionists out there, but we are a small force trying to bring our abilities to the public without getting ourselves killed. Our country has already had one giant witch hunt. We don't need another.

It was my turn to stand, and I got up from behind the desk. I'm tall, but I usually wear cowboy boots with heels. Gives me the height to look down on these assholes so they know a woman is the one putting them in the grave for good. I have long black hair I wear straight, past my shoulders, and skin that appears perfectly tanned year-round. Not my choice, but my mixed ethnicity. It's my eyes, though, which are an odd shade of muddy green with yellow flecks, that give me the advantage over the nut jobs I deal with. Some say it's like looking into hell when I give them the right stare. Frankly, I don't believe in hell anymore, so I don't know what they are talking about.

"How you doin', Rufus? You ready for all this?" He was a weasel of a man, not much to look at. Dark brown eyes too closely set, a short, wiry frame and the disposition of a rabid coyote. Probably has a dick the size of a baby dill, too. I've discovered the meaner a man's disposition, the smaller his dick. Hmm. Wonder why?

"Fuck you," he said and spat at me.

"Sorry. I don't fuck dead guys." As if.

"You're gonna pay for what you do. Someone's going to take you down." He made the sign of the cross as well as he could in shackles. Kinda tough, though.

The guards on each side of him just laughed, and that makes me smile. As close to a warm fuzzy as I'll ever get. I'm not warm, and if I'm fuzzy I need to shave my legs.

"Really? Well, it ain't gonna be you." I let my eyes wander over his hot pink jumpsuit. I took a cue from that sheriff in Arizona who makes the inmates wear pink underwear and live in tents outside no matter how freakin' hot it is. Unfortunately, pink is not a good color for most men, unless they're gay or less than three years old, and Rufus was neither. "Let's go, boys. We don't have all night."

The guards are equipped with a bulletproof, four-wheel-drive van. One drives, one rides with a shotgun trained on the life-swapper, and I mentally prepare for what I'm about to do. My main man, Sam Lopez, is unavailable tonight, and I actually miss his strong,

hunky presence at the 'yard. He has secrets I can't penetrate even if I wanted to, and I suppose he's entitled to
them. I don't own him, and he isn't obligated to have
share-time with me, but his presence at the graveyard
gives me strength I didn't know I needed until he said
he couldn't be here. Each ritual takes a lot of energy,
and I'm usually too wasted to drive safely back from
the 'yard. Maybe it'll get better the more resurrections
I perform, but for the time being, I have guards. Men
like to drive anyway, so I don't mind having them cart
my ass around once in a while.

The next morning, I felt as if someone beat the hell
out of me when I wasn't looking. Obviously, I hadn't
had enough meat yesterday. This girl needs loads of
protein just to function in a normal manner. Well, my
normal anyway. My stomach roars to life the second
my eyes open. Dammit. I am so ruled by my appetite.

The life-swap had taken way longer than it should
have last night, and as a result I was more ragged out
than usual this morning. Having Sam present for the
rituals obviously makes a difference, so I'm going to
have to make sure he's not out dancing naked under the
full moon for the next one. My energy stores last only
so long and must be replenished frequently.

After a shower I put on some jeans and a black
T-shirt. The crystal amulet on a chain never leaves my
neck (a little gift from the other-siders), so I tucked it
inside the shirt. They didn't give me direction on the
crystal, but just said it was a source of power. Maybe it
wards off bacteria, too, 'cause I haven't been sick since

I began wearing it. I tugged on scarred black cowboy boots I wouldn't give up for anything and shoved a pair of sunglasses over my burning eyes. When I'm depleted of nutrients, my eyes turn funny colors. Scared a waitress half to death the first time that happened, hence the shades.

Coffee sustains me in my hour of need, which is every bloody hour of the day, so I swing by the coffee shop for a couple of those gallon-size coffee boxes. I keep one and share the other with the cops in the office.

They love me.

And I love 'em right back. They're the good guys in blue. Entirely too many of them have lain down their lives for others and not been returned to this plane. My never-ending project is getting a few of them back on the force and sending their killers to the nebula instead of a cushy jail cell for twenty-to-life. Two good cops had been killed a few years back by a psych patient, and it's been a high-profile case ever since. The venue for the trial had to be changed several times because there was such a public outcry on both sides. Fortunately, the cops have been on ice in my cryo lab since their deaths in anticipation of future resurrection, but I don't know when, if ever, it's going to get straightened out. Figuring out the legalities of this case still gives me a headache.

Can the mentally ill who murder be considered for life-swaps? Do they have real quality of life as they exist now? If not, then I'd like to play swap-a-cop for this particular bad boy. But how is one to know?

That's the part that has always given me pause and a lump in my gut that won't go away with an antacid.

Truly mentally ill people may or may not be held responsible for their actions, no matter how heinous. If that's the case, then I could not in good conscience perform a life-swap with this afflicted man and the two cops, no matter how much people begged. My personal moral code wouldn't allow me to proceed. As far as I know, there are no *Resurrectionists Guidelines* to refer to in this kind of case.

Psychiatrists will fight to the death to defend either side of the fence, which leaves me sitting in the middle of it with splinters up my ass. So that's where we sit until someone more important than me makes a decision. I've been trying to get the court to pass some new legislation that will speed up the decision, but so far I'm having no luck getting them even to look at it.

These are the issues we resurrectionists ponder every day. They may never be solved in my lifetime, however long that is, but I've got to try. Something won't allow me to walk away from a situation I might be able to help with. Maybe it's the way I'm made or part of being a resurrectionist. Others in my situation have few answers, either. Those of us who have heard the battle cry for resurrections always feel alone, even though there is a small group of support available.

"Hey, Dani." A deep voice that gives me shivers at night got my immediate attention. Though I could have just sighed and listened to him talk, I have a reputation to uphold. Tough chicks aren't just born. They're cultivated.

It's a lot of work.

"Hey, Sam, what's up?" I usually leave the door

propped open with a large piece of petrified wood, about the size of a bowling ball, I had found in my yard. Here in the desert, the stuff's everywhere, and someday when he's being a butt head (and you know he will be no matter how hot he is now), I'll probably have to clobber him with it.

"Just reviewed your notes on the cop-killer case." He held several files in one hand that contained my attempts to outline the legislation. In his other hand was a cup of coffee I'd brought. See? Bringing coffee is a good thing, no matter what it costs my budget. Makes for good relationships with smart men who carry big guns. Here was one with a 9 mil on his hip, and he ain't afraid to use it. That's yummy, in my book.

"Take a seat and tell me what you think." Although I have my suspicions, I want to hear it from him. My powers don't extend to mind reading, but I know Sam pretty well, and he's giving off a negative vibe. Could be his years as an army Ranger, though. He's one tough dude. That makes him a good resource for me, but he's hell on relationships.

With a sigh he sat and parked the files on my desk. "I'm not a lawyer, but I don't think they're going to make a decision. At least not yet. The public isn't ready for it."

"Yeah." Running my hands through my hair is a habit, and one I engage in now. One I'll probably regret down the line when I experience androgenic alopecia and there's more hair in my brush than on my head. "I wish there was a way around this. It could be the start of something big here. I hate waiting for New York and

California to set the bar, and then we catch up later." I wanted this, bad. Not just for me and setting a precedent in New Mexico, but setting one for all resurrectionists. We need to know. The families of those we resurrect need it, too. I tried not to think of how badly the families of the cops needed it.

Sam's dark, dark gaze roamed over my chest and lingered for a second before his attention returned to my face. Not that I dislike that sort of attention, especially from him, but we have bigger things to focus on than the bumps under my shirt.

He pushed the files back to my side of the ugly desk that was a recycle from the precinct. "Sorry, babe."

You know, I'm a fully liberated woman, but for some reason, I don't mind him calling me babe. Mostly because he does it with affection, and knows that if he ever gets in my pants we'll set the desert on fire. If anyone else tries it, I'll rip their tongue out. Sometimes the sparks between Sam and me are visible at night. In a graveyard. Woo-hoo. How romantic is that?

"Thanks for taking a look at it." Trying not to be disgusted and impatient, I shoved the file into a drawer.

"Did you get any sleep last night?" He's got dark, dark eyes that don't miss much. Of course the bags under my eyes are probably as big as *sopaipillas* and just as puffy.

"Some. I never get enough." Never, never enough rest. Someone needs to invent a pill to replenish lost sleep. I'll buy stock in the company.

"Did you eat this morning?" He was starting to get bossy, which I didn't like. I'd gotten out of a controlling relationship with my ex-husband. I didn't need a lecture from Sam. Having been born the oldest in a house full of women, he was born bossy. They let him get away with entirely too much and ruined him for any other women, hence his track record of disastrous relationships.

I shrugged, noncommittal. Something I learned from him. "Yep. The usual."

Sam grinned. The man has a smile that could set me on fire. I must resist. "You're the only woman I know who has steak for breakfast."

"Is that a bad thing?" Hardly. I know better, but can't resist teasing him sometimes, and my irritation disappeared. There's so little joy in my life, I have to take it where I can get it.

He rubbed the back of his neck as if it ached. Having known him for a year or so, I picked up on little nonverbal signals, and this was one of them. Something was up that he didn't like and didn't want to talk about. Wonder what it was? He'd eventually talk, but until then, he'd stay clammed up. I should start calling him Sam-The-Clam.

After getting up from the chair, he strolled around to my side of the desk and leaned a hip on the edge. Hmm. Our flirtations over the past year have always been restricted to arm's length. This was new. Wonder if it had anything to do with that neck issue of his and the one growing between my shoulder blades? There was either something coming, or my gallbladder was having an attack.

"You need more sleep." He ran a finger down the

side of my face. "The rings under your eyes aren't going away."

"I don't wear much makeup, so they're easier to see." Maybe that makeup sale was still on. I could pick up a spackling tool on the way back.

"You're beautiful with or without makeup, but you're also damned tired. I can see it every time you walk in here that you're burning out. Can you take a week off and get out of town? Relax on a beach with a fruity drink and a book somewhere?"

"Could you?" As if. We're both chained to our work.

"Is that a proposition?" There was that damned grin again and a new tingle in my stomach to go with it. Interesting, but it ain't gonna happen.

"Hardly." I shoved him off my desk. When he's too close to me I get distracted, and sometimes I think that's what he's after. "Go arrest someone, will you?"

He took a step away and rubbed the back of his neck. "No rituals tonight?"

"None so far."

"Make sure you call me if anything comes up." That dark, guarded look was back in his eyes. There was something behind it. Something he hid that crept out at times despite his efforts to bury it.

"You're taking the bossy thing to a new level today." I glared. I didn't need a babysitter.

"It's my job, babe." Serious now, he held my gaze as if he wanted to say something else, but held back. Yeah, he was a man of secrets, and I wasn't likely to penetrate that barrier he erected every time I asked him a personal question. Sometimes I just can't help myself and must ask. Just makes my day to irritate other people.

"So what's going on with you today? I'm getting a weird vibe from you." I raised my brows and waited for the answer I knew wasn't coming.

"Nothing." Slam. That door in his eyes closed, but I knew something was bothering him.

"You're lying, I can see it. If something's up, I need to know. If you don't share, dude, then neither do I." That broke all the rules of my agreement with the P.D., but right now I didn't care. Something was up.

Narrowing his eyes, he tried to stare me down, but failed. I know his tricks, and he sighed. "There's something I can't get a hold on. Something in the air."

"In the air? Could you be vaguer?" My turn to frown.

He stood and spun away. "Never mind. If anything concrete shows up, I'll let you know."

"If you've got a feeling about something, I want to know, even if you think it's nothing."

"Like I said, when it's concrete, I'll let you know." His hand drifted to his neck again, but I kept silent. Miracles do happen. Sam gave me a crumb.

He's my assigned protector from the P.D. I've been through private training like you wouldn't believe. I know a thing or two about guns and how to protect myself, but when I perform the rituals my focus is internal. That's when I'm vulnerable and need someone to watch over me. A big, bad, hunky cop like Sam will do. Sometimes I resent that I need one, but it's become obvious I do. The security guards offer some protection, but there's something about Sam in particular that needs to be there. I don't know what yet, and it's pissing me off.

"Like I said, it's my job." He gave that tight little smile he has when he has to do something he doesn't want to. Talk about control issues.

"Yes, I know. You're the liaison, blah, blah, blah." I get so tired of the blah, blah, blah sometimes. "But you're off your game, and that affects me whether you know it or not." Well, I guess he knows now.

"Yes, I am. One of these nights we're going to have more trouble than we bargained for." Concern emanated from his eyes and a little something twisted between my shoulder blades. That's my signal something is wrong.

I hope it isn't an omen. Not that I believe in them, not seriously, but I sort of wish for a bit more protection at times. Something small and inconspicuous, like the Spear of Isis. That's all.

With a nod he left, and I tried to return to the work in front of me, but it didn't keep my attention.

I'd had a sense of foreboding for a week now and didn't know why. Maybe that's what I was getting from Sam. He has senses finely tuned from his military service that I'll never get close to, but he's so damned closed-mouthed sometimes, I just want to strangle him.

I must resist.

Chapter 2

The sound of a skateboard on the sidewalk always gets on my nerves. I never know whether I'm going to get run down by a herd of teenagers, or if there is a message from my mentor, Burton. This time it was Burton and the muscles in my back tensed. I'm going to need a painkiller by the end of the day if this keeps up.

"Where you been, *chica?*" He knows that any reference to my ethnic backgrounds will get my immediate attention. When I went to nursing school, I applied for scholarships based on my three ethnic groups, but was denied two of them. Bastards.

"Oh, get off it, Burton. What do you want?" Sometimes I have no patience for the man. Sometimes I want to cuff him just because he's such a piece of work. Any spiritual entity that's four thousand years old shouldn't be such a smart-ass. There's just something wrong with that.

"Just wanted to make sure you're okay."

"Okay? I'm fine." I narrowed my eyes, immediately suspicious. Him, I never quite trust. "You've never asked me how I am before. What's up?" That niggle between my shoulders was aching again.

"The other-siders have a sense something's changing in the universe. They want to make sure you and other resurrectionists are unharmed."

"Unharmed?" Maybe that was why Sam and I had had uncomfortable feelings we couldn't name. "Who would want to harm us?" Aside from the obvious.

"The Dark."

"What the hell is that?" As if I needed something to screw up my life more. The judicial system was enough.

"The entity who has disrupted the balance, and grows larger and more dangerous every time evil wins out over good. It is a congealed group of dark souls that has banded together from the deepest part of the nebula. They had been banished for their misdeeds while earthbound and have gathered to form a darker, stronger being. It's made a declaration to stop the resurrectionists, but most especially you."

"Me? Why me? What about the others out there?" He said it as if this thing had challenged me to a game of checkers. Was he serious?

"Of that we are uncertain. They ask that you take no unnecessary risks until the threat has passed."

Jeez. Could they be more nebulous? Unnecessary risks? What the hell was that? Every day I take on a case, and the risk I take with my body and my life to send killers to the nebula is a huge risk. What about that seems unnecessary? I thought they were out there to help me. And I know that most threats generally don't just pass by without slapping you upside the head.

"Uh, how will I know when that happens?"

"That is unknown. At this time we are offering the warning to all."

"Well, that's some comfort, I suppose."

"Do not underestimate the power of this entity. It has been dormant for millennia and now seeks its vengeance." For a moment I saw every one of his four thousand years revealed in his eyes, and a chill rose over me as the full effect of his warning got to me. Then the moment was gone, and the teenager with a goofy grin returned. "Man, this is just too much fun." Hopping on his board, he was off in a flash and a whoop of delight. Too bad more people aren't pleased so easily. I'm certainly not, though a big gun and a frozen margarita come close.

"I don't understand what you see in that kid. He's nothing but trouble." Sam was right behind me, and I nearly jumped, but I controlled the urge to clobber him. My instincts are finely tuned, and I could have given him a bloody lip just then, or driven his testicles up into his eye sockets, but I restrained myself. Turning, I gave him a glare instead, but the sunglasses made it less effective. Sometimes I'm just too nice.

"What are you doing? You shouldn't sneak up on people like that." Especially now with universal warnings of doom and gloom on the horizon.

"I know, but with you?" The shrug said it all and his army Ranger training proved it. He liked to live dangerously around me. "That kid's trouble."

If he only knew. "He's harmless. He's probably just like you were at that age." Yeah, right.

Sam glared down at me, and I was surprised his shades didn't melt. "Don't ever compare me to that kid. Ever."

O-o-o-*kay*. An unintended arrow hit a tender spot I hadn't known existed. "Why not?" I just had to know.

"Don't go there, Dani. It's none of your business."

"You're the one who made it my business by giving me a bone with nothing on it."

"Forget it. I heard him mention not taking any risks right now. Is he threatening you?" Sam stepped forward, violating my personal space and trying to pressure me into telling him something I don't want to. Won't work on me. I'm immune to that sort of pressure.

I almost laughed. Burton? Threatening me? *Pfft.* But this new thing? Had me thinking. "It's fine. See you later." Some secrets are mine to keep, and I don't have to explain them to anyone. Not even the man who watches my back.

"Dammit, Dani, if something's going on I need to know about it. If I'm to protect you, I need to know what's going on." He followed me at the pace I set.

"You need to trust me, that's what you need to do." I won't be controlled. After one disastrous relationship like that, I was never doing another, not even with Sam.

He said nothing because he knew I was right and wouldn't admit it. He didn't trust anyone. Me more than most, but not enough to sit down and have share-time over coffee. That pissed me off, so this conversation was over. We were at a stalemate on the issue, but at the moment it didn't matter. I knew he had his reasons that were related to his military service and probably his life growing up in the *barrio.* These were areas of his life he spoke little of, and I respected that, but I didn't like it. "Catch you later."

As I walked away I felt Sam's eyes watching my ass, *not* my back, so I put a deliberate saunter in my stride and took a quick look over my shoulder. There he was, feet spread apart, arms crossed over the chest I'd like to spend some time crawling across. Seriously, there ought to be a cartography class for women who want to map out a man's geography to remember fondly later. Then, I caught his gaze over the rim of my sunglasses, and there was nothing except complete male apprecia-tion in those eyes. The look said he'd have me on my back with my feet in the air if he thought he could do it without getting his jewels crushed. That made me laugh, and I turned around again, leaving him with his tongue hanging out.

It's good to know that there are some consistencies in life I can depend on and for some men to behave like men. That thought made me smile a little bigger, and the tension of the day eased a bit. Sam was nothing if not dependable.

There's only one thing I hate worse than weepy women, and that's weepy men. Today, I had 'em both. They're manipulative, whether they mean to be or not.

People come to me all the time to resurrect their loved ones, but if it isn't for the right reasons, I won't help them no matter how much they cry. I *hate* being manipulated.

A young couple, Juanita and Julio Ramirez, sat across the desk from me in my office. The pain in her eyes reached out to me. "Please, please, Miss Wright. You have to help us."

"But this isn't what I do. You need a psychic, not me. I come in at the end when everything is settled. I don't find lost people." I charge in on my white steed and send the bad guy away, but not till all the shootin's done.

"No one else can do it. He's our only child, and he's gone!"

That did it. I was on the job, whether it was normally my job or not. I couldn't not help, even if all I did was offer comfort.

I have an unfortunate kinship to these people, but they'll never know it. My personal loss must stay buried in order for me to work successfully with others like me.

Before I could move away, Juanita took my hand in hers. Unable to remove my hand from her grip without looking totally stupid, I had to sit there while she cried onto my skin. My nerves are raw and the sensations I pick up are extreme. That's why I don't touch people very often. I pick up their vibes, their emotions, and their life force if I'm not careful. The skin reveals a lot in the sweat, the texture, the nerve endings that send out little pulses, and we just don't realize it. If people knew others picked up all of that information, we'd never touch each other. Don't get me started on the bacterial transmission.

With Juanita hanging over my arm and sobbing on the desk, I had no choice except to ingest the energy she put off, and I tried to resist it as much as possible. It was like being simmered in *menudo.* A greasy soup of animal parts you don't want to have identified.

"Juanita." I tried to focus and push away the overload oozing out of her. She was a terrified mother, and I felt every emotion, every pulse of her terror knifing through my head. I had to get the woman off me or we were both going to be on the floor sobbing and nothing would get done to save her son. "Sit up and tell me what's going on."

After one last wail, she sat and released my arm. Oh! What a relief. I could breathe again. I couldn't think without having her emotions bleed into my brain. It was sad enough in there. It didn't need any help.

Juanita was one of those unfortunate women who were too caught up in appearances. At around age twenty-four or so, she was truly beautiful, her skin flawless, her hair shoulder length and a thick, dark brown. It was the makeup that killed the effect. She'd shaved off her brows completely and drawn them in with a pencil in an unnaturally high arch on her forehead.

Maybe she thought it looked good. Maybe Julio liked her that way, but the effect made her look overly alert, as if she were questioning everything you say.

"Well." She looked to her husband, who had yet to say a word. "Our son, Roberto, has been missing for two days. Two days! The police are too slow. He's out there by himself." The implication being that if he weren't found immediately, he was going to die. The bigger implication was that he was already dead. I recalled hearing something about this case and feeling the urgent energy of the cops, but I tried not to watch or listen to the news too much. It overwhelms and depresses me.

With trembling hands, she slid a picture of an engaging-looking, happy little boy, about the age of six or so, with one front tooth missing. I didn't touch the photo because I was certain I would end up on my knees in pain. I don't like to do that in front of clients. Kinda puts people off when the expert loses her mind.

"When did you last see him? Is it possible he's simply run away?" The truth is, if the cops don't find a kidnapped child right away, the kid is probably already dead or out of state and unlikely to be recovered.

"He didn't run away. He didn't *come home* from school. My cousin, Filberto, was to get him because I had a dentist appointment, but Roberto never came out of the school." She covered her face with her hands. "He's gone!"

Never came home, my ass. If I had hackles they'd be standing straight up. You didn't need to be a resurrectionist to smell something foul in the story. "Was Filberto questioned by the police?" Something in me sizzled when I said his name, and I jumped as if I'd been stuck with a cattle prod. Bad sign for Filberto's team.

"Oh, sure, I know what you think, but he'd never hurt my baby. Never." Wiping her eyes with a tissue, she was careful not to disturb the black mascara topping off her wide-eye look.

The skin on my back began to itch and crawl, as if maggots had already begun to eat my flesh. Not a good sign, either. Everyone has a sixth sense; some are just more highly developed than others.

Mine was on fire.

"I need to meet with your family. Can you set that up for tonight?" I looked at my watch. It was almost 6 p.m. "In a few hours, please. We have to move fast." I was fairly certain it wasn't going to be fast enough.

"We'll do anything to get our baby back."

Leaning forward over the desk, I focused on Juanita, cupped my hands around her face, and held her gaze for a few seconds. At first she was startled, but then she held my gaze. That's not easy. I'm a little scary sometimes. She was true, and I released her. "Are you certain you'll do anything to find him?"

"Yes." She hadn't blinked and neither had I. You'd be surprised what shit could happen in the blink of an eye.

"I'll see you around eight." I slid a piece of paper across the desk. "Write down your address."

I walked them to the door with a mental sigh. It was going to be a long night. Calling Sam occurred to me, but after our conversation this morning I was feeling ornery. Besides, I wasn't doing a resurrection. Just information gathering, so technically I didn't have to call him.

I just love technicalities when they work in my favor.

I arrived at the Ramirez house a few minutes early. I like to watch a house for a little while before walking in. Opening the door for a person I didn't know got me killed once. It ain't happening again.

Instincts on full alert, I approached the door. Letting my senses reach out, I felt for imminent danger, but found nothing, so I rang the doorbell. Burton and the other-siders had to be mistaken. There was no big, bad darkness out to get me, just a missing boy who needed to be found. Looking overhead, I saw no threat. I was just a simple resurrectionist doing a job. I wasn't any threat to a universal force.

But I kept my right hand free to grab my gun, anyway. I carry a 9mm semiauto. I also tuck a derringer in the top of my boot, but that requires a little extra maneuvering to get to. Most people aren't used to women carrying weapons openly, so I wear a light blazer over my shirt and shoulder holster. Basic black, goes with everything. And hides the dagger strapped to my left wrist too.

"Miss Wright, please come in." Julio opened the door and ushered me in. Here, everyone says Miss, not Ms., but it means the same thing. "We're here, like you said. Tell us what we need to do."

Oh, he might not like what I was suspecting he had to do. "Thank you. How about I just talk to everyone, and we go from there?"

"I don't know if it will help." He swayed slightly as he held on to the door, and I detected the faint odor of tequila leaking from his pores. After what he'd been through, I couldn't begrudge him a shot or two of fortitude.

"Someone knows something." He shrugged, but led

me to the kitchen table, which was the hub of the family activity. This was a typical Catholic-Hispanic household with crosses of various sizes around the house and a small shrine in the living room. My grandmother's house is nearly identical, except she has a shrine to Buddha. No matter, same deal.

"We're here because I believe someone here may have information about Roberto they haven't told the police. On his own he's not going to survive for long."

"You think he's still alive? After all this time can he be alive?"

This question was posed by one of the family matriarchs. Although only two days had passed since his disappearance, I was certain it felt like an eternity. Anger and grief warred for control in her eyes. She was afraid to hope, afraid to believe he would be found, and terrified something she didn't want to think about had already happened. I wanted to help this family, but I knew I was going to bring more bad news. That part wasn't my problem to deal with. Recovering a child was. I hoped.

"That's what I'm here to find out."

"Are you a *curandera?*" she asked, watchful and suspicious.

That's the Hispanic version of a witch-woman or a healer, depending on the interpretation. Not my gig, but most people, especially the highly superstitious, are more comfortable with that term. "No. I'm a nurse, not a healer in the way you mean." Once a nurse, always a nurse. We're kind of like the marines that way, but without the firepower and snappy haircuts. "Tonight I'm

here to see if I can help find Roberto." I looked away
from her and the grief pouring out of her. That kind of
energy messes with my mojo. "I need everyone to go
outside and form a circle in the yard."

This family understood the need for ceremony and
rituals, so there were no complaints. I entered the circle
the family created. Turning, I moved toward Roberto's
parents and held my hands, palms out, toward them.

I don't have the power to see energy or auras that
other resurrectionists do. I feel them, sense them, and
almost taste them if they are strong enough. Not very
palatable, but it's not as if I have a choice. I'll brush
my teeth later.

The little charge of energy that flowed from Juanita
and Julio was clean. I don't know how else to explain
it, but it wasn't tainted with evil or deception. I guess
I have an evil-ometer in my hands. I have to be careful of whom and what I touch because my senses pick
up things when I don't want them to. One of the undis-
closed perks of coming back from the dead.

I focused on the present and the possibility of finding this child. Alive or dead, I wasn't sure, but at least
we could find out what had happened to him.

I moved around the circle with my radar on full alert.
It was as if I had a bubble of energy around me with
tendrils that reached out for information and drew it
back to me. Kind of like an electrical octopus feeding
information instead of fish. I felt the vibrations flowing around and over the bubble and absorbed some of
the energy. Not unlike static feels when you rub a bal-

loon against your hair. Assuming you have hair. You know what I mean.

One of the women shivered as I approached her and made the sign of the cross, then rubbed her arms. Whatever makes you feel better, I guess. She wasn't my target, and I moved on. Women were rarely the perpetrators of crimes against children. Sure, you got the ones who murdered their entire families, but those people were mentally ill. They had to be or I couldn't sleep at night. I was in search of a male. And I had found one. Possibly abused himself, but had never dealt with it.

My hands nearly glowed with golden light, and I began to sweat. Damn. I hate being right sometimes. "Filberto?" I asked. Fear and shame oozed out of this thin young man. In his early twenties, he still carried that uncoordinated stance of a teenager who hadn't quite found his place in the world. Filberto was going to find his place in the world, and it wasn't going to be to his liking.

The hairs on my arms stood up, and my evil-ometer went nuts. This was the guy. I knew it. Looking into his eyes, I knew that he knew that I knew it, too. He stepped back, scared shitless of me. My eyes must have been going wild again. I'd have to work on that.

"Get away from me." He backed up. I stepped forward.

"What did you do?" I didn't want to touch him and see every blasted detail of it in my mind. I wanted him to confess to these people. Making him tell of his crimes was so much more powerful on the universal scale. It wouldn't balance the scale, but at least it would help add a stone or two to the side of justice. There needs to be equal parts of good to counter the evil in the world.

Gasps and screams filled the air and broke the circle apart. Juanita wailed the way only a wounded mother could, and the sound set my nerves on edge. I had made that sound once. But now I couldn't let it or my memory interfere with what was going on in front of me. Filberto continued to back up until he stepped against a large cottonwood tree. "Get away from me. Witch!" he cried and held out his hands. *Pfft*. As if that was gonna stop me.

I stepped into his personal space, and we both began to glow. From my feet all the way to the top of my head, I was encased in a golden light. It was both healing and protective. Filberto, however, glowed sort of a dark green. Bad news for him. So maybe I'm seeing auras after all.

He broke into a run. Shit. That meant I had to chase him. I hate running in boots. Fortunately, all of the yards in Albuquerque have some sort of fencing. To keep things in or out, I was never sure. So I had to chase him only a few feet and caught him as he was trying to climb over the fence using the trumpet vine like a ladder.

I grabbed him by the back of his jeans and yanked. He came flying, and we landed in a heap. Screams and hysterical Spanish, most of which I didn't want to have interpreted, landed on us as the family descended. Filberto was ripped out of my hands, and I was left in a heap all by myself. That's sort of hard to do, so I got up and went after them.

I had to stop them before they killed him. We needed information, not another murder. That wouldn't be justice for Roberto, and it wouldn't balance the scale, giving evil more weight. The Dark's been growing enough from what the other-siders have said. "No! Wait." I squeezed through the mob and landed on my knees. Crawling forward, I maneuvered myself closer and stood again. How could I stop this before they killed the only person who knew what had happened to Roberto? I could shoot my gun into the air, but in this part of town it probably wouldn't get any attention.

Fortunately, my years of martial arts had given me some muscle, and I used it now. Elbowing my way through, I nearly fell on top of Julio, who was pummeling his fists into Filberto's face. The men of the family, some of whom were certainly armed, stood in a protective half circle around the two and let Julio wail on Filberto.

"Stop it!" It was like talking to a couple of pit bulls who had their teeth into each other. I tackled Julio. What else could I do? We fell to the ground, and Julio pulled back with an elbow that landed in my chest. That was gonna hurt later. "If you kill him, we'll never know where Roberto is." I didn't say I thought Roberto was already dead and we needed to recover the body, if possible, for a resurrection and life-swap.

Julio stood abruptly, then I realized he had help. Sam had yanked him to his feet and shoved him into the arms of his cousins. "Hold him." He pointed to two of the larger men. Without question, they complied and held on to Julio. Now, why don't men react like that to *my* direction? That's just disgusting. Machismo at its finest.

I grabbed hold of Filberto's shirt, yanking him to a sitting position. He was bloody, and his eyes were swelling shut. Most of his wounds appeared superficial, like a fat lip that bled as if he'd bitten through it, but who knew about what was going on in his brain. He could have damage I couldn't sense.

"Don't touch me," he cried and put his hands up like a girl.

"Oh, please, give it up. You're caught, so just can the innocent routine." I hated touching him, even by the shirt, but had to.

"What are you doing here?" I asked Sam, who glowed with his own sort of angry-red aura.

"I followed you." Sam moved closer to me. "You were supposed to call me if something came up."

"Had a late case come in."

"What did you do to my son?" Julio cried and strained against the arms of his cousins. Though he wasn't the biggest man in the yard, he was fueled by the need for vengeance and to tear something apart. That's different from the need for justice, which is where I came in.

"Where's my son?" Juanita collapsed on the ground at his feet, sobbing. The night was alive with cries.

"Yeah, Filberto. What did you do to Roberto?"

Chapter 3

Filberto swayed back and forth. Sam and I had to hold him upright. He might be more hurt than I first thought. Although I had not been gifted with X-ray vision, I was a nurse, so I could keep his ass alive long enough to get some information out of him. He wasn't really hurt. Not hurt like Roberto. I shook him. "Where's Roberto?"

"Gone."

In that word, I knew everything. Just once I'd like to be disappointed and have a happy ending, but that's apparently not my karma this time around. "Dammit." Focusing, I heaved out a sigh, then took a deep breath and steeled myself against the pain that was going to saturate me the second I touched his skin. I placed the heel of my hand on Filberto's forehead and let my fingers fall over the top of his head. This was the only way I knew to access another person's memories. It hurt me to do this. Physically, emotionally and spiritually I would suffer for days, trying to get the stench of someone else's mind out of mine, but I had to do it. For this family to recover their loved one, I had to do it.

After a glance at Sam to link myself in the present, I closed my eyes and let it wash over me.

Flashes of light hit me first. Then I sort of saw a slow-motion movie playing, and I was the only one watching it. Filberto had picked up Roberto at the school. They got into a car and drove away. Filberto sweating and cursing himself all the way as memories of his own molestations filled him. So many years, so many hidden secrets and lies had finally bubbled up out of him. He couldn't help it, or that's what he told himself, as he choked the life out of Roberto's little body and tucked it away at the edge of a rock outcropping. Then he raced away and returned to Albuquerque before he was missed.

Pulling myself out of the memory, I gritted my teeth against the impulse to pick up where Julio had left off. My stomach cramped, and I wanted to vomit.

"I know where he is." I removed my hand from Filberto's forehead, then wiped my palm on my jeans. They were going in the washer as soon as I got home.

"He's alive?" Julio asked, the fragile hope in his voice staggering.

"I'm sorry, Julio." I hated this part, but it had to be done swiftly if there was to be a chance of recovery. "No. His body is out in the lava fields between Laguna and Grants." There was little hope of us finding his remains, but we could try. Many people had been lost out there and never recovered despite massive search operations. How was little ol' me going to find him? *Help?*

"Where's my baby?" Juanita screeched and raced at Filberto with a knife in her hand. Before I could think of moving, she reached out and struck Filberto across the face, blood spattering from the wound. "Where's my son?"

Sam and two others tackled Juanita and divested her of the weapon. I grabbed a fistful of Filberto's hair and held his face up as anger, hot and bright, coursed through me. "You look at these people, at that boy's mother, and tell us what you did."

"I killed him." He squinted through eyes already narrowed to slits by the beating he'd taken. I wanted to reach into his head and pull his brain out through his nostrils. "I didn't mean to, but I had to."

"What do you mean, you *had* to kill him?" I asked, really not wanting to know the answer to that, but pretty certain I was going to be sick once I heard it. A quick image of The Dark flashed in my mind. Could this be the influence Burton had talked of? Could The Dark have made Filberto act when he wouldn't have otherwise?

"He would have told. He would have told!" Filberto breathed through his mouth, as his nose was most certainly broken, if the swelling was any indication.

"Did you hurt him?" I knew he had, but I wanted him to tell the family.

Sobs made Filberto's head wobble, and he cried, feeling sorry for himself. Not what I wanted to see, but confession was supposedly good for the soul. I'd just rather hear the story than have all the blubbering along with it. "I couldn't stop. I couldn't stop myself."

"Did you touch Roberto in a way you weren't supposed to?"

"Y-e-s."

Anguish as you've never heard ripped the night to shreds. Sam and I looked at each other as we were shoved out of the way. There was no reasoning with an angry mob, and certainly no reasoning with a family who was rightfully justified in tearing apart one of their own.

"We have to stop this." I held on to Sam's shirt. He tried to put me behind him, to protect me. He's such a guy. But I hardly needed protecting. After dying once, I learned what to really fear, and these people weren't it.

We shoved into the group. We needed to get to the middle of this, where the action was, and prevent them from killing him.

Dropping onto my knees, I was able to crawl through and around the others. Not as dignified as I would have liked, but I got through and pulled my weapon. "Stop it." Sam joined me, on his feet, and drew his gun, too.

"We need him alive," Sam said.

"He doesn't deserve to live! He killed my baby." Juanita dissolved into a puddle on the ground. The women surrounded her and held on to her. The atmosphere in the yard was changing, becoming darker and malignant. A dark cloud or mist appeared overhead, but failed to manifest into anything I recognized.

Julio's fists were a mess of blood and raw flesh. He breathed heavily as the murderous light finally left his eyes.

"Julio, see to your wife," Sam said and motioned him back with the gun.

"I will see this done now. I don't care if I have to die for it. He'll pay for what he's done to my son!"

"We need him alive if there's any chance to bring Roberto back." I didn't tell them I wasn't sure I had the skills to do it, whether it could even be done, depending on the amount of decomposition that had begun, let alone animal involvement. Ew. "If you kill him now, there's no chance, and you'll die, too." I reached out to Julio and touched his shoulder. I tried to resist the vibrations coming off him. I was contaminated already by Filberto, so what was a little more? "Do you want that? Your family needs you now."

He collapsed beside his wife, and they wept together and clung to each other. I was unable to offer any solace.

Reaching out to Sam with my hand, I nearly fell face-first into him. He would have liked that too much, so I settled for dropping to my knees from fatigue.

After things settled down and a small plan for recovery took shape, Sam led me to his truck parked down the street. I got in and let him drive to the nearest diner we could find. "That was damned stupid." Anger crackled off him, nearly lighting the night around him.

Yeah, yeah, yeah, I know, but I didn't need to be reminded. I survived, and no one died in the process. Bonus. "I got the information I needed." Filberto had taken a beating, but he deserved it. Almost instant karma.

"At what cost?" he asked. "I've never seen you so

wasted, Dani, not even after a tough life-swap." Sam
was never outright angry; he's too controlled for that.
What he does is simmer. It's not brooding, because
that's too much like a pout for a man. But he simmers,
and stews, and makes me wonder what's going on in
that mind of his. I might have to do a mind-meld someday, but not now.

Right now, I didn't care. I needed flesh and lots of
it. For whatever reason, it's what I need to keep going.
I don't need just blood, though I do like my steaks rare.
It's not just protein, either. I tried plenty of whey protein shakes and granola bars at the beginning, and they
didn't do squat. I now despise granola. But something in
a good, bloody steak does it for me. Who am I to question it? Maybe it's in the chewing and grinding of the
food in my mouth that makes it work, or part of the di-
gestive process. Do you know what's going on in your
stomach when you're not looking? I don't know and
don't care, as long as it fills up whatever is depleted.

We inhaled the meal and headed out the door. This
was a fuel stop for me. I was so depleted of energy, I'd
have chewed my own leg off soon. We had to get to the
lava fields near Grants. About an hour away, depending
on who was driving. I could make it in forty-five. We
had to try to recover the body tonight. Preventing further decay was essential to a successful resurrection,
but as always to fully restore the body would require
some sort of blood sacrifice, and there was no way to
know how much blood the ritual would require.

I didn't know if I had enough. I was exhausted
enough already. However, Sam had volunteered for

this duty. I didn't want it to be his sacrifice either. Perhaps our combined forces would be enough to get the job done. There was something special about Sam that helped make the resurrections successful.

The unmistakable sound of a skateboard approaching made me step back into the doorway, into Sam, and his hands were on my hips to steady me. What I wouldn't give to be able to really reach out to him, but I couldn't. Touch, skin to skin, made me feel things I wasn't prepared for, so I hung on to the wooden doorway and gasped for air.

"Hey, you okay, *chica?*" Burton asked and flipped his board to a stop beside us. My little mentor. At first I was always surprised to see him, but then I figured he knew things I didn't and let it slide.

"Yeah. I'm good."

"Don't you listen to anything I tell you?"

"Huh?"

"I just told you not to take any extra chances. Maybe your brain is going bad or something."

"Hardly. But I couldn't not take this case, you know that." Or at least he should. "Go away. I'm fine."

"Cool. But heed the warning." He tossed the skateboard onto the sidewalk and leaped onto it, disappearing into the shadows as only he could.

"That kid drives me crazy. How did he know you were here? We didn't even know we were coming here." Sam stepped up beside me to watch Burton zip away.

"I don't know. I think he has some sort of radar." Yeah, four-thousand-year-old radar.

"Has he been following you?"

"What, like you did?" Bingo.

Sam didn't answer, but just stared down at me with a perturbed glint in his eyes. As a rule, I do *not* enjoy being looked down upon, but with Sam, I make the exception. When he looks down at me, I almost feel petite and feminine. I need to avoid that feeling. I'm not petite or particularly feminine. I'm strong and in charge of myself. Softer feelings aren't in my job description and could get me killed again if I allow them.

"I tell you that kid is trouble."

"How can a kid with his pants halfway down his ass be trouble?" I mean, really. Who takes a person like that seriously?

"You do have a point," Sam said and watched as Burton skateboarded back to us.

"Later, dudes," he yelled.

"See ya, Burton. Pull your damned pants up!" I called over the rush of the night. He raised his arm and flipped me off. Typical teenager. "He's harmless."

Sam shook his head, not convinced with my judgment of character. If he only knew how far I'd come, he wouldn't question me now. "If you say so, but that's the future of this country riding away on a piece of wood."

If he only knew. Burton was a piece of the past trying to hold on to a future for the entire universe, and I was helping him. No wonder I was tired all the time.

"Let's go."

Two nights later we were back in Albuquerque. We had searched for two days before finding Roberto's remains. It was a shame, too. All I could do was put what was left of this young boy on ice and see if we could figure out how to bring him back. The reverence that surged through me as I touched the small bones, placing them into the little cooler that would become his temporary coffin, surprised me. I pulled back and closed the lid as a wave of unwanted emotion washed over me. There was no time now for emotion.

The balance in this case was only partially restored. The crime had been committed, the criminal caught and the body recovered. Filberto was in a coma on life support with a significant brain injury and not expected to survive. I suppose that made my job easier. This was one case where a life-swap was certainly warranted, but the method by which to create the swap wasn't in my hands yet. Paperwork and red tape. It all came down to who could argue better, your lawyer or theirs. I was betting on Liz, my little Chihuahua with the heart of a Rottweiler. All I had to do was wait.

I hate waiting.

Sometimes, I simply don't understand the universe. Today is one of those days. Before I left the house, I spilled water three different times and in three different ways. That either meant something significant or my kitchen was more cluttered than I thought. But I made it in, coffee in hand, ready for all of the really important stuff I do around here.

I sat behind my desk trying not to laugh at the plight of the poor woman sitting across the desk from me. She could have been anyone's auntie or grandmother, sitting there all prim and proper with her Sunday best on, and her glasses shoved pertly on her nose. There she sat, with pictures of Fluffy, her four-legged canine companion. Recently deceased. This wasn't boding well for an improvement in my day.

"I'm sorry, Mrs. Chapman, but I simply can't help you." Not entirely certain I would, even if I could. I wasn't trying to be mean; it simply comes out of me that way sometimes.

"But you can do it. I know you can." She held out a flier I had mistakenly made when I first started out. It was somewhat unclear, and I now regretted ever putting those pages together. One came back to haunt me now and then, and this was one of those times. Maybe this was where the spilled water came in. An omen. "It says so right here." She shoved the thing across the desk to me.

"I know what it says, but this is old and the wording was poor. It doesn't say that we life-swap animals."

"It doesn't say you don't, either. I want my Fluffy back." She was on the verge of tears, and I pushed a box of tissues toward her. Here we go again with the tears. "I'll give you every last penny I have. My entire savings, if you'll bring back my dog!"

"Please calm down, Mrs. Chapman, and take a few breaths." I didn't want to have her stroke out right in front of me, 'cause then I'd have to go back to nurse mode and do something heroic. I wasn't in the mood. "Even though we know who killed your dog, in this case, Cesar, the Doberman next door, and you've kept Fluffy in your freezer, that doesn't change anything. I simply don't perform canine resurrections." That was to the point and not quite as tactful as I could have made it, but the woman was wearing me down. I should have done it just to get her out of my office.

"It was my neighbor's damned dog." Her lips pressed tightly together. No love lost there. She'd run him down if she got the chance.

"Yes. Weren't there numerous noise complaints made by that particular neighbor about Fluffy's incessant barking?" I had the file in front of me and pushed that toward her, too. Not that she picked it up. She knew what was in it.

"It doesn't justify murder. Fluffy was a terrier, and it's part of the breed. Anyone who owns terriers accepts that." She said it as if everyone in the world ought to know that terriers are barking maniacs. As everyone knows that fast food makes you fat. (Everyone knows that, right?)

"Yes, I know, but it doesn't mean your neighbors do. And it still doesn't give me the power to bring him back." I stood. Fortunately, Mrs. Chapman took the hint. She gathered her tote bag against her middle as if it were a priceless object. The bag was about the right size for... Oh, gag. The smile on my face melted as another thought occurred to me. If she had Fluffy in there, I was gonna puke. After the last night I had, it wouldn't take much. I was still trying to clean Filberto out of my brain. "If our conditions change, then I'll be in touch." I patted the file, indicating I had her contact information. I was going to shred it the second she left.

She nodded, didn't say thank you, because she had

nothing to thank me for. I wish she'd just go to the pound and get a replacement dog.

Kind of like boyfriends were for some women. When you lost one, you just went to the pound (the bar) and brought another one home. He could make you happy for a while, but may have a straying problem and some were better trained than others. There was just that pesky neutering issue...

I sat and dropped my head into my hands, closed my eyes and groaned.

"Tough day?" Sam asked from the doorway.

I didn't even have to look up, but I did. "Understatement of the century."

"Wanna go shoot something?" There was a grin hiding behind that well-controlled expression of his. There was a little secret behind his eyes, too, and I definitely wanted to know what it was. The temptation of having him around for so long was beginning to wear on my defenses.

"You got a new toy?" He'd mentioned something about it.

A twitch of the brows was all I got. Intriguing.

"Get me outta here before I shoot something I'm not supposed to." I stood and grabbed my bag that was equally as large as Mrs. Chapman's, but there was no frozen dog in it.

The firing range was a great place to let off some steam. It was a safe environment where no one was going to shoot back, and you could pound the hell out of a flimsy paper target. I love that.

Sam got out his new toy, and it was a doozy. A forty-five millimeter with a nice weight in the hand. I love a man with a smokin'-hot piece of…*steel* in his hands. Makes me shiver all over. Not that I'll let Sam know that. Too many times in my past I let a man have control over me, and it is never, *ever* going to happen again. Control is something that is mine and mine alone. I don't care how illusive it is. Denial has gotten me through many years of my life, so I don't see a reason to stop using it now.

Now, I've gone through a number of weapons training courses, so I've shot many different kinds of weapons. Never stopped me from salivating over a new one, though. Kind of like some women are over shoes. It's all about the accessories, right? Mine just happen to be loaded.

Sam looked at me through that sexy, protective eyewear in a bold, jaundiced color and raised his brows. He really didn't even have to ask, but I *so* appreciated it.

"Hell, yeah, I want to shoot that thing." He grinned and handed me the weapon.

"Give it a whirl."

"Where'd you get this thing, some online shooting shop?"

"Yeah, right."

He knows I want his contacts and insulting him is one of the ways I'm trying to pry the information out of him. Not subtle, but then, I'm really not known for it. I tried the direct route for a while by just asking politely, or as polite as I get, but he just dissed me, so I was reduced to insults.

He went over a few specifics before I loaded the thing, then leaned against the wall beside me. I think he likes watching me shoot. Probably gives him a hard-on. He didn't stand behind me or try to put his hands around me or treat me like a girl, which I totally appreciated. I am *so* not a girl.

Without a word, I squinted through my equally sexy eyewear and popped off one shot, just to get a feel of it before I unloaded the clip. "Recoil's a bitch."

"Did I forget to mention that?" The man had wrists of steel, so recoil meant little to him.

"Uh, yeah." Squinting my left eye, I focused on the target again and squeezed off five shots.

"Nice, Dani. Very nice," he said, admiring the way I so sweetly took out the target.

I returned the gun to Sam and shook out my hands. "Gonna have to work up to that bad boy." Not that I was weak, but my wrists were tiny compared with Sam's. I had supernatural powers, but not supernatural strength. Maybe I could put an order in with Burton, but I doubted it. He'd just laugh.

We picked up our spent shell casings and cleared the way for someone else to shoot. There was never any shortage of cops, P.I.s or gun fanatics practicing at the range. After we left the shooting area, we removed our ear protection. He used an over-the-head earmuff type, and I used the squishy things in my ears. They were cheap and didn't mess up my hair. A woman's gotta watch out for these little issues in life.

"That's a nice piece," I said and meant it.

"Feel better now that you've shot something?"

Oh, the man knows me too well. "Yeah. Sometimes the grind of the job just gets to me, and I want to kill something. Better a target than a person, ya know?" Since I came back from the other side, controlling my anger has been an issue. Kickboxing and margaritas help keep it under control, depending on the situation. They are *not* interchangeable coping mechanisms.

"So, you want to tell me what's really bugging you?"

We headed outside into the parking lot on the south side of the big square, cinder-block building out in the middle of nowhere. Guess the desert has its perks. There are a lot of open spaces that no one wants to build on, so this was perfect.

I told Sam about Mrs. Chapman and the stupid dog she wanted resurrected.

"My grandmother would have loved that one." Normally, Sam is your typical, well-controlled, serious cop-type guy, but now, he wiped his eyes beneath his reflective sunglasses. He was laughing so hard, it brought tears to his eyes. I'd never have bet money on that happening.

I tried not to smile, but couldn't help it. Laughter is nearly as good as sex as a tension reliever. There has been little of either in my life of late, but then sex was what got me killed in the first place. Not mine, my ex-husband's. He's the one who couldn't keep it zipped. "Did she have a dog like Fluffy?" I asked. I knew his grandmother had passed into the beyond, but other than that, I knew little about her.

"No." He shook his head and put his hands on his hips. The laughter was still with him, and it was good to see. I love police officers, and our men in blue have little to laugh about on the job, so a snicker here and there does them good. "Oh, no. She'd have never had a dog like Fluffy."

"She liked big dogs then, like the killer Dobie?"

"No."

"Then what?" I couldn't see what was so funny now.

"The irony of the underappreciated. Like you. Like her. I never told you, but she was like you," Sam said, and all humor between us came to a screeching halt.

My smile faded. "What do you mean, just like me?"

"A resurrectionist." Sam removed his sunglasses. I saw his eyes, so I knew he spoke the truth. "That's why I volunteered for the liaison post with you. I have some experience with it."

"Are you kidding? Why didn't you tell me?" I yelled and slugged him in the chest. Touching people gives me too much information about them, but now and then I put up with it if I get to punch someone. Like now.

"What was the point? She was gone already, and I don't know how to do that stuff."

"The point was that…well, hell, I don't know, but I would have liked to have known."

"She was gone, Dani, years ago."

I sighed, not satisfied with that explanation. It was as if he had insider information and had kept it from me. "I would have liked to have known, that's all. Maybe you could have helped me in the beginning. Maybe you could help me now get some things figured out." I know there are others out there like me, but finding them is not easy. It's not as though we have an online newsletter or a blog like other, more populous states do. I'm going to have to work on one for New Mexico, because no one else is doing it.

"I don't know anything about what goes on during the rituals, other than what I've seen you do."

"Didn't she raise you?" As if that meant he knew everything about her life.

"Yes, but she kept that part of her life very secret when we were kids. It was only by accident that I found out."

Sam put his glasses back on, and we walked to his car. It was an unmarked police vehicle, and it looked like one. In the dark, no one would know, but in the daylight it screamed *cop car*. Just needed a cherry on top. The dashboard was outfitted with more technology than a small plane, and the two hundred antennae on it was a dead giveaway. It looked like an insect on steroids. But I got in anyway. I had to unless I wanted to walk back to the office, some forty miles away. I didn't. "How did you find out?"

"She didn't think my sisters and I were old enough to understand. Our family and the neighborhood were very superstitious. If there had been any implication of witchcraft in her house, the state would have taken us from her. It's different now that there are others out there." He shrugged. "So I did what every kid does. I followed her."

"So following people has been a lifelong endeavor?" Explains why I didn't hear him sneak up on me the other day. Bastard.

He didn't answer that and just gave me a look. "I was

about twelve, but looked older, so I could be out on the streets and no one said anything. Back then the courts hadn't sanctioned resurrections and life-swaps, so it was very underground. Only the family of the victim was present, and the killer of course."

"You were such a wiseass, even at twelve, weren't you?" The image I had of him at that age was funny, all legs and feet and not quite grown into his attitude yet.

"Yeah. I was a piece of work. Got into more trouble than I was worth. Until the Rangers, anyway." He looked away. That's where his secrets lay, in his past, but here was an opportunity to find out a little more about him.

"Did she have a fit when she found out you had followed her?" I could just imagine. My grandmother would have kicked my ass from here to Sunday.

"Oh, yeah. My ears rang for a week. She could carry on like no one I've ever known." He grinned as if it was a good memory. Having good childhood memories is a sign of a balanced life. "Kinda miss that now." That was good. We usually have too many bad memories from childhood that are stuck in our brains. I never understood why the bad ones always come through first and the good memories are left behind. It would be nice to have that in reverse. If I'm ever elected Queen of the Universe, that's the first thing I'm changing. "I had to clean the chicken coop for three months after that."

"Oh, man." I pinched my nose shut. "Just the sound of that stinks." I released my nose with a giggle, then remembered why we were talking about her. "Do you know how she came to have her powers?" I'd heard stories that were different from mine. People who weren't murdered, but born with the abilities.

"No."

"I wonder if you could have inherited something from her." Could this affinity for raising the dead be passed from one generation to the next? Would Sam develop powers of his own? If he hadn't already, it was unlikely that they would surface now. Dammit.

"I don't think so." Sam maneuvered the car through the desert on the dusty, rutted road with casual ease, his long-limbed body relaxed, yet in control. The jiggling of the vehicle over the ruts was about to shake my liver loose, but he didn't seem to be bothered by it. "There's never been any impulse for me to do what you do."

"You have three sisters, right?" Maybe there was some hope in them. Some traits were passed from female to female.

"Yeah."

"Any of them?"

"Not to my knowledge. They'd have told me."

"Oh." It would have been nice to know that there was someone else I knew well who could have helped me.

"Sorry." He reached out and patted me on the arm once, then returned his hand to the wheel.

"I'm thinking about Roberto's case. I don't know if I have what it's going to take to bring him back. In all of my other cases, I've always had intact bodies. Not as far gone as this one is." Something in me just knew this was going to be one of the toughest cases I'd ever been involved in, emotionally as well as physically. Admitting that to myself, let alone to Sam, is a big step for me.

Admitting vulnerabilities only makes you responsible
or gets you a weekly date with a therapist.

"Have you checked with the hospital lately? What's
Filberto's condition?"

"Same. Brain-dead. Waiting on the court order."
Sometimes it takes hours, sometimes it takes days.

"What happens if you can't bring Roberto back?"
He gave me a glance.

That was a good question. A really good one. And
one I didn't know the answer to. I hated admitting that.
In the world of nursing you must know the answers for
every question. Saying *I don't know* isn't acceptable.
It's no more acceptable to me now than it was then, but
I said it anyway. "I don't know."

I just hoped we didn't have to find out. Thankfully,
Sam didn't give me any meaningless reassurance to
make me feel better. It wouldn't, and he knew it.

Chapter 4

There are days when the past haunts me entirely too much, and this was one of those days. Being around pregnant women unnerves me. I admit it. I should have no problems dealing with the condition of women who are growing new life inside of them, but I do.

It's what got me killed.

I hate thinking that I'm weak and vulnerable when I've worked very hard to be as tough as I can be. Certain things set me off, and seeing a happily pregnant woman on the arm of her police officer husband is what did it today. This is a joyous time for them, but for me, it does nothing except bring back haunting, hideous memories that still have the power to make me shudder.

After they passed with a happy smile and a wave, I closed the door to my office. Usually, I keep the door open unless I'm consulting, but now, I need some privacy to have my nervous breakdown. In an office that sits in the middle of the police station, there is no such thing as privacy. Or quiet.

One by one, I pulled the horizontal blinds and closed off the windows. Was I hiding? Yes. I'd hide until it's safe for me to step out again. Until then, the memory of my life in the past overwhelms me in sloshes of emotions that build into pounding waves, and I allow it. Crawling onto the small couch against the wall, I tucked my feet beneath me and clutched a pillow to my middle. Closing my eyes, I let the memory, the horror of it, wash over me. I've learned that resisting only puts off the inevitable and gives more power to the pain. If I give it the time it needs now, then life will go on much more quickly.

I had been happily, blissfully, ignorantly, pregnant. My husband hadn't been as thrilled about it as I had been, but I don't think men can ever have the same connection to a baby as women do. Just the nature of how we're put together.

Anyway, my husband, Blake, and I had been headed for divorce when we decided to give it one last go. He'd been carrying on with a woman for several months and had tired of her clingy, demanding ways, so he let her go and went back to his wife, who wasn't so clingy and demanding. Maybe I should have been and things might have been different, but now, we'll never know.

So, giving it the old college try at reconciliation, the husband and I had a nice dinner with requisite margaritas, enough that I became a little intoxicated. Okay, a lot intoxicated, but I wasn't driving, so who cares? And we screwed our brains out all night long. We hadn't done that since we were dating, so we indulged in an all night bang-a-thon.

And I got pregnant. My family was thrilled because I was finally fulfilling my reproductive obligations inherent to any large family that seemed to want to take over the earth, one generation at a time. The playboy-doctor-husband was not thrilled. Although he said he wanted children someday, to him, someday meant years into the future, when he had a more secure practice, blah, blah, blah. What he really meant was *never*. He wasn't the fatherly type who could, or would, be there for his child.

In the old days, T&A's meant tonsils and adenoids. Now it was tits and asses, making them bigger and smaller in that order. There was serious money to be made in elective plastic surgery, and he was going to make his killing now, then retire to an island in the Caribbean and work on skin cancer late in life. Or something equally brilliant.

As my pregnancy progressed and my belly grew, I was happy. Even though the spousal unit couldn't be bothered to come to checkups and ultrasounds with me, I was content in knowing that I was growing a new life I could love and cherish. One that would love and cherish me, at least until the teenage years, and then it would be all over for a while.

Although my growing abdomen housed a new life, and that was good, it also threw my center of gravity off, and that was bad. I was in an awkward stage at the end of my third trimester when the doorbell rang and without thinking, I opened it. I'd been shopping for baby things and had taken a load into the house and was ready to return for another, so I was right there by the door. An unfamiliar woman stood there, and the smile fell from my face when I noticed the gun in her hand. She grabbed me by the shirt and dragged me out of the house toward my car with an open back door just a few feet away. I tried to struggle, knowing if I got into my car I was dead. It was the middle of the day and my neighbors all worked, so screaming wasn't going to help. I had to save myself or die trying.

She clobbered me on the head with something that felt like an anvil, and I collapsed onto the backseat. She shoved my legs in, and away she went with me unconscious in the back. I finally roused, but had no idea where we were or for how long I'd been out. My legs were numb from being folded up in such an awkward position. I had to move, but if I did, she'd know I was awake. I eased my weight up slightly so my legs got some circulation, and they screamed in pain as the blood flow returned.

"Dammit, where is this place?" she grumbled aloud. I heard the shuffling of papers, so maybe she was looking at a map. There was no GPS in my car. If she didn't know where we were, I wasn't going to find my way out of there either. Panic as well as my position was making me dizzy.

She turned off the car and got out. As quickly as I could, I shifted to my back. Not a comfortable position when you have a watermelon in your belly, but when your life was on the line, you coped. She opened the back door and reached in. I kicked out with both feet as hard as I could, and she went flying.

I knew I had hurt her, or at least surprised the hell out of her, but I was certain we weren't done yet. With any luck, she'd left the keys in the ignition, and I could get out of there. I scrambled out of the car as fast as any nine-months-pregnant woman could scramble, which wasn't too sprightly.

"You're a dead woman," she yelled. "Fucking bitch."

She was on her knees and clutched her front. Hopefully, I'd broken a few ribs. I didn't know who she was or why she thought kidnapping me was going to improve her life.

"What do you want?" I tried to slide against the car toward the front door.

"You. Dead."

The words didn't make sense, but as a nurse, I knew that things many people thought didn't make sense. She might have been an escaped psych patient who was on a mission from above or listening to the voices in her fillings. Or just off her medications. In any case, keeping her talking and away from me was my first step to survival. "I see, but why? Who are you?"

"You're the only thing standing between me and Blake."

Oh, shit. She was his mistress, who was supposed to be a *former* mistress. And she was freakin' nuts. Good going, Blake. If I got out of this alive, I was going to put certain of his body parts in the blender.

"Are you out of your mind? What the hell are you doing?" Anger overcame fear for a moment.

"Blake went back to you." The idea that Blake was married to me seemed to have escaped her. "If you hadn't gotten pregnant, none of this would be happening."

Oh, yeah. As if this was my fault. Another sign of pathological nuttiness. Blame everyone else for your personal failures.

"Now, just a damned minute. I have the right to sleep with my own husband. You are the one who doesn't." This was pissing me off. Now that I could see what was going on, I was damned mad and some of my fear wore off, which wasn't necessarily a good thing.

"We were so good together," she said with a wistful tone to her voice. "You should have seen us." She spoke to me as if we were girlfriends sharing secrets. Definite lack of reality attachment.

"I would prefer not to." I didn't need anything else to make me nauseated.

"Bitch." She reached for a large knife on the ground beside her and dove for me. I ducked, but that's hard to do with a big, fat belly. The knife missed me, but the impact of her body against mine thumped me between her and the car. The air went out of my lungs, and I couldn't breathe. A pregnant woman has a hard time breathing to begin with. When one is body-slammed by an insane woman, it's all over.

We collapsed into a heap on the ground, and she clobbered me again. Back then, I didn't know how to fight. Every woman ought to know how to defend herself, and this was one reason why.

When I woke up there was a knife sticking out of my stomach. I screamed, not certain if it was from pain or from the sight of the butcher knife protruding from my body.

The woman obviously intended to cut my baby out of me.

"Stop!" I reached out to the knife. Adrenaline and the heat of a white anger so deep I felt it in my bones surged through my marrow. I was going to remove that thing and stick it into her. I was not going to die. I was not going to lose my baby to this psychopath.

Unfortunately, I did all of that.

She reached the knife before I did and pulled it toward her, my left. "I'm going to take your baby and watch you bleed to death." She laughed, as if she was surprised she hadn't thought of it sooner. "And there's not a damned thing you can do about it."

Clenching my teeth against the pain that penetrated every cell of my body, I felt as if I were on fire and there was nothing I could do about it. Pushing up with a hand beneath my hips, I bore the weight of my body on my left hand and reached for the knife with my right. Breathing was next to impossible, and my chest burned with the need for air. I had to win, I *had* to win. This woman was going to kill me and steal my child. "No." It's all I could manage. "No." She was not going to win. I would not let her win.

Digging deep into a place I didn't know existed within me, I grabbed her hand on the knife and pushed with everything I had in me. Although I'd never hurt anyone before, I was going to kill this woman.

Somehow I got to my knees with her trying to shove the blade deeper into my side. In the movies there always seems to be a lot of noise in fight scenes, but it was eerily silent. Only the groans of pitting my strength against hers broke the night.

Abruptly, she let go, and stood, her breath coming in and out of her in harsh gasps. "You bitch!" Then, she kicked me in the stomach, and I crashed to the ground, the pain incapacitating me. Stars and bright lights swam in front of my eyes and seemed as though they came from all around us. Then she tackled me and straddled my body, her knees forcing my hands down, trapping them at my sides. My strength was fading. I knew it and so did she.

She grabbed the knife with both hands and pulled, spilling everything inside me out onto the ground. A scream echoed off the canyon walls, and I realized it was mine.

"Come here, little one. You're so precious," she said in a sweet voice as she searched for my baby.

"No." Reaching up with one hand, I tried to save him, but I was too weak. My vision blurred, and I was certain shock was overtaking me. Shock isn't such a bad thing. It keeps us from remembering the horrors that are happening to us, and at the moment I welcomed it.

She extricated the baby, and held it up. It wasn't moving and it was purple. "Oh, that's right. I have to cut the cord before it will breathe." Talking to herself, she retrieved her knife, slicing through the umbilical cord. Blood spurted, then she looked at me, as if I had the answer to the stupid thing she had done. "It's bleeding. Why won't it stop bleeding?"

I looked at my limp baby that she held out. I could see that it was a boy, and tears pricked my eyes. It wouldn't have mattered to me. I would have loved a girl just as much. She'd cut the cord close to the abdomen and hadn't tied it off. Now there was nothing left. If the baby could have survived, it would surely now die. It was going to bleed to death, just like me. "Didn't tie… the cord." It was all I could manage as tears for him and for me closed off my throat.

She looked down at the baby and tears flooded her eyes. "Dammit! I worked so hard on this. And now, just look at the mess it is."

My legs went numb, and I knew my end was near. I felt my breathing become labored.

She'd won after all. She laid the baby down beside me, wiped her hands on her jeans, got into my car and drove away, leaving us alone in the darkening desert. I had only moments left.

Pulling the baby toward me, I cuddled him as best I could, tucking the little head under my chin, and I let my tears flow. I sobbed and my baby fell out of my arms.

A light, the brightness of which I've never seen, appeared a few feet away. It wasn't a person, or an angel, though it could have been. I knew I was dying, and who knew what was coming to get me? I wasn't particularly religious. At least until that moment. For a second, I reconsidered what I knew about religion.

And then I took a breath, and it sighed out of me for the last time.

"Come, child." The other-sider, for that's what I have come to know it as, reached out to me. How I knew it was from beyond, I don't know, but I realized it was trying to communicate with me, even though no words were spoken aloud. All I could hear was a loud ringing in my ears.

"No." From above my body, I looked down at the baby, who had never begun to live, and touched it with one finger. I wanted to stay with him. He should go with me.

"He is gone to the source now. Your time here is not finished."

"Yes it is." It was. I knew it. I'd accepted it. Closing my eyes, I waited to be taken too. Waited for that irresistible pull from beyond I had heard about.

"You will go back. The call for help has gone out, and you will be saved."

Saved? How could I be? Did it not see the condition of my body? It was too late now. "No." I looked down at the mess that had been my body. It was almost beyond recognition. I don't know if I said it out loud, but I thought it and the other-sider heard me. My condition was beyond saving.

The being moved toward me, and the glow of it burned through my eyelids and into my brain. I wanted to let go, to leave this plane of existence, but couldn't. Something was drawing me back inside. I felt a pop in my physical body. I don't know how else to explain it, but it was as if someone or something had yanked on me, only I felt it at a visceral level. I had returned.

I began to glow, just like the other-sider. The life force had returned to my body, not floating around as it had been moments ago.

"You will return. You will survive, and you will right

the wrongs committed against you, against humanity, and against the universe."

"Who do you think I am, Wonder Woman?" I managed to ask with my mind. Something was changing, something was reforming inside me. I could feel it. Reaching down, I placed my hand onto my abdomen and realized all was not as it had been. Things were returning to my body that had just been on the ground. I didn't want to think about infection or how much dirt was coating my internal organs. Should I survive the injuries, I'd die of septicemia for sure. No antibiotic could cure this.

"You are indeed a wonder. Each step of your life has prepared you for this moment. Your life-threatening wounds are repaired, and you will fully heal, be stronger than you ever were. You will return to your life, gifted as no other." The light that I had thought was bright went nuclear. In that moment, that nanosecond, my life was changed, whether I wanted it to or not.

I screamed from the deepest part of me, and the sound of it echoed off the canyon walls. The smell of wood fires and the murmur of my ancestors crowded my mind. I had been gifted with knowledge from the ancients, and the power of justice. Just as I had come back from the dead, I would assist others to return, to restore the balance of the universe.

Now, I pulled myself out of the musing at the sound of a scuffle outside my door. In a police station, there is always a scuffle of some sort going on.

The clock face slowly came into focus, and I decided my day was over. Though it was early, four o'clock or so, I was whipped. Nothing else was going to get done today.

I grabbed my bag and stood just as the door opened.

"You look like someone beat you with a rock," Sam said. Charming as ever. Where was that damned petrified wood? I could use it about now.

"Yeah, I feel like it, too." Shouldering my bag, I avoided looking into his eyes and shoved my shades on. They protected me somewhat, but he was so friggin' observant that nothing got past him. Damn cops anyway.

"I'm buying," he said and stepped sideways in the doorway to let me pass.

That meant I had to touch him with my body and slide intimately against him, smell that cologne of his that always made me want to forget my mission and lick my way from one end of his body to the other. Right now, I was too tired, and tried not to sense the way his body felt, the firmness of his chest and abs as I slithered past him. "You coulda moved." I threw a glare over my shoulder. With the sunglasses on, it was less effective. Sam wasn't very susceptible to my glares anyway, which pissed me off. I wasn't in the mood, so he was on his own for chow.

"Coulda." He fell into step beside me. "Garduno's?"

It was the one word I couldn't resist. My mouth began to water in anticipation. Guacamole, margaritas and meat. "You're such a bastard," I said and hung my head. I was defeated already. My stomach ruled my life, and he knew it.

"I am, but that's why you like me." With his hand

on the middle of my back, he gave me a playful shove toward the main doors. "Let's eat. I'm starved."

In less than thirty minutes I was surrounded by the things I loved and needed to get through the day: an excellent margarita, a flat-iron steak, rare, and a hot-blooded man across the table. It was a feast for the taste buds and the eyes. Okay, so I didn't really need the margarita to get through the day, but it was a nice touch at the end of a sucky one. And I really, really didn't need the hot-blooded man across the table from me, but boy, the eye-candy factor was too hard to resist sometimes. He was buying me dinner, after all. Who could argue with that?

I know Sam was interested in me in a way I couldn't return. My life was so complicated, it was all I could do to get through it. I didn't need any more complications. So for the moment, I just sat there and let him ogle my body, enjoying the rush of it. I knew he wanted to, and if this was the only control I had over a man, I had to take it. Gave me a shiver just thinking about what it would be like to have Sam naked and pressed against me. I gulped my frozen-no-salt-on-the-rim drink, trying to cool off my brain and the burn in my crotch. Didn't work though. Next time I was having salt. I didn't care what my blood pressure did.

Fortunately, our orders arrived quickly and I grabbed my knife, ready to stab it into anything that didn't move.

"You're the only woman I know who likes her steak bloodier than mine." Sam cut into his meal.

"I feel so feminine and dainty when you say things like that." Me? Ha. Not even on a good day. After I was resurrected, I burned every feminine thing I owned. Except for that one pair of pretty pink thongs with a matching bra. Someday…

"We never finished our conversation the other day," Sam said.

Uh, what conversation? We had so many that got interrupted with phone calls and firearms that I couldn't keep track. Always on the move, always busy doing something for the station or my office, we never seemed to have a moment to allow our brains to catch up. "Which conversation was that?"

"About my grandmother and her job in the underground."

I had to laugh. That's certainly one way of putting it. "Yeah." I looked at Sam. I liked the way his smile sort of slid over his face slowly just then. The man has a face that isn't pretty or handsome, but it is compelling. His hair is that dark, dark black that Latin men have, and his is cut very short. Not quite a buzz, but a little longer. He is clean shaven, but I've seen pictures of him with a 'stache, and it's nice, too. The most compelling part of his face is his eyes, which sort of pull everything together and make it come alive. His eyes were the shade of espresso, dark and fathomless, eyes you could get lost in. Kinda like now.

"Dani?" He waved his hand in front of my face, bringing me back to the present. Doh!

How embarrassing. "Sorry." I cleared my throat and speared a piece of grilled jalapeño. Maybe setting my mouth on fire would keep me focused. "Didn't mean to stare."

"No problem. You just seemed lost for a second." The espresso in his eyes percolated a little warmer.

Yeah, I was lost. In his eyes. It's that damned cologne he wears. I swear there's some sort of chemical in it that puts me in a trance. Kinda like catnip for women. Ugh. Back to the convo at hand.

"We were talking about your grandmother and Roberto's case the other day, weren't we?" Back on track. That's where I feel best, with a job in front of me, a purpose and a mission to accomplish, not just drifting around like those in the nebula.

"Is there another resurrectionist who can help you?"

Sadly, no. "Not right now. I know a few, but not well enough to step into this kind of job." Something occurred to me, though. Something I've been doing just to get the events of the day out of my brain is something Sam's grandmother may have done. I have a computer and the internet, but she had access only to books and papers. I frowned and leaned closer to him across the table. Intent. Assistance might come from the other side in a different form. "Did your grandmother keep any records, any sort of journals, papers, anything about her work? I write some things, keep a journal of sorts, so it clears my brain and records some of what I do in the rituals. She might have done the same thing." That would be a huge bonus, to have information from such a source. I never know if the internet information is legit.

Sam thought a minute, then frowned. "If she did, I don't know of any, but my sisters might."

"She could have had a journal she kept hidden, if, as

you say, she was at risk of being accused of witchcraft."
If nothing else, I had to have a little hope.

"That's true. She had so much stuff though, something like that might have been overlooked. She was a Depression-era survivor, so she never threw anything away." My grandmother had also survived the Great Depression, and she has a garage full of toilet paper and plastic water jugs. The two things she can't live without. Oh, and soap, too.

"Would you ask your sisters if they found anything like that?" Desperation led me to ask Sam for such a favor. The weight of it got to me sometimes, even with my jovial outlook on life. Even if his *abuela* was dead, at least I might connect to her through her writings. Burton might be helpful, but he's unreliable and difficult to contact. Sam, I know I can count on, no matter what it is. He is a man who keeps his word, keeps promises he makes. I just didn't know why.

"Sure." He searched my eyes, and I wondered if they had returned to their normal color. After eating, my need for protein and blood is satisfied, and externally, I look normal again. Hesitating, he reached out and placed his hand over mine. He knows that touching is difficult for me. It isn't something I can easily control, and I can get sucked into the feelings of the person I'm touching. Occupational hazard. But right then, it was simply nice. "I'll help you any way I can. Sometimes you seem so lonely in what you do, that it takes so much out of you."

There was no other way to acknowledge that very astute observation. "I am, and it does."

Chapter 5

Two days passed and the resurrection order finally came in. We were given the go-ahead to perform the life-swap between Roberto and Filberto. I was a nervous wreck. I wasn't certain I had what it was going to take to make the swap successful. I had no one except myself and Sam to rely on. I kept dreaming of the movie *The Fly,* where the scientist tried transporting an animal and it came through *inside out.* Even for me that's got a high ick-factor.

Burton was no help. The bastard. Sometimes he just annoyed the hell out of me and took the teenager persona entirely too far. He's involved in a skateboard competition today and can't be bothered. *Dude.* I hope he leaves some skin on the sidewalk.

I was on my own. Again. I should be used to it by

now, but sometimes, the times I felt most vulnerable, were the times I needed someone, and there simply was no one except Sam, and he could do only so much.

Details, details, details. Sometimes I thought I was going to get sucked into my phone, ear first, as I made arrangements to have Roberto's remains thawed and prepared to travel to the hospital. Then all the hoops I had to jump through at the hospital, I felt like a tiger leaping through flaming hoops and getting my tail singed. Having worked in the hospital system, I should have been used to the flak, but it continues to amaze me that any patient walks out of the hospital alive, because so much documentation has to be done first. Oy!

If I had more time, I'd sick my Korean grandmother, Suzie, on them. She'd get some results pretty damned quick. She's small, but she can be very mean. Maybe that's where I got some of my enhanced traits from. I'm descended from several mixed cultures, of Anglo, Mexican, East Indian, with a little Korean for extra spice. That's makes me perfect for this wonderful melting pot city of Albuquerque. Here, no one sticks out because there are so many different cultures mingled together. It's great. Don't get me started about the unbelievable variety of food here. If I didn't take kickboxing three nights a week, I'd have an ass as big as a sports car.

Finally, things were moving in the right direction, and I called Roberto's parents.

"Now, I know you're going to want to have the whole family there for the ceremony." People reacted better to that word than *ritual*. Too many ghosts and references to the occult regarding the word *ritual,* even though it's a bunch of crap. "It would be better if everyone stayed at your house. Just you and Julio come to the hospital. Normally, it would be different, but we have to obey the hospital rules while we're there."

"Sure, I understand. It will just be us."

I heard the tears in Juanita's voice, the questions that she hadn't asked. This woman's happiness rested on my shoulders, and disappointing her would be painful to both of us. "Don't worry," I said, trying to reassure myself, as well. "Things will turn out the way they're supposed to." I hoped that The Dark entity was going to take a powder tonight. The ritual was going to be difficult enough without adding an unknown threat to the scenario. This was so out of my comfort zone, I didn't really want to think about it.

"My son wasn't supposed to die." She burst into tears, and I felt the burn of them on the back of my tongue, but forced them down. I'd shed my tears long ago.

"I know." I know. Believe me, I know.

After ending the call, I headed out to the parking lot. I had to go home for a while, gather energy, gird my loins and do all the stuff it takes to perform a ritual. The sun was just beginning to head off the edge of the horizon, so I watched for a second or two as the sky turned a deep peach, frosted with magenta hues, as if someone had dragged a spoon through melting sorbet. Lovely. I wish I could breathe those colors inside myself and feel what it's like to be so alive on the inside that the hues are deep enough for others to see on the outside.

* * *

When I arrived later, there were fifty people in the hallway outside the ICU waiting room. Could no one follow directions? I was surprised security hadn't tossed out the lot of them.

Sam was already there, looking strong and silent by the doorway of the ICU. Now, his presence was comforting rather than stimulating, which was what I needed. I'm never more vulnerable than when performing rituals, and having him at my back relieves a stress I don't need. My energy and concentration can go where they're needed.

At least the ICU's visiting policy kept most everyone out of the room. I nodded at Sam and pushed open the stainless-steel double doors. Two of my guards came along with me. One pushed a cart covered with a white sheet. Beneath the sheet were Roberto's remains, which I dearly hoped would fuse together using the energy from Filberto's dying body.

There's only so much I can do, and then energy from the source, the nebula, the other side, or whatever you want to call it, takes over. Every resurrection was a little different, so I wasn't exactly sure what was going to happen tonight. With any luck, we'd all come out of this unscathed and the Ramirez family would have their son back. With even greater luck, he'll have no memory of what had happened to him.

Even before the ritual began, I felt the charge of power surging within me. It was like a small pulse growing stronger and stronger, as if something inside me had just awakened and was slowly humming to life.

In a way, a piece of me remains dormant until I call upon it.

Filberto's parents were at his bedside sobbing their eyes out. I couldn't help them. No one could. For now, their son was gone. And who knew if I could do anything more than just make that really final?

One of the physicians, Dr. Ernest Cooper, was an older man and one I had worked with in my days as an E.R. nurse. Seems he'd snagged some extra time in the ICU tonight. "Dani, how are doing?" he asked and patted my shoulder. He's been with me on a few cases and knows that since my change, I can't touch his hands the way I used to. He leaned over and gave me a fatherly kiss on the temple.

"I'm doing well." I glanced at the white sheet on the cart and shrugged. He knew what I meant. He'd been around far too long not to.

"I hate to ask, but do you have the paperwork?" I know the man has a job to do, and I'd rather it be him than some physicians I know. Most don't have the temperament for this work.

"Here it is." Sam handed him the paperwork packet, and he removed his glasses to read it. I never understood why some people take their glasses off to read. I have to put glasses on to read. Go figure.

He sighed. I understand the depth of that sigh. It's an unfortunate event that has brought us together. We're caregivers, trained healers, we work our asses off to save people and return them to their lives unscathed. The two primary players in this drama are already dead, but we, the living, are charged with carrying out the task of returning the balance to the way it should be. It's a heavy load to bear, and sometimes my shoulders ache from it.

"It's okay, Doc. We're going to get through this and go have a midnight snack at The Frontier." They have the best home-baked cinnamon rolls smothered in butter ever made. Sign me up for another kickboxing class.

Without a word, his fatigued blue eyes met mine. Time to get moving.

Sam ushered in Roberto's parents, who were understandably freaked out. If this ritual was a success, they'd have their son back and lose a once-trusted cousin in the process. They'd already lost Filberto anyway. If the ritual didn't work, then they stood to lose their son all over again. I could feel the energy pouring off them, and it invaded every corner of the room. Sam slid the glass door shut, closing off distractions from the other parts of the ICU, and closed the curtain.

This was a private party and no one else was invited. A stretcher had been brought into the room, and I moved the cart carrying Roberto's remains beside it. After removing the white sheet, I looked at what had once been a happy, thriving little boy and was now just a pile of bones. I had to put rubber gloves on to prevent contamination of his remains and prevent me from feeling anything just yet. Totally focused on my task, I moved the remains onto the stretcher.

The pulse that had begun inside me increased in vibration to a hum. This is the time where people usually started to freak out. That's why I hired a few guards to help keep the families focused instead of running away screaming in the dark. I usually perform the rituals in graveyards at midnight, so you can understand why some people run.

Sam unzipped my kit of tools and placed them on the cart. There were several lethal-looking knives, but most were ceremonial in nature. A picture of Roberto, provided by his family, was placed here with several candles. Lighting the candles in a building with a sprinkler system might be a problem, but the ritual can't be done without them. They're white, sacred and specially made by a *curandera*.

I held my hands over Roberto's remains, took in a deep breath, closed my eyes and began to glow.

Power surged down from the universe, swirled within me, and I became the conduit through which the souls passed. Practice makes a perfect resurrection, but the circumstances here were difficult. I had been right—I would need to bleed hard for this one. Even then, I lacked the confidence to say everything would work out the way we wanted it to.

"Peacemakers of the universe, hear me now." My voice rose over the whoosh and noises of the life-support system, the heart monitor and other extraneous sounds in the room. All I could hear was the voice inside me and my heartbeat throbbing in my ears. "Death is bitter, and worse when a child is taken. Tonight, spirits of those beyond, we gather to right the wrong done to this soul. Hear me now and let it be." I took the dagger that had been given to me at the time of my recovery and drew it across my forearm perpendicular to the bones. A line of red appeared and droplets formed.

Shaking my arm, I flicked the blood onto Roberto's remains. "Take my blood offering and restore this star to his proper state."

I looked at Dr. Cooper and nodded. It was time to remove the life support from the criminal. Dr. Cooper turned off the ventilator, silenced the heart monitors and removed the breathing tube from Filberto's throat. In minutes the body would die anyway without it, but the ritual hastened the process.

A whirlwind developed inside the room. Paperwork scattered, and the ends of my hair rose up with the energy of it. I touched Filberto's arm with one hand and placed the other over Roberto's bones. Energy filled me, flowed through me, electrified me. Tears filled my eyes as the surge, the power within me, drove everything else from my mind.

Then everything stalled, and I opened my eyes. The energy dropped down through my legs and out my feet. I didn't have enough power to bring Roberto back. Dammit. Filberto was going to die, and Roberto was not going to return.

This was my worst nightmare.

Scrunching my eyes closed, I dug deeper inside myself, searching for the power I needed. But it was no use. I shook my head. Denial wasn't going to help me this time.

"More," I said. "I need more." Panic began to overwhelm the energy surge.

"More what?" Sam called over the torrent of energy in the room. He placed his hand on my shoulder, and I opened my eyes. Then I knew. An image of his *abuela* flashed in my mind.

"Blood."

Juanita rushed forward and thrust her arm toward me. "Bleed me dry if it will bring back my son." Sobbing, she pulled her sleeve back and reached for my blade. She'd slit her wrist and it wouldn't help, then where would we be?

"No. It's not right." I turned to Sam. "It's you. It's your blood I need. Your *abuela* was powerful, and I need the blood of another resurrectionist." I couldn't make the right words come out, but I knew it was right.

"I'm not her." Thank you, Captain Obvious.

"I know, but you have her blood." I hoped he wouldn't make me tackle him.

"Do it." He stepped closer and offered himself to me as no man has ever done. Although he'd volunteered before, part of me was still shocked that he'd stepped up to the plate for me. The color of his eyes was dark, brooding and intense. Part of me that had shielded myself against him eased. This man was going to bleed for me, and I was humbled by the gesture.

I took the ceremonial dagger and sliced it across his right palm, not too deep, but enough to make a pool of blood well quickly in his cupped hand. Next, I sliced the dagger across my palm. This was a man who understood the sacred and understood the need for rituals. The blood of his grandmother, the blood of another resurrectionist, ran in his veins, and that was what was needed to complete the circle here. I needed her power to blend with mine. I sliced our other palms, and we joined hands, mixing our blood, pooling our power together.

The second I touched Sam's hands to mine, the sensations I've always tried to avoid pulsed from him into me. The beat of my heart beat in time with his as our energies melded, becoming one, more powerful agent. I gasped, and Sam's eyes widened as intense heat flowed between us. Snatches of his memories flittered through my mind, and I'm sure he saw parts of my past he never expected to.

An energy I'd never sensed in Sam now surged upward. Unable to look away from his face, I spoke the final words needed to complete Roberto's restoration and return his spirit to his physical body. Calling this spirit to return from the nebula took some doing, apparently. Having been injured so badly in life, the reluctance I felt from him was understandable, but returning him righted the wrong.

"We, together, join our bond and sacrifice our blood for this child. By all that is right, by all that is true, restore the balance." I took a deep breath and closed my eyes, pulling on every ounce, every speck of energy and power in me. I squeezed Sam's hands, and he squeezed mine until they hurt, but it was the final requisite joining our blood cells together to create something bigger, something deeper between us. "Hear me now, and let it be."

A blinding white light glowed in the room, similar to the one that had approached at my dying time. It was a spirit from beyond, and I knew it was Roberto, waiting. His body had reformed and glowed with a beautiful white light. It began to move, and everything returned to its proper place.

Roberto breathed.

At this same time, Filberto's body gurgled out its last breath. His body ejected his spirit as if it were trying to vomit up a large, sticky object. A chasm of darkness opened in the ceiling of the room.

Some of the tension left me, as I knew the ritual was going to be completed the way it should be, and I had not failed. Failure in myself was something I would not accept. Not when so many people depended on me. My death grip on Sam's hands relaxed slightly, but I didn't let go of him. I still needed his strength to hold me upright.

In contrast to Roberto's light, glowing spirit, Filberto's spirit was a dark, nearly black light. Maybe it was an indication of the color of his soul. The innocent are light and clear and wondrous. The evil are nearly black, dense and cloudy.

Drawn toward the chasm of darkness, Filberto's spirit hesitated. I knew it would be punished, and it deserved that for the acts it had committed while in physical form. The spirit would return to the nebula for an undetermined period before being allowed to return to physical form. I don't believe in purgatory, but I do think there are waiting periods for certain souls, allowing them time to think.

Finally, it was gone and the dark chasm swallowed itself, then disappeared with a small pop. I breathed a sigh of relief and looked up at Sam, relieved the ritual had worked.

"Mom?"

Screams and cries filled the room. Juanita and Julio enveloped Roberto in hugs, kisses, tears and babbled words. My breathing came in quick gasps, and I squeezed Sam's hands again until his nails dug into my skin, the pain grounding me in this time, helping me avoid the pull of the nebula. It's easy to see why souls want to leave this plane and go there. The pull, the sense of peace, is overwhelming. The familiarity of the place is nearly too much to resist, and one that's hard to give up for the corporeal body and the earth plane.

Tears filled my eyes as I watched the grateful family bundled together. Roberto sat in Juanita's lap and Julio's arms were around both of them. Tears streamed from his eyes, and he pressed his cheek to the top of Roberto's perfect head.

"A pediatrician is waiting to examine Roberto." I cleared my throat, trying to choke down my emotions.

"Thank you, thank you, thank you." Julio started in English, then reverted to Spanish. He looked to Sam for help.

"He says he doesn't have the right words to tell you how grateful they are." Sam cleared his throat, his voice deeper than usual, choked with the same emotions swirling inside me. He wasn't as unaffected by this ritual as he would have liked.

"I know. I know." I released Sam's hands because his emotions were beginning to leach into my skin. I hugged Julio, and I thought he was gonna crack my ribs. "Take care of him and each other. This restores the balance. So let it be."

"If you ever need anything, I mean *anything,* do not hesitate to come to us. We will do anything for you, Miss Wright." He crossed himself and then grabbed me again into another hug, kissed both my cheeks, then released me and grabbed Sam. "My family is yours. We'll do anything for you. You have my word." His voice cracked. "Anything."

"Restoring your family is enough." He needed to stop or I was going to cry. That would totally defeat my tough-chick persona.

"What's going on?" Roberto asked and peaked through his mother's arms. "Mama?"

Juanita looked at me, panic in her eyes. She'd apparently not thought of what to tell him. I stepped forward, careful to hide the blood on my hands from Roberto.

"You've been sick for a little while, but are doing much better now." It's the simplest explanation for someone of his age. Kids understand what sick is. His parents could decide what to tell him later, when he was older. I'm older and still don't know if I understand everything. "You're going to go home tonight and sleep in your own bed. You probably won't remember much from your time away from home, but if you do, be sure and tell your parents about it." Counseling is always available to families of the newly resurrected. Families heal, but it takes time. Time they now have together.

"Okay." He closed his eyes and sighed against his mother's chest, his little arms wrapped around her as far as they could go. "I'm tired."

Everyone in the room gave a small laugh, and the tension eased. "Me, too." I was beyond fatigued and was grateful that someone was going to drive me home. I looked at Sam. He looked as bad as I felt. The guards ought to drive him home, too.

Turning away from them, I faced Dr. Cooper. "Thank you." It was all I could manage. After scenes like this, my brain forgets how to operate for a few hours.

"This was a good thing you did, here, Dani." He met my gaze for a few moments, then looked away. "Want to come back to the E.R.?"

I had to laugh. "No way." This is my job now. "This is kind of like E.R. nursing, but with better weapons."

The man chuckled, opened the sliding partition and walked out.

"Why don't you go meet the doctor who'll examine Roberto?" I didn't want Roberto lingering in the area and speculating who or what was under the sheet in the bed next to him. "Dave will take you there."

The group of three followed my guard out of the room, leaving Sam and me alone with a corpse. Did I mention that we have such romantic moments between us? Yeah. This was another one.

"What now?" He was looking down at me, his energy vibration flatter than usual.

"Now we wash our hands." It wasn't the answer he was looking for, but I didn't have one. Instead, I approached the sink and motioned him over. We scrubbed the blood off our hands in silence, then dried them on paper towels from the dispenser.

I dug in my bag of supplies and retrieved a tube of antibiotic ointment, squeezed a bit onto my fingers. "Let me see." I wasn't exactly avoiding his question, but I wasn't tackling it head-on either. We exchanged blood during a ritual. That might do nothing, or it could tie us together forever. There's no way to find out, other than to wait and see what happens.

The wounds on Sam's hands weren't deep, but they were going to hurt a little bit. I rubbed the salve across both cuts, careful not to press too hard, then finished with a one-inch-wide gauze, hooking the thin wrapping around his thumb to hold it in place. Nursing experience does come in handy sometimes. I gave his other hand the same treatment.

"Yours now." The touch of his hands on mine was tender, careful, as if he thought he could hurt me. My hands didn't hurt. They were actually numb. I wasn't sure whether that was good or bad, or made no difference whatsoever. My circuits had probably overloaded and wouldn't reset until after I'd had some sleep. Being unconscious was restorative, as long as you woke up again.

After he was finished, he pressed a kiss to each wrapping. Surprised, I looked up at him. Some of my emotions must have shown in my face, because he gave that sideways smile of his that always lit me up. At that moment, I was too tired to get lit up, but it still warmed me inside. I appreciated the gesture and tried not to read anything into it. Sam was a protector, and he included me in the circle of people he protected. But I couldn't imagine him being so tender with his sisters. "Let's get out of here."

I led the way, and we took the employee elevators to the back door by the loading docks. Facing crowds of family, curious onlookers and possibly the press was not something I could cope with now. Sam would try to shield me as much as he could, but we were both wiped out from this one, and it was better just to deal with it later.

We were on the way to my place when the inevitable happened.

My stomach growled.

"Time for food?"

"'Fraid so." I hate being at the mercy of my stomach, but I have no choice. "Rats."

Chapter 6

Erotic dreams are generally not part of my imagery. At that moment I didn't care what the rule was, I was so diggin' the exception. I knew it was a dream, yet I didn't care. The world could wait for a few minutes while I got off on my nice, safe dream. There's no sex safer than that. Rolling onto my stomach, I dug deeper into the dream.

Strong hands rubbed the small of my back. That's exactly where most of my tension ends up, and the man in my dreams knows it. The sigh that rolled out of me was pure bliss. Pressed against the soft sheets, my nipples tingled, and I was certain an orgasm was on the way. Since I had been celibate for years, it wouldn't take much. Restless, I couldn't stop the moan lodged in my throat. I wanted more of this dream.

The hand of my dream man eased up my sleep shirt, and his skin touched mine. More bliss.

Then the scratch of something unexpected dragged me away from Nirvana. The rough texture of his hand was interrupted by something soft, but different from skin. Strange. Frowning, I opened my eyes and blinked, looked around my bedroom. Everything was the same. Except for the hand.

Whipping around, I turned to the other side of the bed.

Sam lay there, his eyes intense, serious and wanting. Oh, by the gods, how had the man ended up here? I remember passing out over coffee, but that was it.

"What are you doing?" I tried to sound mean, but as turned on as I was, the effort was totally lame.

"I was rubbing your back." He moved his hand upward, then cupped my breast, and it seemed to fit perfectly. My throat tightened and my lungs burned. Breathing would have been helpful. "Now that you've turned over, I'm finding this to be a much better place to touch." Thumb stroking lightly over my nipple that now felt heavy and swollen.

"You can stop anytime you want to." I reached for his wrist. Before I knew what he was planning, he had me on my back, arms pinned to my sides, his hips pressed against mine and his weight holding me to the bed. Fighting him off seemed like a really bad waste of energy, but there was no way I was going to give in to the lust brewing in me.

"I don't want to." Lowering his head, he opened his

mouth over my nipple and suckled it through the satin of my shirt.

Men simply have no idea how good that feels or how instantly nipple sucking can turn a woman to mush. If they knew, they'd skip kissing on the mouth and go straight for the nipples. Whoever invented going from first to second to third base was stupid. Women need a long pause at second base before there's going to be any action at home plate.

I am so not a morning person, but this could inspire me to be one. That, and the feel of his cock pressed hot and heavy against me, making me wet in places that hadn't been moist in entirely too long. Morning testosterone levels had something going there. Get a little action in the morning and start your day off right. I'd take a good lay over breakfast any day.

Without a word, Sam released my nipple and moved his oh-so-lovely mouth to the other one. Struggling against him occurred to me again, but I simply couldn't find the resistance. I didn't know why he was there, but at that moment, I didn't care as long as he kept it up. (Well, you know what I mean.)

The alarm clock buzzed, and we both jumped. Sam raised his head and looked into my eyes. I knew this little romp in the park wasn't over, simply delayed.

"We have court in an hour." I hated myself for speaking aloud and breaking the aura of sexual arousal surrounding us. My mouth ached for the first touch of his, but it wasn't gonna happen today. Especially not before I brushed my teeth.

"It won't take an hour." He moved one of my hands

to his groin. Through the fabric of his shorts, I felt the
hugeness of his erection, and my mouth, as well as other
parts, began to water. I remembered sex. I simply hadn't
had any since my comeback. That was a long time to
go without intimacy, without satisfaction, without the
craving of skin to skin, flesh to flesh. The temptation
of him was nearly too much, and my resistance wavered a smidge.

"I know it won't take an hour, but parking is a bitch."
Distraction, that's what we needed. "We've got Epstein.
She makes Judge Judy look like a puppy."

"This is far from over." He pressed a hard kiss to my
lips and left it at that, then pushed off me and sprang
up from the bed.

"I know." Like a coward I ran into the bathroom
and slammed the door. Only frigid water was going to
keep me from unlocking that door and inviting him in.
Ditching my nightshirt, and tossing my panties on top
of it, I turned on the taps and jumped in.

I screamed. Son of a bitch, it was cold. But it kept
my mind off the hot man outside the door. Rushing, I
let the water run over my body. The goose bumps were
so big, I looked as if I had puckered nipples all over my
body. Great. As if two weren't enough already.

A quick rinse, and I was so ready to get out of there.
I dried off, wrapped the towel around me and opened
the door.

Sam stood there, rumpled and sexy, holding his
clothes in front of him. "You screamed?"

"Uh, yeah. Water. Cold." Squeezing past him wasn't

going to help my state of turned-on-ed-ness, so I waited for him to move.

"I hope you saved some for me."

That made me feel better. He had it as bad as I did. "I did, but if you scream like a girl, you're on your own."

With a nod, he moved back, obviously realizing the precariousness of touching me again. I stepped past him, and he entered the small bathroom.

I needed clothing and coffee for my armor. What's a woman without her accessories? Just as I reached for the coffee in the freezer, my phone rang, and I silenced the secondary alarm I had set. The Grim Reaper ringtone usually gives me a little laugh. Right then, I didn't care. I was horny and hungry, and that was not a good combination when there was a naked man in my bathroom.

Sometimes the gods were crueler than even they knew.

Somehow we got through that awkward morning-after feeling though we hadn't had a night-before to justify it. Kinda wish we had, but it could ruin our working relationship, and *that* we both needed, no matter how hungry we were for each other. We made it to court on time.

"Your Honor," my lawyer, Elizabeth Watkins, began. I sat behind her, and Sam was beside me. There were quite a few seats taken by people interested in the case, especially the family of the mentally ill killer. He, however, was not present, and I was grateful for that. "We'd like to introduce new legislation that is being presented in other states right now, which will help us toward a decision on the cop-killer case."

"Give it to me." Judge Epstein motioned it forward. The bailiff retrieved it, then passed it along to the old bat for review. She took three seconds to look at maybe the first paragraph, then set it down and folded her hands over it. We were hosed before we even began. She'd already made up her mind before our court appearance.

Dammit. If she's ever killed, I am so not resurrecting her.

"When the legislation is complete you may come back to my courtroom to petition for a reopening of this case, but until then, forget it."

In that moment, I hated her. Or at least her position on the issue.

"Your Honor," Elizabeth began again. I could feel the frustration pulsing off her. I wanted to reach out to her, to try to stop her, because we were not going to win this one right now, but I kept my hands clenched in my lap.

"Forget it, counselor. There is no precedent in *this* state, and I'm not starting one." She banged the gavel, and that was the end of that. Bitch.

Elizabeth turned to me, anger blazing in her blue eyes. Her hair was blond and done up in a French twist, which only made her eyes more prominent in her thin face. "Dammit. She didn't even listen." She slammed her briefcase on the table and stuffed the paperwork back into it.

"I know. This was a long shot anyway." I sighed and looked at Sam, who looked as irritated as I felt. That made me feel somewhat better, and I choked down my disappointment. Getting hopeful had been just stupid.

"This is the process for getting new legislation looked at here. We aren't the first state to have to go through this."

"California and New York have had this in place for three years without one single adverse incident. We're not in the backwoods, and she shouldn't treat us as if we're stupid." I knew Elizabeth hated that. Her husband had always called her stupid. She divorced him, put herself through law school, and when he continued to publicly demean her, sued him for libel. That was a smart woman. She didn't get anything out of him financially, but the humiliation factor was priceless.

"Let's get out of here," Sam said and stood. "I have something to show you. We can go back to the office later." He shook hands with Elizabeth, and we left the courtroom, our quest and our moods thoroughly doused and the morning had only just begun.

As expected, there were cheers and jeers to greet us on the courthouse steps. Fortunately, I was immune to most of that now. Nothing could compare to what I had been through in my life.

"Come on, I'll drive." I followed him to his truck, his really big four-wheel-drive truck. Don't get any ideas that Sam's got a little winkus or anything. Just this morning, I had had evidence to the contrary. Almost everyone, or every other person, drives a truck in New Mexico. It's like the token vehicle. Never know when you're going to have to haul something, or use the four-wheel drive to get out of a flooded arroyo that two seconds ago was dry. Here, even in the desert, we get floods. A storm in the mountains above Albuquerque can send your feet out from under you thirty minutes later, and you'll be floating down the river before you know it. That's just one good reason to have a truck around here. I stepped up onto the running board three feet off the ground, and hauled myself into the passenger side.

"What are we doing?" I trusted the man with my life and my firearms, but I wasn't certain about my body. This morning's incident had left me a little on edge. I was still aroused to a point the frigid shower hadn't curbed. Buckling up and staying on my side of the truck seemed like a good idea, so I did.

"Going to my grandma's place."

"Elaborate, please. I thought she left the house to one of your sisters."

"She did. The place belongs to Elena, but out of habit, it's always grandma's place." He looked my way, or simply checked for traffic on my side of the truck. With the sunglasses, I couldn't tell. He may have copped a visual feel while he was checking out the traffic. My nipples tightened as if he had.

I straightened and cleared my throat. "Did you find something? If you found journals I'm going to kiss you."

"Actually, Elena found them, so you might have to kiss her."

"Ew. Not on your life."

Sam barked out a laugh, and I felt as if we were back to our old snarky relationship. Maybe it really had been a dream. Except that there were two wet towels in my bathroom. Yeah.

"What's in the journals? Did you read any of them?"

I hadn't allowed myself to get hopeful, so this was exciting stuff.

"Down, girl. You'll just have to wait."

"Dammit, Sam." I punched him in the arm, even though he was driving. "You're taking all the fun out of having an anxiety attack. Don't make me shoot you so early in the morning."

"Only ten o'clock and you're threatening my life. You're ahead of the game, babe." He pulled onto I-40, the interstate that cuts east to west through Albuquerque. Or west to east, depending on how you look at it. In the western regions of the state lay vast high deserts and Indian pueblos interspersed with an occasional outcropping of the Rocky Mountains. To the east, past the city limits, the interstate winds through the canyons cut from the mountains by ancient glaciers, passes a few small towns, then straightens out in the high desert of eastern New Mexico, the badlands, and on into Texas.

We were headed west, to the old part of town where the earliest of the Spanish settlers created their lives. Not that I'm a historian, but I believe it's important to recognize and appreciate the cultural varieties of wherever you live. Here, it's old neighborhoods and even older superstitions.

After making a series of turns and losing me completely, Sam pulled the truck onto a dirt lane that ran alongside a large, relatively modern house by Albuquerque standards, and parked beside the adobe home. It squatted between a couple of ancient cottonwood trees with gnarled and scarred bark. It looked as if the larger house had been plopped down in what might have been a corral for livestock. A frayed rope, which might have once been a swing, hung from a high branch and drifted, caught by the wind or the push of an unseen hand.

"This is her place. Where I grew up." After cutting the engine, he sat a moment, looking through the windshield at the small house, seemingly lost in memories.

This was perhaps a greater task than I'd understood when I asked for the favor. "You okay?" Although it didn't take a trading of blood to understand he was bugged by being here, something else brewed in me that helped me see something was up.

"Yeah. Just been a long time."

"When was the last time you were here?"

"The day she died."

"Ouch." Guess that should have occurred to me before now. I tend to get a little self-focused at times. Like right now. The journals were right there. Fifteen feet away. I was almost salivating. Please, can't you suck it up a little longer for me? "Sam, if you're not cool with this, we'll figure out another way to get the journals." I was dying inside. There could be something in there about The Dark and how to defeat it. I needed there to be information in there. At some level, I knew there was information there. There could be information about how long I'll live as a resurrectionist, and why I don't get sick anymore. After my recovery the first year, I've never had a cold or been ill in any way. Maybe my immune system has been supercharged too. I just want to know! There could be so much in there that she wanted to pass on, but didn't have the opportunity to.

Or there could be no answers to any of my questions, and I was basing my expectations on a dream.

"Nope." He opened the door. "Elena's at work, so she left them on the table for us."

I followed his lead. If he said he could handle it, it was the truth. Small rocks crunched beneath my boots as we walked across the gravel driveway. The cry of a Mexican jay screeched overhead, the echo of its call ceasing suddenly, as if it had been snuffed out. A foul wind stirred the branches above and a chill fell over me, though it shouldn't have. This wasn't the weather for it. Something lingered here, and I didn't like the feel of it, even though I didn't know what it was. I wasn't precognitive, but something was literally in the wind. Perhaps I was just being paranoid, uncomfortable in this part of town that I wasn't familiar with, but a sensation, an instinct or intuition I hadn't felt before, nagged deep in my gut.

I recalled Burton's warning at that moment. Maybe we really ought to pay attention to that, rather than blow it off as I wanted to. I'd been dead once, so it's hard to fear more than that. At the next stirring of the leaves overhead, I expected to see a monkey that had escaped from the zoo or some sort of giant lizard hiss at us. Weird, but I couldn't shake the sense that we were being followed by some unseen force. I'd have to pay more attention.

"Jumpy?"

I almost jumped at the word. "I'm getting a weird vibe here. I know this is Elena's house, but something is raising the hair on the back of my neck." And twisting that knife between my shoulder blades.

He paused and looked down at me, considering my words, and his hand reached for the back of his neck. "It ain't just you, babe. I thought it was because I hadn't been here in a while." If I had been paying more attention to him, I would have seen the tension in his shoulders, the stiffness of his movements and the subtle alertness, as if he were sending out his own senses. I was glad that he and I were tuned in to the same thing.

"I think there's something here, Sam." I glanced overhead again, convinced we were going to be experiencing a boreal attack at any second. I hate monkeys, and if any had escaped from the zoo I was going to shoot them. The *Wizard of Oz* had scared the crap out of me when I was a kid. And the skeleton monkey scene in *The Mummy Returns* made me want to hide in the closet for a week. Nasty little bastards. Don't get me started on sock monkeys.

I hate monkeys.

The jingle of Sam's keys directed my attention away from my dreadful primate fantasy. We approached the home, which was probably one thousand square feet. And she'd raised four kids in this little place? I suppose they spent a lot of time outside running wild. Knowing Sam, I'm sure that was true.

Sam unlocked the door with an old key on his chain. "Elena never changed the locks. Felt like she was locking grandma out if she came back to visit, you know? The door was always open for us kids, no matter how old we were." He gave a sort of sad, sideways smile, as if he were remembering something bittersweet.

"Does Elena…see spirits?" How does one ask that question without sounding like a kook? Maybe that was the sense I had had outside, but somehow I doubted it. I didn't think his *abuela* was evil, just dead.

"No."

"That's good."

"She hears them."

"Oh." Not good.

"Sometimes she smells them. She swears she's smelled grandma's perfume, especially right after she died." Sam avoided looking at me while he said this, so I couldn't really figure out how he felt about it. Potential primate attacks were still creeping me out.

"Maybe she did come back for a while. I've heard stories of others being visited by the newly dead and fragrance was one of the indicators." Whether he believed it or not wasn't important. I was certain his grandmother did visit until she was ready to go to the nebula. A strong spirit like hers would have had more control than others. She's been around awhile, of that I'm sure. She had all the signs of an old soul. I just wish I had met her.

"She sounds like a wonderful woman."

"She was the best."

"So, you've never told me how you and your sisters came to be raised by her."

"No, I didn't." He gave me one of those sidelong glances I've seen him use on suspects he's annoyed with.

"And I take it you're not telling me now, either, are you?"

"Nope."

Who says I'm not precognitive? One of these days I was gonna get something out of him. One day I'd figure out how to get Sam-The-Clam to open up.

We stepped into a surprisingly modern kitchen. I'd expected avocado-colored appliances from the 1970s. The house had received an upgrade, and all of the appliances were white. Lacy curtains hung in the kitchen window, framing a wooded view of the land behind the house, bordered by the bridle trail. I could imagine Sam's grandmother on lazy weekend afternoons watching people ride their horses and thinking of times past. As I looked out at the beautiful scene, I could imagine Sam's grandmother sitting here, but I couldn't shake the effects of the evil sludge that tainted my skin. Something was coming for us, but I had no idea what. It seemed that entirely too many bad things had happened in a short time. Could there be some pattern to it? Was it The Dark again? I hoped we didn't have to find out anytime soon.

"Here they are." Sam drew my attention to a cardboard box on the table. It was stuffed with old journals, turned on end, spines out.

There were about a dozen notebooks of varying sizes and types. Some were old black-and-white composition books. Others looked like handmade leather volumes with fragile, yellowed pages in the middle. A fine layer of dust covered their spines.

"I'm almost afraid to touch them." I wiped my hands on my thighs.

"Well, I'm not." He reached in and pulled out about five of them at once.

"Sam!" So much for reverence and respect for our elders and their legacies.

"What?" He gave me such a man look. "They're books. They aren't going to bite you." He took two, gave me three and sat at the table. "Get started."

"You're such a charmer." I sat opposite him, and opened the first one. Anticipation swirled through me, and I was nearly giddy. I didn't do giddy, but if I had, that's what I would have felt like. Then my giddy bubble burst.

It was written in Spanish. With a sigh, I frowned and ground my teeth together. I was entirely too dramatic sometimes, but now I didn't care.

"What did you expect?" he asked as if he could read my mind. After our blood exchange, maybe he could. "Spanish was her first language, *gringa*. You didn't expect everything to be laid out, did you? You're going to have to work for what you want."

"Dammit. I can get by speaking the language when I've had enough to drink, but not with the written word." My mother is so disappointed in me. She's from Old Mexico, too, and enjoys an affinity for languages that has escaped me, even though I genetically belong to three ethnic groups. My father, who is the sole white guy of the family, attempted to learn Spanish, but always sounded like a backwoods drunk with a bilingual dictionary asking for another round. Perhaps I inherited my affinity for languages from him. *Dónde está la margaritas!*

I tried to glance over the first page, but glancing brought me nothing. Sam was right. I was going to have to work to decipher these writings. Struggling to hide my disappointment, I frowned harder, as if it would help, and focused on the words I knew. Didn't help. Too many holes.

"I'll make coffee. We're going to be at it awhile." Sam set about the task. I needed the caffeine to sustain my blood. Blood chemistry was a fine balance. I hadn't had nearly enough coffee this morning between rushing from the house and to court. Bastards, messing with my coffee addiction.

Journal entries ran together in front of my eyes after a while. Plodding on, I pulled a small notebook from my blazer pocket and wrote a few things down, but none of it really helped. I was so disappointed.

"There's nothing that jumps out at me." Except every word I couldn't understand.

"Sorry there isn't more here to help you." He waved at the stack of journals spread out over the table. "There are pages and pages of cooking, canning and preserving. I think she wanted to record the old ways, hoping we would use these someday, but we've all gone away from that life." He closed his journal and opened another. "I thought there would be something in this."

"Me, too." More often than not I'm afraid to hope. To hope means risking disappointment and pain. I've had enough of those to last a lifetime. "Would you mind if I took these back to my place for a while?" I could go through them at my own pace and perhaps learn something more, something not obvious to the casual reader.

This wasn't going to be an easy discovery. In the end, there might not be anything helpful in here. There might just be her *sopaipilla* recipe.

"Sure. I'll let Elena know." Sam was such a doer and a fixer. Frustration didn't set well with him. I could just imagine him riding hard on his sisters and their dates. Probably made their lives a living hell. That image made me smile, and the knot between my shoulder blades eased a little.

"I'll take good care of them. Promise."

Sam took me back to my truck. I transferred the journals and gave him a quick salute. "Later."

He went on his way, and I returned to the office. I called Roberto's parents to check on them. Juanita didn't answer the phone, so I left a message. I was sure they'd turned their phones off to find a little peace after what they'd been through. I hoped Roberto wouldn't remember a thing, believing that he'd simply been ill. It was easier that way.

Could this incident have been connected to the threat of The Dark? Burton seemed to have no clue how the thing was going to harm me, but maybe it could influence people. The Dark certainly seemed powerful enough to have an effect on people. Could this entity have influenced people to commit atrocities against each other in order to get my attention? I hoped not.

Chapter 7

Distracted by paperwork and irritated I'd forgotten to pick up coffee after Sam dropped me off, I answered my phone without looking at the caller ID. Normally, I liked that nanosecond of brain recognition to get all the cells moving toward the caller.

"Dani." I still can't believe I forgot the damned coffee!

"It's Liz."

Brain function came to a screeching halt. "Did she change her mind?" Oh, this was great news after such a sucky morning.

"What? Oh, hell no. This is something else. I've got a case for you."

"Oh, goody. Another gangbanger who hosed a bunch of his friends?" It would be fitting for today.

"No. A lot more complicated than that." She sighed. Liz rarely sighed like that, so I knew we were in for some serious shit. I was glad I was sitting down. "What is it?"

"A compassion killing."

"Dammit." I ran a hand through my hair, thinking of alopecia again, then rested my forehead on my hand, tried not to anticipate. "Tell me."

"An elderly gentleman killed his wife, who had been suffering from Alzheimer's for years. He shot her, called 911 and waited for the cops. He even took a video of it, so there would be no questions."

"Jeez." Can't imagine the gore.

"He read her medical power of attorney and her living will, said she wouldn't have wanted to be kept alive, and so he took care of what Mother Nature didn't."

"She's going to be awfully pissed off."

"Who, the wife?"

"No, Mother Nature." She's not one to mess with.

"Very funny. Will you take the case?"

We talked about the particulars. He'd plead no contest in court, sentenced to life, no parole and all that. He was ready to return his wife to the living if that was what she wanted, but if she didn't he was content to end his days behind bars.

"I'm going to have to think about this one." The space behind my eyes began to throb. Going blind. Need. Coffee. Now.

"There's going to be a huge amount of press, probably worldwide, on this, whether you take it or not.

You're the best one to do it." She paused. "There could be some good PR with the judge, too."

The caffeine headache I had was nothing compared with what this was going to be. "Let's have lunch and talk some more. I'm gonna need a drink for this one."

We met at my favorite lunch spot, kind of halfway between my office and hers. Nice shady trees overhead, great to eat *al fresco*.

"Albuquerque's going to be in the world focus for this one, and so will you. Are you ready for that?" Liz speared a piece of avocado from her salad.

"Hell, no. You're my lawyer. You can do all the PR, nicey-nice stuff, can't you?" Nicey-nice ain't in my bag of tricks, and I preferred to stay behind the scenes, rather than being out front like a cheerleader for the team. I wasn't very good with pom-poms.

"Sure, I can, but people want to know who does the rituals, how does she do them, what happens and all that crap. You know there are more resurrectionists out there who are too afraid to come forward. This could do it. We could turn this into the world's biggest reality show, but we won't." She held up her hand to silence me, knowing as soon as she said those two words I was gonna blow. I hate reality shows. The one I live in is bad enough.

"Well, hell." I swirled my *margarita de oro*. Next time I'd just get straight tequila and a long straw. "There's so much that's appealing about this case, but there's so much that's gonna drive me nuts, too." The PR alone could do it. I understood the need for it. I just didn't like it.

"I know you don't want to be the poster child of resurrectionists, but in this case you're going to have to be. Might even bring some closet resurrectionists out of hiding to help. There aren't enough of you here to present a united front to take on the judicial system." She leaned forward, her blue eyes bright with eagerness and righteous passion for her subject.

She was thin, but well developed, the epitome of a modern, successful woman. Sometimes when I look at her, I just don't know how she could ever have been an abused woman. Then I recall my own previous life and know it sometimes takes an earth-shattering event to bring about change in people.

"I know." I sipped the remainder of the drink and broke off a piece of tortilla chip and stuck it in my mouth, chewing slowly. This restaurant makes the most delicate, homemade chips in the city, and I adore them. Doesn't matter how full I am, there's always room for one more chip.

"Look at it this way—it could bring your business more recognition, more legitimacy and frankly more money. You can't do everything pro bono, like that kid's case. It's great for the PR, but screws your budget all to hell. You have operating expenses, and security doesn't come cheap." Reality check.

"Brings out more protesters, too." They've begun showing up lately. One here and one there, but eventually they'll get organized. There are the pro-lifers scaring people at family planning clinics, and we have the anti-deathers. Both ends of the spectrum are now covered. Yippee.

"Dani," she said with a slight reprimand. "Nothing's perfect."

"You're right. I know." I hate that. I perform the resurrections because they're the right thing to do and they right a wrong, not because I get piles of money for them, or immense recognition. I perform resurrections because the balance of the universe is truly in jeopardy. I owe the other-siders for returning me here instead of letting me die by violence. As I now knew, those kinds of acts only fed The Dark and gave it strength. In the early days of my recovery I had hated them for returning me, but time has soothed that pain to a dull ache, and for the most part I understand my purpose here.

"I had to take the Ramirez case. I couldn't not." Squirming in my seat a little, I fidgeted, not wanting to go into explanations.

"I know. There are cases that call to you, and you have to heed that call. That's what made you a good nurse, a loyal friend, and what's making you a great resurrectionist." She reached out and patted the back of my hand, then picked up her water. She knows some of my quirks and respects them, just as I respect her right to check each and every one of the five locks on every door and two on every window and the security system of her house four times before she can fall asleep at night. Some things we can't change about ourselves. We just accept them, figure out how to deal with them and move on.

"I'll take it. Who's funding it?" She'd mentioned budget, so I figured someone had to be putting up the cash for it.

"He is."

"What? He's funding his own life-swap?" This was a first and a rare surprise. Little surprised me anymore, but this was a shocker.

"He's ready to die. He has no quality of life, no family and few friends. He wants to go, if coming back can heal his wife."

Put like that, it sounded simple. When things sound that simple, they rarely are. "I gotta talk to this guy." Was he a nut job looking to go out in a blaze of glory, or could he truly be what he said he was? People rarely were.

Liz gave such a Cheshire cat smile, that I was beginning to think I'd been set up. "Good. We have a three o'clock appointment at the jail with him and his lawyer."

I had to admire her bravado. I laughed and for the first time all day, felt a little joy seep back into it. "What if I'd said no?"

"You wouldn't. Who else was going to do it?"

"Really." As if.

She grabbed the check and I let her. Next time I'll grab it. I finished what was left of my drink, then added sweetener to the iced tea I had also ordered and guzzled that down too. I'll take caffeine in just about any form today.

Surrendering my weapons, even if it is for a good reason, makes me itchy. I don't want to have to depend on others to defend me should the need arise. Given the situation, that we were meeting with an elderly man in shackles in the middle of the county jail, I should have relaxed, but I didn't. There was more to this case than I knew, and my radar system was whooping it up in my gut. It wasn't just the bean burrito I'd had for lunch, either.

Liz shook hands with the lawyer, but I refrained. The only lawyer I touch is Liz. "Mr. Vernon." I resisted the urge to call him Mr. Vermin, which was what he was. He took the most absurdly horrific cases there were to be had. Drug dealers, rapists and murderers were his norm. Don't know why he was on this case, other than for the publicity.

Introductions to the prisoner, Harold Dover, were made.

"What's your offer?" Vernon asked and placed his forearms on the table, laced his carefully manicured hands together and waited. I never trust men who have professionally manicured hands. I don't know why. Too much the perfectionists, I guess. Usually they're far from perfect, but like to keep up the illusion. My ex-husband was that way. Deliberately deceptive, so my hackles were up already.

"Our offer?" Liz scoffed, leaned back in the chair and extended her legs in front of her and crossed her ankles. All she needed was a cigar, and she'd look like a CEO in a bad movie. "I'm not the D.A. We're here to listen to *your* offer."

"Don't listen to him, ladies. He's an asshole," Mr. Dover said. He was gray of hair, of course, since he was in his eighties. Though soft around the middle, his arms looked strong and so did his hands. He wore silver rimmed glasses, nothing special. Clear, intelligent, amused blue eyes connected with mine. I smiled. I was gonna like this guy. Too bad I was gonna have to kill him.

"So what's your deal, Mr. Dover?" I asked. I know I'm supposed to be silent and let the lawyers duke it out, but I've never been the silent type. Opening my mouth has gotten me into a lot of trouble, but keeping silent hasn't kept me *out* of trouble either. Go figure.

"Please, call me Harry. My deal is that I'm done here. I've murdered my wife, and she deserves to come back to life."

"No regrets?" Curious.

A fleeting look of what could have been regret passed his face, then was gone. "I just wish I hadn't had to act."

"I see." I leaned forward, unconsciously mimicking the same posture as Vernon. Ick. So I placed my hands under the table on my lap. "You do realize this is no guarantee, right? There are rules about resurrections. You have to go through the psych eval first. We'll also consider your wife's disposition and mental state."

"She'll be better then, right? She'd be…normal again?" Eagerness and hope oozed out of him in a rush, as he clung to one thought. If she were better, it was all worth it.

I had to look away from him for a second and think how to say this. "Unfortunately, no. She would return to her former mental state with the dementia intact. The resurrection won't remove any medical conditions." Sad, but true. There were entirely too many high expectations by the family of the waiting-to-be-resurrected.

They got the person returned to them. That was it, but for most families, that was enough.

Harry deflated. The eagerness, the positive energy surrounding him, simply vanished. Damn.

"She wouldn't be better?" Though he asked me the question, he looked at his lawyer, who simply shrugged. The idiot didn't want to admit to his client that I was the expert here. I just love when that happens.

"No, I'm sorry. As you know, she was suffering. I can't in good conscience return her to a suffering state. What I can do is wake her up a little and ask her what she wants. That will satisfy the law and my conscience." I reached out to touch his shackled hands on the table. I wasn't supposed to touch the prisoner, either, but I wanted to read him. Some people, even the elderly, are master deceivers after a lifetime of practice, and the only way I can know for sure is by using my senses.

The second my skin contacted his, I was yanked into the death scene. He had been so calm, so sure in his convictions, I knew he was telling the truth, and I released him. Any more contact would pull me away from my control, which I will never give up. "Harry, I need to do some research, and then we'll go in front of a judge. It's not a simple request you've made." Not a slam dunk by any stretch.

"I thought it would be all right. She didn't want to live that way." He shook his head, and I hardened myself against the emotion in his voice. "We made a pact years ago, since it was just the two of us. We were going to look out for each other." He glanced down and cleared his throat. "I promised to protect her."

I stood, unable to bear any more. "We'll be in touch soon."

Liz followed me out the door, and I recovered my weapons, which made me feel much better. Once you're used to being your own personal security system, being without any part of it is like going out without earrings. Such a naked feeling.

Thinking is easier for me when I'm hitting something. Kickboxing is not just exercise. It's fitness for my mind. Saturday mornings are my favorite classes. Tom Ju, my instructor and owner of the gym I belong to, works my ass off, gives me time to work the body and the brain without asking me about my job. Focus is the key, focus on what's right in front of me.

Right now what's right in front of me is a very muscled instructor who doesn't give any regard for my gender or station in life. He tries to beat the crap out of me, and I give him the same treatment for half an hour. Exercise should always be this much fun. Otherwise, what's the point?

After a hot shower, I was ready to face the day, and it was only 10 a.m. What to do on a Saturday? Before I left the gym, I checked my phone. Something was nagging me, and it wasn't the muscle in my ass I pulled on that last series with Tom. My phone is a lifeline to my schedule. If I lose it, I'm hosed. What at first had been a complete annoyance has now become a way of life. I am so lame. A techno-babe.

The sound of skateboard junkies heading my way made me step off the sidewalk. I looked up, expecting to see Burton, but it was just a bunch of nameless kids whooping it up, and they sailed by.

"Waiting for someone?"

Startled, I flashed around and let Burton have it. I knocked him off his feet with a right-handed shoulder punch that hit him in the center of his chest. He landed on his ass in a heap. Fortunately, my phone was in my left hand or I could have crushed it. They are so fragile. "Dammit, Burton! When are you going to stop doing that?"

I reached down and helped him to his feet. For his advanced age, he's really not very smart.

"That hurt." He rubbed a hand to his chest and looked at me, shock in his eyes.

"Oh, shut it. It did not. I can't hurt you."

"If I had been truly human, that would have hurt. How about that?" He grinned.

"Fine, but you should know better than to surprise someone who has just left a martial arts studio." Duh.

"Oh, right."

"What do you want?" I stuck my phone back into my purse. In case I needed to whack him again I'd have two hands free.

"The other-siders have been observing the compassion-killing case and would like you to take it without hesitating. They are old souls who wish to return home."

Who says I can't shoot the messenger? I have a gun, and he deserves it. "I'm not hesitating. I'm considering all the angles, and since when do they get to tell me what to do?" That always makes my claws come out.

"Uh, since they're responsible for returning you."

He directed his gaze away for a second, as if he were listening to someone speaking in his mind. "They are old souls who are tired and need to return home to the nebula to rest and join their energies with the others. This fight with The Dark has only begun, and they are needed at home."

"I am grateful, but the decision must be mine to make. As always." Free rein on earthly decisions is mine and always has been.

"Dude, I know. I'm just giving you the information."

I'm so not a dude and despise it when I'm called one. My *chi-chis* may not be very large, but they are there, and they work just fine.

"Although they wish you not to take unnecessary risks, this one is vital to the old souls."

"Thanks. Now go annoy someone else. I have work to do."

"On a Saturday?" He tossed the skateboard down and was off again.

Yeah. There was never truly a day off for me. I had journals to decipher. The thought of asking my mother to assist me in the translation occurred, but that meant I'd actually have to see her and get a lecture I didn't need. A pain shot through my head, reminding of my caffeine quest. I'd think about the mother bit. Sam could always help me. He was easier to deal with than my mother, and better-looking, too.

I went home, got the journals and my Spanish-English dictionary and headed to the coffee shop.

In about an hour I was ready to tear my hair out. This so wasn't working. There was information here, and I knew it. I was going to have to call Sam a lot sooner than I'd anticipated.

"Where are you?" I almost screeched into the cell phone.

"None of your business, and why are you calling me on a Saturday?" He was in as foul of a mood as I was. Not a good time to ask a favor, but I live dangerously.

"Starting over. Hi, Sam, whatcha up to today?" The brightness of my tone was enough to make me want to hang up on myself.

"I'm gonna puke if you keep that up. I liked surly better."

"Fine. I need help." How's that for surly?

"Like I didn't know that."

Bastard. I could almost hear him laughing in my head, but keeping me humble was part of his job. "With the journals, I meant."

"I figured you'd be calling me instead of your mother. Dinner, tonight. You feed me, I translate for you."

"Done." He was so easy. Apparently, so was I.

"Six. Steaks on the grill, your place. Rare."

The line went dead. I pretended as if I had ended the call just to make myself feel better and shoved the phone into my pocket. I checked my watch. Time to get moving and get shopping. The kind of meat I had in mind ideally should be marinated for twenty-four hours, but I didn't have that kind of time now, so I was gonna have to pound the hell out of it with a hammer. That ought to make me feel better.

Sam arrived looking as if he'd stepped right from the shower, put jeans and a T-shirt on, ran his hands through his hair and got into his truck. Yummy. I love a man with good grooming habits.

"Where's the food?" He walked past me into the kitchen. He'd been to my place dozens of times, so it wasn't as if he didn't know where to go.

"Yeah, come on in, why don't you?" I slammed the door with a flair, just because I could, and followed him. I needed a beer, too, so I got out a couple of cold beers, quartered a lime, tossed a squirt into each bottle, then handed him one.

"Moving."

"What?" I blinked. It's rare that I'm caught off guard, but I had no idea what he was talking about.

"When you called, you asked what I was doing. I was moving my sister's house full of stuff. She bought a new house, and of course, being the only male of the family with a pickup, I get to help." He shook his head and muttered something ugly in Spanish. That I understood.

"Lucky you. Now you get to kick back, drink a beer, have a steak and help me."

I turned away to check the meat, and Sam slapped me on the ass. "Get me some food, woman. I'm hungry."

Yet another shocker for today. "Did you just…" Incredulous, I looked at him and gave him the stare I usually reserved for souls that were about to head to their graves permanently.

Sam laughed and sipped his beer as the look in his eyes changed to something I couldn't quite read, but might have been a flash of desire. I shook my head and headed into the kitchen. I gotta work on that stare. His immunity to it was growing or our relationship was changing, big-time. Not that it would be bad, but it would certainly be different.

Later, after a few more beers, a belly full of steaks with grilled green chilies on top, and *calabacitas,* a side dish of corn and squash with green chili and cheese, we finally dug out the journals. I hoped I wasn't placing too much faith in something I wasn't certain would be of help, but for a woman to have preserved journals like this, something of great importance had to be contained in them.

"I've placed them in chronological order, I think, but double-check." I gave him the first one, pulled a chair beside him and got out my notebook and pen. There was no way I was going to remember all of this stuff, so I had to take notes.

"Let's go outside. It's a nice night." He stood, took the journal and the beer with him.

"I'll put on coffee first." Always gotta have that damned coffee. Someday I'll wean myself off, but at that moment I was ready to drink it straight from the pot with a curly straw.

My house was down by the river. It was originally a caretaker's house in the back of a horse property, but the land had been divided some time ago, and I got the little cottage-size house. I loved it. Massive trees surround the property. There's no garage, but there was enough sun protection from the trees, and winters here are mild enough most of the time so I don't really need one. Evenings outside in the small yard are what make this place so worthwhile. The original owner had laid a flagstone patio big enough to have a party on, so I put a wicker set of furniture out there and called it good.

Of course, Sam headed straight for the hammock strapped up between a couple of trees, and flaked out. I had strung little white holiday lights around the perimeter of the yard, so it was festive as well as functional. I think I read that in a decorating magazine in a hardware store somewhere. Move over Martha.

Right now, all I could do was wait until Sam found something I could use.

Okay, so I admit it. I'm not a very patient person. I took the second journal outside with me to slog through, gave Sam a giant mug of coffee that matched mine, sat at the table and tried to work on my translation.

After being watched for several minutes, I couldn't take it anymore and glared at Sam. Hmm. He was engrossed in the reading and didn't look up from where he swayed in the hammock.

Weird.

But I couldn't settle down. Something kept bugging me, as if some perv was watching me undress. I looked over at Sam, the only possible perv in the area. His jeans remained zipped, both hands on the journal.

"You getting it, too?" he asked without looking up.

"Yeah." Sometimes we were so tuned in, it was scary. I was beginning to think the blood exchange had made us more in tune to each other. I positioned myself sideways in my chair in case I had to move quickly. My gun was in a shoulder holster today, so it was handy. Sam was armed, but didn't have his usual open display of firepower.

He closed the journal and stood. "Got any more coffee?" Though his eyes were keen and assessing, his voice remained casual.

"Sure. Come on in."

He pretended to stretch, and I stood too, waiting, watching, anticipating. My nerves were taut, straining and about to snap. Dusk was hovering, just minutes away. We'd be dead if we were attacked outside in the dark, and Sam without enough weaponry.

Sam took one step toward me and gave a nod to the trees overhead that began to shake violently, as if something had been poured out of the sky onto them. Mummy monkeys, I knew it! My worst fear brought to reality in my own backyard.

The sound, like the advent of a hard rain coming on, approached. The sky blackened, and the wind roared.

"Dani, go!" Sam raced hard toward me and nearly flattened me into the back door. Splatters of black rain hit, sizzling as it pounded the patio. This storm hadn't been there moments ago. I got the door open, and we burst into the house and slammed the door shut behind us. It was one of those heavy metal security doors, but had a window made of double-paned bulletproof glass. Nothing was getting through it. Not even the skeletal monkeys pressing their ugly little faces to the window. I was gonna have nightmares for sure.

"Get out of my yard!" I hit the glass with the heel of one hand, but they just turned away and headed for the trees. The things were really monkeys, devoid of flesh, and they were ripping my beautiful, lush yard to shreds. How could my greatest fear from childhood have manifested so hideously? The only answer was The Dark had invaded my fears and fed on them. Somehow, The Dark had been inside the place where I keep my fears locked away, and I hadn't even known it.

"What the hell is going on?" Sam caught his breath beside me and looked out the window. All we could do was watch as a herd of evil, skeletonized monkeys tore branches from the trees, ripped the shrubbery from the ground and bent my patio set into shapes it wasn't meant to be bent into.

"I have no idea. I had the same feeling when we were at your grandmother's place. Like we were being watched, and all I could think of was the monkeys from a horror movie." I looked up at him. Concern and confusion filled his dark eyes as he looked into my face. He looked at me as if I held the answers, but I didn't. We were lost in this together. We needed each other more than ever. I trusted Sam, but this was a whole new level we were heading into.

"There's been something going on since the Ramirez resurrection, hasn't there? Like someone's deliberately watching us and throwing things in our path." The tension in his shoulders changed, and his energy focused totally on me now.

"I feel it, too." I felt more than the danger outside the house now. There was danger circling between us, closing the gap.

His eyes searched mine, nearly pulled me into some deep place where you dance naked and pull the petals off daisies. I couldn't go there ever again. But I would consider a place where we were both naked and entwined in certain positions to achieve mutual sexual satisfaction that we had not yet explored. *That* I could get into. I let my gaze drop to his mouth and watched as he talked.

"Don't look at me like that." His eyes darkened, and his voice thickened.

"Like what?"

"Like you want me to touch you."

The heat of his breath fanned my face, and I didn't need any help in the heat department. Tension flared between us, grew taut, and I swallowed, wanting to stay in the moment.

"Sam, I…" I watched his mouth as I salivated in anticipation.

He leaned closer. "Tell me what you want."

Chapter 8

The man had a mouth that I'd like to have wander all over me. But not now. We had Mummy monkeys to contend with.

"I say we shoot them all." I was in the mood for it, too. Sexual frustration of this magnitude didn't sit well and needed some sort of outlet.

"Like that's gonna work against supernatural spirits from the underworld, or wherever the hell they're from." Sam snorted and took his shirt off over his head in one swift move. Obviously it didn't set well with him either.

"What are you doing?" My mouth had gone dry at the sight of his smooth, tawny chest. Although I had seen many a chest as a nurse, this one had me intrigued.

He held up the shirt. The back was filled with holes. If, indeed, something can be filled with empty spaces.

"It wasn't like this when I got here, babe. That rain burned. Didn't you feel it?" He turned me around to inspect my clothing.

"I felt something, but I didn't know what it was." Now, I was pretty certain it was his assessment of me that burned, not the friggin' rain.

"You have a few spots on your shirt and the back of your jeans, but I think I got the worst of it." He balled his shirt up and tossed it into the trash.

"The hell with the shirt, how's your skin? Turn around." His skin was covered with tiny wounds, and I cringed. "Oh, Sam! You need to shower and get that stuff off you." If raindrops burned holes in his shirt, they could burn holes in his skin. "I don't know what to put on them, though. Antibiotic ointment?"

"Baking soda and water." He turned around.

"How do you know?" I was the nurse here.

"It feels kind of like a bee sting, right? I read in the journal about an episode where she treated an ailment like this. She didn't mention acid rain when being attacked by Mummy monkeys, though. I extrapolated." He shrugged. "Can't hurt to try, right?"

"Smart-ass. Get in the shower, and I'll mix up some goop."

Burton and the other-siders had never mentioned anything like this. The frustration level I thought I had before was nothing compared with this.

I got the baking soda in the ugly box that couldn't decide if it wanted to be yellow or orange, and poured a bunch in a small bowl, then added some water and mixed. I added more water, then got it too soupy, so I had to add more baking soda to even it out. Guess it wouldn't hurt. Caveman chemistry at its finest.

I heard Sam leave the bathroom as I stirred the goop at the sink. "I used your scrubber thingie. Hope it was okay."

"Sure." I gave the stuff one last stir and turned toward Sam. "Christ!" I nearly got a case of whiplash trying to stop quickly.

"Nope. Just me," he said with a very male grin.

"You're standing there naked and aren't expecting me to say anything?" Tremors that had managed to remain hidden now found their way to my brain and turned it stupid. My salivary glands screamed in anticipation of taking a big bite out of him.

"What? I'm covered." He reached for the precarious knot of the towel around his hips. "But if it bothers you…"

"Nice try." With a smirk, I regained some of the sass and confidence that had momentarily evaporated. "Turn around and show me your ass."

"Gladly." Sam flicked the knot and dropped the towel.

"Sam!" I screeched and clutched the cereal bowl to my chest, spilling some of the goop down my front. "What are you doing?" The tone of my voice was unnaturally high, and I sounded like a teenaged girl who had gotten her first good look at a naked man. I wasn't far from it at the moment. I'd never seen Sam naked and wasn't sure I ought to be seeing him in such a state now. It could make our professional relationship a bit precarious. Interesting, but precarious.

"Oh, come on. You're a nurse. You've seen plenty of skin." He turned his back to me, and I swallowed.

"What? Skin?" Was I supposed to be doing something? I looked at my hands and saw that I held a cereal bowl. What was that white stuff on me? Oh, yeah. Sam's injuries. I looked up at what had once been flawless skin that had turned angry red, but at least wasn't as bad as his shirt. "The shower helped. I was afraid it was going to eat holes in you, but it's just red now." I wanted an excuse to touch him. I needed an excuse to touch him. Now.

Regaining control of my libido and my tongue that hung out of my mouth, I dipped my fingers into the paste and applied some to the speckles on his shoulders. His very defined, broad shoulders that I wanted to surround me. The muscles beneath my hands bunched, but other than that, he held still like a good little patient.

Continuing on to the marks on the center of his back, I applied the paste again, then down farther on his hips, then his nicely sculpted buttocks. Ooh la la. Mama needs a new pair of shoes!

The skin and muscles were firm and warm beneath my fingers. I licked my lips and swallowed. I hadn't had my hands on any man's buttocks in such a long time. I hesitated, trying to control the lust that seized me. I was a professional. I was a trained nurse.

I was so drooling over his ass.

"Dani?" He leaned both hands on the table and parted his feet. He looked as if I were about to frisk him. Sweat formed on my upper lip, and I licked some of it away. An image of him naked, hands cuffed overhead to the wooden slats of my headboard, hit me with an almost painfully vivid picture. A shudder passed through me, and I remembered to breathe. I wanted to reach out to him.

"Are you in pain?" I frowned, hating to hear the answer.

"Yes." The word hissed from between clenched teeth.

I grabbed another beer and gave it to him. "This might help. I have tequila or whiskey if you want." Frankly, the thought of a shot of tequila was extremely appealing right now. Anything to put out the fire smoldering inside me. If I didn't get it under control, Sam was going to be experiencing a sexual assault at any moment. As he chugged the beer, I reached for the tequila. I already had the limes cut, so I licked my hand between my thumb and first finger, and sprinkled it with salt.

My hands shook so badly I got salt everywhere. I drank straight from the bottle. Half the liquid drizzled down my neck and into my shirt. I was so not a shot drinker. Coming up for air, I bit into a lime and gasped as the flames shot higher. Note to self: never toss alcohol onto a smoldering fire, of *any* kind. "Oh, gods, that was good." I blew out a long breath and gasped for another one.

Sensing Sam's presence beside me, I looked up. He was standing there, all male, and naked, and gloriously aroused.

"Did that help?"

"It's not that kind of pain." He grabbed me by the shoulders and held me facing him. He leaned over and pressed his tongue to the skin over my breasts bared by the V-neck shirt I wore. He licked upward, cleaning up the tequila spill I made. I was paralyzed. I couldn't have moved if I had wanted to, and I certainly didn't want to anymore. I wanted Sam with everything I had in me, and he was in obvious agreement. The feel of his tongue on my skin was exquisite and made me want more of it. He roamed his way over my jawline to my mouth. My heart raced, staggered in my chest. My breathing was uneven in anticipation of more, more, more. I wanted his mouth. I wanted to taste him. But he didn't kiss me.

He licked the remaining salt from my hand, raised the tequila bottle and guzzled. I watched the muscles in his throat work as he swallowed, spilling much less of it than I had. With a wet slurp, he released the bottle from his lips and returned it to the counter. Apparently, he didn't need the lime.

He cupped my face in his hands and licked the excess salt from my lips and then swallowed, as if he were taking a part of me down inside him. That was the most erotic thing I've ever seen, and I was lost to him. Tipping his head back, he growled, deep in his throat, as if I were the most wonderful thing he'd ever tasted. When he looked at me again, I knew we were in serious trouble. Neither of us was turning away. Neither of us wanted to move. I don't think either of us could have.

Maybe it was the blood we'd shared or the emotions of our shared cases, but I sensed things in Sam I hadn't before this moment. Maybe he was just more open to me now standing naked in my kitchen. I didn't know, but I wasn't going to destroy whatever was going on by moving, or speaking. I craved him with every resurrected cell in my body and knew he felt the same. Unmasked desire sparked off him and torched something deep inside me, some female part that needed this moment. With him. Only him. I needed Sam's hands on me, his skin against mine. I needed to be a woman again for just a while, and I knew Sam could take me there. I trusted him. My defenses broke.

"We've been circling this moment for a long time," he said.

"I know. I know." It was a truth I couldn't deny.

My hands didn't know what to do with themselves as we stared at each other, so they drifted down and landed on his hips. The full contact with his skin was something I'd forgotten about trying to avoid. The instant I touched him, rockets of desire filled me, and my knees buckled from the power of it. I actually cried out from the intensity of feeling, emotion and unbridled desire scorching the air between us. If lightning had erupted inside the house, I wouldn't have been surprised. The vibrations were from somewhere deep inside him I hadn't known existed. He'd blocked them from me, and I hadn't even known it. I felt like an idiot standing there with my mouth hanging open, but I'd had no idea the depth of his wanting of me. And it was intensely arousing.

It reflected mine for him, that I had somehow, insanely, managed to suppress until this moment. There was much of myself that I didn't want to reveal to him. I had scars inside and out. I didn't know if I would ever be prepared for a man to see me naked again. The visible scars were evidence of my fight to the death and of my struggle for survival. The hidden ones, no one would ever see. Would seeing my physical imperfections douse what was going on between us? There was only one way to find out, and I had to trust Sam as I hadn't ever trusted any man.

"Don't fight it." He drew me closer. "I don't want to fight it anymore, either." Looking down at his cock, hard and straining toward me, I could find no deceit in his words, or his erection.

What could I have said? Let me rephrase that. What could I have said that wouldn't have been an outrageous lie? Denying what was going on between us had been amusing for a while, but now, there was no more denial I could rely on. He'd stripped it away as swiftly as he'd stripped away the towel, and he was as vulnerable as a man could get.

I looked at his mouth and finally, thankfully, he kissed me. He still had my face cupped in his large, gentle hands, and he pulled me to him by my face. Oh, the man knew how to use his mouth. Surprisingly soft, his lips covered mine, and he eased his tongue forward. Since my mouth had already been hanging open, this was an easy task. Responding to the silky softness flared my need from desire to outright lust.

A moan began deep inside me and surged upward. He touched me as if I were a precious thing, and at that moment, I felt it. For once in my life a man touched my soul. He opened his mouth wider and devoured me. After that, things got really hot, really fast.

My hands, the hands that had avoided touching Sam's skin for so long, now roamed over every inch of him that I could reach. Pulses of energy surged from him into me through my hands. Images of me, as he saw me, flooded my mind. He'd pictured me naked more than once, and his desire for me was overwhelming. He tucked me into his shoulder and leaned me back over his left arm. I was in a foggy haze of desire, and I knew nothing except for the feel of him against me and filling my mind. His right hand left my face and drifted down to my ass. His splayed fingers dug in and pressed the front of my crotch against his raging erection. I was so lost to him. My feminine body that had been dormant for years now pulsed to life. Surges of desire filled me. I was wet and ready for him.

Then, I really don't know what happened next, but it was good. Oh, it was so good. I was lost in him, simply lost to his touch, his taste and the smell of him. There came a point where there was no separation between us, and I'm not talking about the physical. It was almost as if we had fused our spirits together to form one being.

He broke away from my mouth and kissed a hot trail down the front of me. Tequila still dampened my front, and my nipples were cold and wet and so hard I thought they were going to tear a hole in my bra. He raised the hem of my shirt and used his thumb to drag the lacy bra down, revealing all of my B-cup glory.

"You are so beautiful." He watched his thumb turn my nipples to rigid points.

What can I say? When a man calls you beautiful, take him at his word, especially if he's standing naked in your kitchen. He leaned over and took one nipple into his mouth. If this type of torture were used on women, the secrets of the world would be revealed in short order.

I adored this man and what he was doing to my body. The rest of the world could take a number.

A bowl of oatmeal was more stable than my legs at that moment. While his mouth was busy, so were his hands—working at the front of my jeans. I wanted this man inside me. Or at least I wanted one very specific part of him inside me.

Then I realized if he got the jeans off me, he would see the scars I'd worked so hard to hide. They were hideous, and I did everything I could to hide them. His breathing came in harsh gasps as I clasped his wrists. Unable to put words to what I was feeling, I turned my face to his, and he rubbed his forehead against mine. Tenderness oozed out of him.

"I know, Dani, I know." He pressed his mouth against mine. "I'll keep your secrets."

I released his wrists and opened the damned jeans myself! It was such a relief to shove that zipper down. With a quick movement, he slid his hands inside the back of my jeans and cupped my bare bottom. In seconds, my jeans and panties were in a pile on the floor.

Sam picked me up, then parked me on the counter. I had to clutch his shoulders for balance, and the skin connection deepened the desire between us. Each finger that made contact with his skin pulsed with the heat of his emotions and shot into me, driving his energy directly into my body. He scooted me to the edge of the counter that was surprisingly level with his hips. I hadn't noticed that before. He stood between my knees, and my legs seemed to remember what to do. They wrapped around his lean hips and tugged him closer.

Oh, yes. That was right. "I want you inside me, Sam. I need you, now."

Groaning, he held me against him and kissed me as if he couldn't get enough. His arms strained with the effort to hold me still, his cock inching forward into my soft and highly sensitized flesh. I was dripping with moisture, and my feminine sheath ached for him to fill it.

"I don't want to hurt you." Precarious restraint directed his movements as he dug his trembling fingers into my hips. He knew that it had been a long time since I'd been with a man.

"You won't," I whispered against his lips and kissed him, teasing my tongue forward into his mouth, and luring him toward me.

Sam sheathed himself deep inside me. My head snapped back at this intrusion, and I gasped at the welcome fullness of him. Digging my nails into his shoulders, I had to hold on or I was going to explode.

Sam stilled, except for his breathing. "You're like a fist around me, so tight, so firm." He stroked my hair back from my face. "You're exquisite."

A rage of desire swept through me, and deliberately I placed my hands around his shoulders, pulling him against me. Tension, the really good kind, pulsed through me. The fullness of him satisfied something that had been lacking and I hadn't even known it. I hadn't had a lover in years. Now I don't remember why I resisted. Sam stretched my taut flesh to the max, and he began to move.

With each surge of his flesh deeper inside me, we became more deeply entwined in each other. There was a connection between us that somehow fused us. We were joined physically, and something emotional had taken over.

I dug my fingers into his shoulders, relishing the feel of his bunching muscles beneath my hands. "More." It was all I could manage. I needed more of him, harder, faster, deeper. He moved us against the door, and used his chest to support me. With his fingers clutching my hips, he let go of any restraint. Oh, by the gods, I needed this. Each movement hit just the right place. My flesh was on fire. Shots of electricity raced from my center, and I was nearing the rocket stage of the evening's program.

Sam's harsh breathing in my ear told me he was close, but at that second I didn't care. The next time he surged into me, I shattered. I dug my nails into his shoulders and screamed. I'm not normally a screamer, but at the moment, there wasn't a damned thing I could do to stop it. Not that I cared, either. Pulses of pleasure erupted. Jets of pleasure surged, and my sheath flexed, clamping down on Sam's cock. The longer he kept up the pace, the more drawn out my orgasm. Sam's cries joined mine, and together we found what we both needed.

Finally, the spasms of my body came to an end. We slid down to puddle together on the floor, gasping for air. At that moment I was really glad I didn't have a wooden door.

Sam lay back on the tile floor and dragged me with him. I flopped over his chest and listened to his ragged breathing and the erratic tempo of his heart. The pounding of my heart finally slowed, and I was no longer in danger of having a heart attack from excessive sexual stimuli. Then I realized he was lying on his injuries, and I tried to get up, but he prevented me from moving away. "How's your back?"

"Perfect. Yours?"

"Oh, I'm good." I smiled against his skin and closed my eyes. "Do you know what we just did?" I was incredulous. We'd just breached every professional barrier in existence.

"Yeah." I felt the rumble of a laugh begin in his chest. "I think we're going to do it again, too."

We spent the remainder of the night in my bed, naked and getting to know each other in a way we never had before. I crawled over every inch of Sam's body, and he did the same to me. The first time we made love in the bed, he turned on the lamp, and I wished he hadn't. As he kissed my breasts and worked his way down my body, I tensed, waiting for him to see the scars on my abdomen and run screaming from the room.

Instead, he kissed each rib beneath my breast on the left side and eased over my abdomen. With a tenderness I hadn't known know he was capable of, he kissed each scar, each stab wound, each imperfection that would never go away and was forever a part of what made me who I am. Tears formed in my eyes as I watched the way he moved over me, the way he touched me with his gentle hands. This man worshipped my body as it had never been before.

When I said he crawled over every inch of my body, I wasn't kidding. He moved down and opened his mouth over my flesh, and I nearly imploded from the hot feel of his tongue on me. Nothing compared with the feel of his mouth or the silken strokes of his tongue. The stubble of his light beard was an extra tactile bonus.

Sam was an incredible lover and took me further sexually than I'd ever been. I never knew such intimacy was possible. He filled me up and gave a part of himself to me that he can never have back. It's mine, and I'll treasure it no matter what happens between us. Some part of my heart that had been forever wounded healed a little beneath the care in his hands. I didn't want to love anyone, but with the connection between us, I was beginning to realize I might not have a choice. Something was changing for us both.

We woke up Sunday morning in a tangle of sheets and limbs. I think I was mostly at the foot of the bed, my head on his lap. I was mostly lying on my stomach, and I was exhausted. Happily exhausted and used up, I sighed. I opened my eyes, groaned and contemplated calling 911 for emergency assistance to get to the bathroom.

"You okay down there?" He hadn't moved, so I figured he was in no better shape than I was.

"Yeah." I cleared my throat because my voice sounded as if something had crawled inside and died. "Yeah. I'm good. Need coffee and steak." I turned my head and came face-to-face with an erection. "Uh, what's that for? I thought we solved the problem of inflation last night." Or was it this morning? "Do you need an ice pack for that?" I thought of the stupid commercials on TV for male enhancement pills. Sam certainly didn't need them. "You know, men sustaining an erection for more than four hours should seek medical attention." At least that's what the commercials said.

"I did. You're a nurse, and you handled it nicely."

I shifted my focus to his face. "I did, didn't I?" For some reason, I was really pleased with myself.

Then the phone rang and shattered the moment. I could actually reach the phone without having to move much, so I grabbed it out of habit. "Hello?" I listened for a nanosecond before squeezing my eyes shut. It was my *mother* calling entirely too early for a Sunday. I returned my head to Sam's lap and refocused on that enticing erection waving like a flag in front of my eyes.

"Things are cool here, Mom." Sam chuckled, but his eyes had turned dark and wanting when I touched him.

"Is someone there?"

Was someone here? "Yeah. I'm having a breakfast meeting with Sam."

His grin widened, but he remained silent. I adjusted my position so I could hold the phone with one hand and clasp his cock with the other. His grin faded and so did mine. "Have a good time, Mom. I gotta go or we're going to be late."

I clicked the phone off and tossed it onto the floor.

"Late for what?" he asked and his eyes drooped to half-mast as he reached for me. "Did I miss something?"

"Yeah. This." I crouched on my knees and opened my mouth over him. He was soft and silky in my mouth, and I swirled the tangy taste of him around with my tongue. Gripping his shaft firmly in my hand, I went down on him and didn't let up until he begged me, in a strange mixture of breathless English and Spanish, to stop. I love it when a man begs, especially when I have him where I want him. Moving forward, I straddled his legs and rose up on my knees. He reached for my hips and drew me closer. With my hips tilted forward, I sheathed him deep. We both cried out at the perfection of the movement. The ease with which he slid home assured me this joining between us was right. I was sore, but it was a good kind of sore, and my hips began to move back and forth, drawing out the pleasure for us both. I leaned back on my hands and clasped his knees. One of his hands moved between my legs, and his thumb stroked my clit in time with my hip movements. I was sweating. I was breathing hard as the tingles of pleasure quickly built in my pelvis. Each touch of his thumb on my flesh took me closer. Each stroke of his cock sealed my fate.

Releasing any semblance of control, I gave my body to Sam and the sensations raging between us. My hips moved faster as I strained toward release just seconds away. With his flesh filling me and rubbing against all of the right places, I crashed. Pulses of pleasure overtook me and spasms rocked my body. I clamped down again and again, milking everything I could from him. His fingers dug into my hips and pulled me down hard onto his shaft. I felt the response of him deep inside me.

Unable to remain upright, I drooped forward, totally wasted, onto Sam. He wrapped those amazing arms around me and squeezed me tight. I couldn't talk and neither could he. We were simply saturated in each other. Then we slept again, content.

Chapter 9

We spent what was left of the day, after a massive breakfast, reading the journals and trying to discover any hidden secrets in them, but there was nothing obvious. I have one of those industrial-size coffee carafes that's usually reserved for funerals or catered events, and I filled it with strong black coffee. We were going to need it for the rest of the day, and I just didn't feel like driving to the coffee shop this morning. Go figure. Didn't know if I was even capable of it today. There were always a few pounds of superior coffee beans in my freezer, so I used some of them now.

Since Sam's shirt was in the trash, I gave him an old shirt that looked better on him than me. It was from a martial arts competition and everyone had received the same outrageously large size. He filled it out better than me, but it was still too big for him. When we went outside to inspect the damage from last night, I was furious. My beautiful yard and private sanctuary had been destroyed by those foul creatures. "Fucking Mummy monkeys." I wanted to shoot something, but the little bastards were nowhere in sight. If they came back tonight, I was going to dynamite them if I had to.

Sam looked down at me, a bemused expression on his face. "Where in the world did you learn to swear like that?"

"ICU nursing." I shrugged. "It was a matter of self-preservation at the time, and I never lost the habit."

"You could embarrass some of the career military men I served with." He shook his head in amazement.

"Ah, you're just jealous I cuss better than you." I elbowed him playfully in the ribs.

"I am. I am." He returned to the hammock and opened a journal.

After a few minutes, the words began to make a little sense with the help of my high school translation book and an online application from www.babelfish.com. The words made sense, but putting them together into a context that applied to our situation took more finesse than I could muster.

"Hey, here's something." Sam motioned me over.

"What, what, what?" I felt like a kid who had just been given a birthday surprise.

"It's vague, but it does reference a dark being. I wouldn't call it an entity, but that's the feel I get. I think this thing has been hanging around for a long time."

Puzzled, I tried to read over Sam's shoulder, but it still looked like a salsa recipe to me. "Anything else?"

"I'll just read it. 'By the truth, by the right, by the power of the chosen will the being be driven back.'" Sam looked up at me. "It doesn't say defeated, just driven back or away."

"Hmm. Makes me wonder."

"What?"

"The chosen. Is that just me, or is it referring to other resurrectionists?"

"Doesn't say." Sam looked down. "I'll keep reading."

I returned to my spot at the table and sipped my coffee, hoping that the caffeine would inspire me to suddenly understand Spanish.

It didn't.

The day was glorious. We spent our time as lovers, discovering each other. A touch here, a glance now and then, and a quick brush of the lips. We were living in a balloon that was rapidly losing its air. Time was running out for us, and we both knew it.

"Tomorrow is coming too quickly." Sam looked down at me as he leaned against the counter. We'd come in for more coffee and were reluctant to leave the cocoon of the kitchen. "We have to go back in the morning." He tucked my hair behind my ears, then slid his hand behind my neck, inching me toward him. I tipped my face up.

"I know." I didn't like it, but he was right. "I know."

"You have to know that our personal relationship has changed, but our professional one has to remain the same or they'll pull me off liaison duty, and I don't

want that." He was intense. "I don't trust anyone else
to protect you."

"What about Romero? He's pretty good with a gun."

"What?" Intense, every muscle in him clenched. Testosterone oozed from his pores.

"Or how about Westlake?" He wore thick glasses
and was confined to desk duty.

"He couldn't shoot his way out of the men's room."
I was teasing him, but he wasn't buying it. He clutched
me tighter. "The only person I trust to protect you is
me. Don't forget that, Dani. Don't ever forget that."

I tilted my head to the side and held his gaze. "Why
is that?"

"No one but me." He dropped his gaze to my mouth,
and I had the feeling he wasn't just talking about protection. Taking a chance, I placed my hands on his face,
wanting to connect with this warrior. I wanted to know
what went on inside him, what made him so fierce.

"Tell me why. Why only you?"

Terror filled him. Each breath, each pulse drove the
panic further. I felt it throb into my hands, and I almost
pulled away. The feelings were so intense. Looking into
his eyes, the memory was right there, nearly on the surface, but he pushed it away again before I could pull it
out. Something had happened to him. He'd never forgotten it and never forgave himself for the aftermath
of it. He was young and people had died. I wish I could
help, but the image snapped away, and I dropped my
hands from his face.

"Listen to me, Dani. I'm the only one who can protect you. We're connected like never before." He couldn't

put it into words any better than I could, but I knew what he meant.

"I know." I felt as though I kept saying that over and over, and I was. I smiled and felt a little sad inside.

Evening had begun to gather on the edges of the horizon and pushed in on us. Pressing a tender kiss to my mouth, he parted my lips with the tip of his tongue. He explored my mouth gently and didn't take the heat any further. Then he lifted his head.

"I'd like to stay awhile and see if the Mummy monkeys return at dusk."

That made me smile. "I'd appreciate it." After all, he has bigger guns than I do. I licked my lips and drew away when my stomach began to clench. I didn't want to get too distracted. We had to end this thing between us now. Neither of us was prepared for more. I'm not sure we were prepared for what had already happened. "I'm wondering if it was a one-time thing or what. I'll ask Burton about them."

"Burton? What could he know?" Sam frowned and drew back.

Dammit. What a dumb slipup. What was I going to tell him? "Yeah, Burton." I sighed. I was going to have to tell him at least some of it. He deserved the truth. At least as much of it as I could tell him. "Grab your cup and sit down." I added a little more sugar to mine. I was going to need it. We sat at the kitchen table, and I kept an eye on the yard. "Burton's not quite what he seems."

"He seems like any dumb-ass skateboard junkie. So what else is he?" Sam sipped his coffee, but kept his sharp gaze on me. I'd not slip anything past him.

Not just because of the new level of intimacy we now shared, but because of the blood we had exchanged.

"He's a messenger, sort of my liaison between me and…" How did I explain them? The other side, the source of my powers, spirits?

"What?"

"You're not going to believe me, so I don't quite know what to tell you."

"Try me. I've seen a lot of things I never thought I'd believe."

"Do you trust me, Sam?"

"Of course."

The answer was too quick. I leaned forward, pressing him more than I'd ever done. "I mean really trust me with everything in your soul, know I would never deceive you."

This time he paused before answering, and I knew he meant it. "Yes."

"You know something really bad happened to me in the past that gave me the scars on my stomach." I hated even mentioning them. "I was kidnapped, and my child was cut from me."

Surprise and sorrow entered his eyes. "I didn't know that was you."

He squeezed my hands, offering me a silent support I needed. "Well, I truly died back then and something happened. It wasn't simply a light from the other side, but a presence appeared and fixed my body so I would survive and sent me back with a mission." I watched his eyes. He wanted to tell me this was all bullshit, but he didn't. He knew me and knew I wouldn't feed him a bunch of crap for no good reason. And he carried the blood of a resurrectionist in his veins.

"What happened?" The emotion in his voice almost made me cry with relief. He believed me. Until now, I hadn't realized how important it was for him to believe me. No one else knew my whole story, and it was a relief to share it.

"I was restored to a living status, rescued and survived. My mission is the resurrections. You've never asked questions about how this all started or anything. You just took the job as my liaison. You have no idea how I appreciated that. I didn't know if I could have answered any questions at the time."

"You were new at it, and I had a little information from my grandmother's experience." That's why he'd fit so easily into the role.

"Anyway, Burton is a very old being who comes in the guise of what you see. He brings information from the other-siders. It's not like I can call them on my cell. When Burton is in physical form, he carries one, but it only seems to work one-way. He calls me."

The rise of the wind drew our attention to the window and the trees beyond. They moved and swayed in the breeze like usual. "I don't get any weird vibes from out there, do you?"

Scanning the yard through the window, he shook his head. "No. Seems like it's going to be okay tonight." He looked down at me, his glance bouncing off my mouth, then returning to my eyes. "Call me if anything changes. And I mean anything."

Always the protector. Sam had his secrets that went

as deeply as mine. Someday he'd share them, but for now, pushing him wasn't going to help. One day he'd have no choice.

"Yeah, I'll call." I thought it unlikely he'd get here in time to help me go target-shooting for monkeys.

Then he stood, and our time together as lovers came to an end. Nervous and jittery, I walked him to the door. He faced it for a moment before turning back to me.

Without a word he reached out to me. With a gasp I reached for him, too. He pressed me against the door with his body, and I was so grateful for the hard feel of him against me one last time. His mouth was hungry for me, and I dug my hands into his hair. There was more desperation than passion in the embrace, as if we knew this was the end, and we could never return to that status of newly found lovers again. Though our status lasted only a day or so, I would miss it, and I knew he would, too. Asking him to stay any longer would just put both of us in more pain.

Finally, he pulled back, and I opened the door. "Call me." I knew that meant to call if anything weird happened, like the monkeys returning, or worse. I also knew if I called him to be my lover again someday, he would be there.

"I will."

Whoever invented Monday morning meetings, especially the mandatory kind, should be shot, drawn and quartered, their entrails flattened by a road paver. Having to be somewhere, awake and pretending to be interested at the revolting hour of 7 a.m. on a Monday, is a violation of the Geneva Convention. I don't care that we're not at war. My right to sleep until sunrise ought to be protected by something, other than my 9 mil. Glaring at the officer in charge wasn't helping, so I rose slowly and filled my coffee cup. When I turned around, Sam was sitting in my chair against the wall and closest to the door for a quick getaway.

Now was not the time to have a hot flash for the man, so I chose to lean against the doorjamb. Standing was a better option at the moment, since my tender parts were getting the raw end of the deal on a folding metal chair. Unfortunately, standing so close to Sam, his fragrance and his energy continued to draw my attention away from the mesmerizing topic. Whatever it was.

My cell phone rang and the Grim Reaper got a chuckle from the guys.

"Hello?" Trying to whisper in a meeting only draws more attention to you, so I stepped into the hall.

"Dani, it's Liz. I know it's early, but can you come to my office?"

I glanced at the stuffed conference room and considered my desire to return to it. "Uh, sure."

"Bring a box of coffee. You're going to need it," she said and hung up.

"Okay, then." I returned to the conference room and crouched beside Sam with a groan. The muscles in my thighs screamed in protest. I'm a kickboxer in good shape, but the kind of sexual antics I'd engaged in over the weekend used an entirely different set of muscles, and they didn't like it one bit. I looked up at him, motioned him closer. "Liz has something going on. I gotta go. Take notes for me, will ya?"

He smirked. "Sure."

"Thanks." I rose like an old woman with an arthritic back, then got the hell out of there.

Half an hour later, I had my bucket of coffee and entered Liz's office. "I'm here. Where's the fire?" I parked the coffee on a side table beside her own silly and insignificant drip brewer that cringed in the presence of real java.

"We're good to go with the Dover case." She sat behind her desk all perky and enthusiastic. She's one of those early-morning people, and I'm surprised our friendship has lasted as long as it has. I do want to smack her sometimes for being cheerful so early.

"Really?" I plunked down into the chair across from her desk and gave an involuntary groan.

"You okay?" she asked, concerned. Did I mention that she's bright and observant?

"Yeah." I adjusted my position and tried not to move too much more. "I worked out a little extra this weekend."

"Oh." She turned her attention to the files in front of her. "I thought you were going to say you spent the weekend having hot monkey sex with a certain sexy police liaison."

"Don't mention monkeys." I shivered with revulsion at the memory of them. I told her about the Mummy monkeys, but kept the rest to myself.

"Are you okay? They didn't attack you, just your yard?" Concern emanated from her.

"Yeah. Want to go shopping for new lawn furniture with me?"

"Maybe, but not now. Dover wants to bring his wife up from the freezer. How soon can you do it?"

I thought a second and couldn't come up with any conflicts, but checked my phone calendar anyway. "I'm good. I could do it as soon as tomorrow." I needed a night to rest after the weekend I'd had.

"The sooner the better, I think." She sighed, rested her hands on her desk and laced her fingers together.

"What am I not going to like?" I'm always suspicious when people take poses like that.

"Press release." She let out her breath in a rush of air and held up her hand to keep me from screaming at her. "I'll be there with you. I'll give the release myself, but you must be present, and you'll have to take a few questions."

"Oh, no. No freakin' way." My mood went from slightly sour all the way to vinegar.

"This is essential PR, and it must be done. The resurrectionists have a lot of supporters out there, but this case is going to hit a lot of people in different ways. We have to be very clear about the intentions of Mr. Dover and our intentions in bringing back the wife."

"Why?" I crossed my arms and pouted like a two-year-old. Liz was making me do something I didn't want to, and I hate that. She's one of the very few people who can make me do things without sticking a gun in my back.

"Because if it works, we can use the attention to get a decision on Vassar and Liebowitz."

I narrowed my eyes. Those were the two cops who had

been killed by the schizophrenic patient. More than any-thing, I wanted to know what was going to happen. They were good cops with families who suffered without them. Every month I received emails from the wives inquiring about the status of the case, and I hated to disappoint them forever. That niggle of morality kept coming up, making me hesitate yet again. I wanted them back, but could we do it ethically and morally? I didn't know, but if this case helped set that one to rights, then I would do what I had to do whether I liked it or not. I narrowed my eyes at her.

"Anyone ever tell you you fight dirty?"

"All the time, but I never believe them." She laughed and waved her hand as if such an idea was preposterous.

"You might consider starting." I scooted forward in my chair and instantly regretted it, as my gluteus maxi-mus screeched. I cringed again.

"You really overdid it this weekend, didn't you? Poor thing." She clucked her tongue in sympathy. "Why don't you go get a massage?"

I didn't tell her that I'd had a massage, inside and out. "I'll consider that."

"At least soak in an Epsom salts bath." She snapped her fingers and nodded. "Those old home remedies are the best sometimes."

"Yeah." I nearly choked. One of those old home rem-edies was what had gotten me into trouble in the first place. Baking soda and water, smeared all over Sam's back. I would never look at one of those ugly orange boxes the same way again.

"So, when are we going to do this dirty deed?"

"Three o'clock this afternoon."

"What?" I started to hyperventilate. "Why?"

"They can have it for the evening news. We'll set up an interview with Dover, so he can say his piece, then off to thaw out the Mrs. and ask her what she wants to do."

"Christ almighty—"

"You'd better watch your mouth around the cameras." She gave me a stern look and pointed her finger at me. "You need this, and the public support, or you'll never move forward. None of you will. Resurrectionists have made great strides in the past fifty years, but public support isn't where it needs to be. Above all, the safety of the resurrectionists comes first."

"I know, I know." I shot out of my chair and tried not to scream. "I just hate being on center stage." I paced her small office, and she let me do it in silence. We've known each other for only a year or so, but in that time, we've become very good friends, a friendship that began with mutual respect for surviving brutal experiences. Survivors recognize each other and form bonds that no one else can understand. "The restraint, I mean. Makes me feel like I've gone back to being Blake's wife."

"I know, sugar, I know." There was that sympathy again. "But you've grown quite a lot since that previous life, as have I. We've moved on, we've become stronger for our experiences, and we are never, *ever* going back." She came across the room, somehow managed to appear to glide on her stilettos over the carpet, and placed her hand on my shoulder. "You can do it. What's ten minutes out of your life? You can live with that, can't you?" She removed her hand and went back to her desk. "Now

get outta here. Go have a massage or go to the gym."
She handed me a card for her masseuse. "Be back here
at two-thirty, and we'll go together."

I took the card from her, grumbled the entire way
to my truck. I stuck the card into the cup holder on the
console. I didn't know what to do with it. Having someone touch my body, even in the most innocent of ways,
so recently after the way Sam had touched me, wasn't
something I wanted. I'd erased the smell of him off me
in the shower, but remnants of his touch lingered on
my skin, and I wanted that to last as long as possible.

That meant I needed to hit something.

Two hours later, I collapsed on the mat beneath Master Tom.

"You're off today." He reached down and helped me
to my feet.

"Yeah. I got something I have to do that I really don't
want to do." I could admit that to him. He'd understand,
make sympathetic noises, and I'd feel better.

"Resistance will get you nowhere. Is it a one-time
thing?" He gave me a hand, then hauled me to my feet.

"I think so." Gods, I hoped so.

"Then just do it. Putting so much energy into the
resistance takes away your energy for other things."
He grabbed a towel from his bag and wiped his face.

"I hate having to do things I don't want to." Always
had, always will.

"Don't we all?"

"I suppose." I parked it on the bench against the wall
for a minute to get hold of myself.

"Here." He handed me a key. "Go sit in the steam

room and sweat out whatever's bugging you. No one else is going to be in there, so put on a towel and drink a liter of electrolyte water."

"Thanks."

"Let me know if you need anything."

"Sure." I undressed, wrapped a towel around myself and went into the sauna. I set the timer for ten minutes, pretty sure that's about all I could take. Jets of steam filled the room, and in thirty seconds I thought I was going to die. Hot air scorched my lungs, and I coughed. After a few seconds the discomfort eased, and I was able to relax on the wooden bench. I closed my eyes, as secure as I could get in there, and tried not to think.

I must have fallen asleep or passed out. Although I didn't remember falling asleep, I startled awake.

It's in the yard.

A voice spoke very clearly in my ear, but I knew I was alone. "Is someone here?" The voice wasn't someone I recognized, so maybe it was just from my imagination or my semi-dream state. It was hardly surprising I'd fallen asleep, due to the lack of rest I'd had over the weekend. If I dreamed, I didn't recall it. Just the voice. A woman's voice. *It's in the yard.* Whatever the hell that was supposed to mean.

The timer had stopped, but I didn't know how long ago. Securing the towel around me, I opened the door. "Holy mother of Christ, it's cold in here." The AC was on in the building, and my skin nearly took off back into the sauna. Needless to say, I dressed quickly.

"Here's the key." Still shivering, I gave it back to Tom.

"How was the steam? Clear your head?" He stowed the key on a hook by the door.

"Yeah. I think." I frowned, wondering about that voice I heard.

"Something wrong?"

"Frankly, I'm not sure. I think I had a hallucination in there."

"You should have had more electrolyte drink first. Did you have any?" He glared at me, suspicious, and he was right. I'd forgotten.

"Uh, no."

"See, there's your problem. You can't take direction from anyone, even when it's good for you." He rambled in Korean, swiveled his desk chair around and opened a small refrigerator, pulled out two drinks and gave them both to me. "Drink them. One now, one in an hour, then two liters of filtered water."

"Thanks. What do I owe you?"

"Nothing. Just go do your thing you have to do and come back in a better mood."

I had had a free sauna and now two drinks. My day was beginning to look up. "Okay. Watch for me on the evening news." I stuffed one bottle into my bag and opened the other one. Kiwi-strawberry. Yum. A little sweet, a little tart, just like me.

"That's all you have to do? A press conference?" He laughed. "I can't believe they're going to let you and that mouth of yours on the news. They do have ratings, you know."

"Maybe they'll save it for the late edition." I cringed and shuffled out the door.

Chapter 10

I looked pathetic on camera, like some hostile Asian bodyguard in a bad martial arts movie. Black looks good on me and hides an abomination of sins, but in this instance, I looked skeletal. Fabulous. Here's the great resurrectionist, who looks as if she's just been brought back from the dead. Again.

I flopped back on my couch and wanted to ignore the phone, but I sat up and read the caller ID. If it was another reporter, I was gonna unplug the damned thing. But it wasn't, and I picked it up.

"Hey."

"Hey. Saw you on the news tonight," Sam said, and I could hear the slight rumble of laughter through the phone. With fiber optics these days, you could hear things you really ought not hear sometimes.

"Not my idea at all." Way not.

"I could see that. Liz did a good job."

"That's why I keep her around. If I depended on my PR skills, my business would have been dead in the water long ago."

"You were fine. You looked serious and respectful, and no cussing on camera."

That made me smile. "Thanks."

There was a small silence between us that wasn't quite uncomfortable, but might have been a yearning we both knew we couldn't give life to.

"Well, I'm going to head to bed." I tried not to think of him there, but the fragrance of him lingered on my sheets.

"No more monkeys?"

"None so far." I hoped to never see those little bastards ever again. I was about to hang up when something weird happened.

"Dani?" he asked when I paused. "What's wrong? I can feel it."

"I don't know yet, but something feels wrong in the house." I stood. A fine mist of blue-black smoke hung in the air. Something definitely wasn't right. "Smoke."

I hung up and ran to the kitchen, because that's where most fires start. Somebody always forgets something on the stove. But this somebody hadn't forgotten anything. That left the barbecue outside, but that hadn't been on since Saturday night. I could see it from the kitchen window. A fire raged in it.

"Dammit." I yanked open the door, ready to charge outside when instinct hit me. My gun was in my hand before I was even conscious of it. I'd almost committed the same blunder that had gotten me killed once. I wasn't about to do it again. That shook me more than the fire blazing away in the barbecue.

Backing up, I slammed the door and locked it. Someone or something was out there. The Dark. I hadn't felt the force of it until I opened the door. My cell phone was screaming at me. I'm sure it was Sam, and that blasted ringtone only added to the chill inside me.

"I'm here." I kept my voice low, not quite a whisper, and I hunkered down in a corner between the cupboard and the back door.

"What's going on? I'm on my way." It was Sam. I could hear the roar of his truck in the background.

"I don't know. Be careful. It's not monkeys, but something is out there and it feels…bigger. Badder." What could be worse than Mummy monkeys? Was this The Dark trying to get my attention again? If so, I was shaking in my shoes, and I hadn't even seen it yet.

"Call 911 on the house phone and then leave the line open."

"Sam—"

"Do it!" The line went dead. I didn't know if he'd hung up or if there was interference in the cell system. I flipped it to vibrate and shoved the phone into my pocket. If I needed it again, I didn't want it to be across the room from me. I flicked the kitchen phone onto speaker and dialed 911, briefly told the operator I thought I had a house fire and needed the fire brigade, but couldn't stay on the line. See? Tom was wrong. I can *so* take direction. Someone just needs to light a fire under me first.

Some people get the shakes during a crisis, some people cry and can't function. I become silent, very focused and deadly. I shake later. Whatever lurked out there was stalking me, and I was never going to be taken down unprepared again.

I moved to the wooden bread box on the counter and eased it open. Bread-schmead, my extra weapons are in there. Why have a broom and dustpan when you can stow a gun by the fridge? And a little derringer for close work should the occasion arise. I stuck that firecracker in the back of my waistband.

The crystal amulet around my neck warmed and pulsed red tones. It's never done that before. Great. I was just a beacon in the night, an illuminated target for anyone who cared to shoot me, but I wasn't taking it off. Ever.

I'm here.

What the *hell?* The words were a whisper in my mind. This was the second time in a few hours I'd had an auditory hallucination. I didn't know how or why I heard the words, but I knew Sam was waiting for me to open the door. I backed up through the kitchen and to the front foyer. Of course, I had a security window, and I took a look through it, just in case I really was losing my mind. I could barely make him out with help from the streetlight a few yards away. I didn't want to turn on the front light and blind him, or alert whatever was lingering outside that we were now opening the front door and it could trot right on in.

There are few home maintenance chores I do, but keeping the front lock and hinges lubed was one of them. The bolt slid back without a sound. Sam turned the knob and pushed. He eased inside, gun ready, then closed the door, and I locked it again. Thankfully, he didn't try to take over the situation, or I'd have had to shoot him, too.

He looked at me, and I inclined my head toward the kitchen. He moved to one side of the doorway, and I took the side opposite. I motioned to the window so he could see the fire in the barbecue.

"Smells like incinerated chicken."

"I didn't have anything in there that could catch." I was baffled.

"Is anyone there?" The 911 dispatcher's voice came through the speaker.

"I'm here." I glanced at Sam, and he nodded. "I don't think we need the police any longer, thanks." I didn't disconnect though.

Sam eased the back door open, and we made our way out. The smell coming from the barbecue was an odd mixture of ozone, charred hair and fried chicken. Maybe the monkeys were tired of being vegetarians and wanted to party.

Trying not to get too distracted by the obvious, we moved closer to the target, but still kept an eye overhead. The night was still. Still, not in a way that's just pleasant with no wind or bugs, but in a creepy way where you knew something was coming for you. Any second. The hair on the back of my neck raised and an instinct I hadn't known I had clenched in my gut.

Foul didn't begin to describe the smell of the new breeze blowing through the yard. Whatever it was hovered above the tree line. If black could glow, then this black being certainly did. It was like a glob of gelatinous energy. I didn't know what the hell it was, and I was pretty certain I didn't want to find out, either.

The crystal amulet around my neck glowed from red to a gloriously brilliant white, brighter than a welding torch. It blinded me, and I panicked. "Sam!" Whatever was out there was going to kill me, and take Sam along with it.

"I can't see!"

Hideous noises roared from the back of the yard and every hair on me stood up. It was like nothing I'd ever heard before, as if something was being torn into bite-size pieces while it was still alive. If evil truly existed, then it was in my yard.

"Cease your interference." The voice boomed, pushing away any other sound.

I nearly dropped from the noise and clamped my hands over my ears. Had I really heard that? "What?"

"Cease your interference and the balance will be restored."

Oh, I get it. "Trying to scare me into stopping the resurrections?" Though I was temporarily blinded by my amulet, I wasn't stunned stupid, too. This was the troublemaker from beyond. "Oh, just bite me." Showing your enemy fear only empowers them. Though I was shaking in my shoes, I couldn't allow The Dark to see it.

"You are indeed formidable." It laughed.

Seriously? It was laughing at me? "You sent your monkeys to destroy my yard, didn't you?"

"Indeed."

"When I get my vision back, you're dead!"

"What you fear will manifest. This is your only warning. Cease."

With that, the being or whatever it was, faded into the back of the yard and disappeared. My limbs started to shake. I was more vulnerable than I'd ever been. I didn't know what the hell was going on.

Oh, gods. *Sam.* "Where are you?" I called out for him, and he pulled me against him. I kept the gun down at my right side and clutched him with my left hand and arm as if I was never gonna let go.

"What happened?"

"The light blinded me." I opened my eyes and things began to take shape again. Trees and objects in the yard all had a white halo around them, as if I had looked at a camera flash too long. I hoped my retinas weren't fried. Being disabled was not in my agreement with the othersiders. We were so going to amend my verbal contract.

"It's your crystal. It's glowing like a solar flare."

I clutched the piece in my hand, but the light still emanated from between my fingers, engulfing us inside it. It was brilliant enough to reach every area of the yard and eliminate the shadows. Nothing could hide in that sort of illumination. Not even the evil thing I had seen.

Damn. "The door. I left the door open." Great. If something was out there, I just gave it an invitation to waltz right into my house.

Before we secured the house though, I had to see

what had been burning. It did smell like chicken, sort of. I looked into the barbecue. Someone had toasted a small animal to get my attention. Surely there were better ways of doing that. Coulda been a cat. Coulda been a squirrel or a raccoon. I gave a full-body shiver and sent healing energy for the unfortunate critter.

Now that my vision had mostly returned and the auras I saw were fading, we returned to the house just as sirens cracked open the silence of the night, and the fire trucks showed up.

"Dammit. I should have called them off sooner." I hated for them to make a wasted trip. The smell of smoke was thicker in the air, and I then realized something was happening inside the house, too. House fires smell different from other fires, and I looked through the kitchen to the table.

The journals were smoldering.

They were still in the box, but the stench of ozone and smoldering papers touched the air. "No!" I holstered my gun and took one step toward the box on the table when the whole thing went up in flames as if someone had dumped gasoline on it. There was actually a whoosh, and my hair blew back from my face. The heat of it made the skin on my face feel tight and crinkly, as if I'd been in the sun all day.

I cringed and turned away from the sight, and felt Sam's hand at my waist, guiding me away from the area. "Let's get out of here. We'll secure the house later."

"But the journals!" I looked back and the flames had shot up to touch off the curtains that seemed to melt against the window.

"They're gone." We both knew that what was in them could never be recovered. That thing out there in the dark didn't want us to finish the translations. That only proved to me there was something important in them we needed. Without a choice, we dashed out the door into the waiting arms of the firefighters.

In my previous life, I would probably have wrapped up in a blanket, sobbed on the driveway and watched my house go up in flames. Now I stalked back and forth and cursed with every breath I took. Amazingly, some of the Korean phrases my cousins had taught me as a kid came back now.

Glaring into the night, I watched as the firefighters extinguished the flames. I hated the violation of my home, what had been my sanctuary. Not by the firefighters, but by the blight that had entered uninvited. I'd have to perform a smudging of the entire place to rid it of the stench I knew would remain long after the dark energy had left. White sage is a sacred plant in the Southwest, and I know where to find it wild. That's the best kind, to pick and dry your own for your rituals. Always makes them more powerful. I was gonna need every bit I had on hand to purify my space.

"It's contained in the kitchen, Miss Wright." The chief, Andy Gonzales, gave me the report. "Seems to have stayed on the kitchen table and the curtains." He scratched his head. "Don't know why."

"Thanks, Chief. When can I get back in?"

"Not tonight, that's for sure. Sorry."

"Dammit."

"You really don't want to be in there tonight. Smells like hell."

"It smelled like hell before the fire started," I said and thought of the thing in the yard. It smelled as if it had come straight from some unclean place.

"Yeah. My wife's always finding something nasty in the back of the fridge. You probably just had something go bad." He scribbled on a clipboard, then handed it to me. I signed the paper, and took a copy.

"Go get your stuff, then we'll secure the house once you're out," he said.

In a few minutes, I had gathered my essentials: the guns and ammo from the kitchen, a toothbrush, sweats and clothing for tomorrow. Just about all a woman like me needed. And my pillow. I have a fierce reluctance to use any pillow except my own.

The fire trucks pulled away just as I closed the front door. The night seemed unnaturally quiet and dark after the sirens and lights faded.

"Want to stay with me tonight?" Sam asked.

"Uh…" How to answer that question.

"No strings, Dani. Just a place to bunk for the night." He took my gym bag and carried it to my truck.

He had read my mind. Dammit. There was no peace for me anywhere tonight. "I'm staying at Elena's. She's out of town for a few days."

"Sure. If you think she won't mind."

"Nope. Let's go."

I followed him in my truck.

Restless and agitated, there was no way I could settle down to sleep, so I dumped my stuff on the couch. Without a word, he grabbed two longnecks from the fridge, opened them and handed me one. "Hell of a night."

I looked at the clock on the microwave. "And it ain't over yet." It was just after 1 a.m., and I was wide awake. That's what adrenaline and endorphins will do for you. "You tired?" I asked him, wondering why we were staring at each other when we smelled like hellfire and were covered with soot.

"Nope. I'm gonna take a shower. Join me if you want to." He took a long swig of his beer and gave me a longer look, then moved away down the hall.

O-*kay*. So much for no strings. He didn't need them. All he had to do was toss me a look like that and my nipples puckered all by themselves. Traitors. My body had been sexually turned off until the other night with him. And now look at it. As hot and horny as a teenager with a new box of condoms. Yee-*haw*.

For several minutes I tried to focus on the event that had gone down at my house. I really tried to keep my mind off Sam naked and wet and fully aroused in the shower, water sluicing down his shoulders and back. Really. I did try.

It was the longest ten seconds of my life.

Then my mouth went dry. I was certain it was from simple dehydration, so I guzzled down the rest of my beer. It wasn't enough to get me drunk or even buzzed, so no worries that I was going to do something I normally wouldn't have, because I'd done just about everything with Sam already.

Except for a shower. Somehow we had missed that. The sound of the shower drew me down the hall.

Part of my personality is an insatiable curiosity about many things, life in general and what one particular naked cop looked like all wet.

Steam escaped through the narrow opening of the ajar bathroom door. Steam. It jogged a faint memory of my time in the steam room, but I didn't want to think about it at that moment. A fresh-and-clean smell wafted from the bathroom, and I had to admit that my hair and clothing held on to the gross fire smell. Sweat formed between my shoulder blades and broke out on my knees.

I pushed the door wider. Rats. Elena didn't have a nice clear shower curtain, but something opaque that distorted the view.

That meant I was gonna have to get a lot closer.

I pulled the shower curtain back about a third of the way. I knew it was steam in the shower, but I felt as if the sizzle between us had finally created real smoke. Time would tell whether there was anything else there.

"You have too many clothes on for a shower." He turned his face toward me. Oh, the man was gorgeous, all hot, and wet, and naked. Better than my imagination. My very own aphrodisiac that was legal and wouldn't make me fat.

"I wanted to inspect your back. Make sure there isn't any infection after the black rain exposure." If that wasn't a lame excuse, I didn't know what was. It was more see-through than the shower curtain.

"I've been meaning to make an appointment for a follow-up."

I removed my smelly shirt and dropped it on the floor. "No need for that, now." Modesty seemed like an overrated use of energy right now. Reaching behind me, I snapped the bra clasp open and it recoiled like a broken slingshot. The jeans and panties weren't much trouble.

After years of celibacy, it seemed I was making up for that lost time in the span of a few days. Now that my body recalled what it was to hunger for a man again, it wanted more, more, more.

Stepping into the shower, I was enveloped in a cocoon of heat, and steam, and hard muscles. Sam snapped the curtain closed and opened his mouth over mine. The smell of smoke permeated the air. It had to have come from my hair.

I pulled back with a frown. "I stink. Sorry." I reached for the shampoo, even though it wasn't mine.

"Wait." Sam took the bottle from my hands. He poured a dollop into his hand and returned the bottle to the shelf. Sensing his intention, I tipped my head into the spray and saturated my hair, then turned my back on him. The hot water blasted my nipples, and Sam thrust his hands into my hair, scrubbing and sudsing until the odor of smoke was gone.

His fingers massaged my scalp, and I closed my eyes to enjoy the sensation and to avoid any dripping shampoo. Now would not be the time to have my eyes burned out by hair care products.

Sam took half a step closer to me, and his cock brushed my buttocks. What a delightful feeling, to know he was as turned on by me as I was by him. Abandoning the scalp massage, Sam opted for a mammary gland manipulation. His hands fit my breasts, and he tweaked my nipples between his thumbs and fingers.

I turned and dragged his head down to mine. Sam's hands stroked me nearly everywhere, cupping my ass hard. My skin was alive from his touch and the stimulation of the water.

Making love in a shower is no easy task, but Sam handled the situation beautifully. He pressed me against the tile wall and I wrapped my legs around his hips. I was gonna have bruises tomorrow, but right now I didn't care. I just didn't want to have to explain a fall in the shower to paramedics. With his face against mine, his chest pressed to mine, he eased the shaft of his swollen cock into me. Hissing at the pleasure of him inside me, I nearly came at that very second. Plunging in and pulling out, Sam set up a reckless pace. Clutching his shoulders, I cried in his ear, "Take me home." And he did.

Naked, we slept curled together in the guest bed. Guess I didn't need my jammies after all. I dreamed about steam. It choked me, tried to strangle me. Then I realized Sam was draped over me in his sleep, holding me tight against him like a body pillow.

"Sam, wake up. You're crushing me." I tried to elbow him, but he woke too quickly and grabbed my arm.

He woke, but didn't move, just alert and tense, then he looked down at me. Inky darkness filled the room, but dawn was just creeping over the edge of the Sandia Mountains.

"What?"

"You're crushing me." I gave him a light shove. "I need my lungs back."

He accommodated my request, but didn't go far, just raised his weight up off me with his hands. "I meant before that."

I thought a second. "Before that, I was asleep and dreaming I was being choked to death."

He rolled all the way to his back. "Guess I was dreaming, then. I heard a voice." With a sigh, he eased me to his side. "We have a few hours yet. Go back to sleep."

I let my head rest in the hollow of his shoulder and stretched my left arm across his middle, my hand in full contact with his skin. The sensations were warm and comfortable coming from him. That didn't bother me in the least, but it made me wonder about where our relationship was going. Were we going to be sex buddies or was there more going on than we knew about? At the moment there were no answers, so I closed my eyes, a sigh on my breath. We slept that way until morning.

I cruised by my house to make sure everything was okay. I wanted to wait for the insurance adjuster, but couldn't. My stomach and dead people waited for me to fulfill their needs.

My cell was still on vibrate and scared the shit out of me when it rang. It wasn't one of those fancy text-until-your-thumbs-fall-off types, just a regular, sleek flip phone.

"What?"

"Down, girl. It's Liz. We still a go for the Dover case tonight?"

I'd wanted a night off, but last night hadn't been in the cards due to the fire. The feel of the atmosphere around me was a growing pressure that I couldn't stop. I was tired, but I could do the ritual, especially since Sam could loan me some energy when I needed it. "Let me check my phone again." Nothing. "Can you get him here before nine?" I paused and sighed. "We'll need to check with the wife, and it ain't going to be pretty."

"Yeah, I know." I heard her sigh on the other side. "She's been on ice, so she ought to perk right up, right?"

Perk right up. Yeah. With half her face missing. I wondered how the hell I was going to talk to her and ask her if she wanted to stay on this plane or go home to the nebula. Not that I had a *Resurrections for Dummies* or *Idiots Guide to Resurrections* book I could reference. Maybe I ought to write one for the others out there like me. That would generate some PR that Liz couldn't argue with.

"Call me when she's ready. Me and Dover's ass-wipe lawyer need to be there."

"Will do." I laughed at her apt description. "Liz, do you realize you made a joke?"

"Yeah, I'm hanging out with you too much." The line went dead. I switched the damned thing from vibrate back to my hackle cackle.

This wasn't going to be an easy case, and I ought to prepare more this afternoon. I tried to call Sam to let him know the schedule. He didn't pick up, so he was either busy or ignoring me. As he had no reason to ignore me, I knew he was busy, so I left a message. We were professionals and weren't going to let a little fantastic fornication get in the way of business.

Time to eat, so off to the Cooperage I went for a slab of rare prime rib. Seconds after I ordered, Sam called. "Hey, I'm gearing up for tonight. Can you make it? It's the Dover case. Nine o'clock."

"Yeah, where are you now?"

"Cooperage."

"Be there in ten." The line went dead. What was it with people hanging up without giving a proper sign-off? I might be abrupt, but that's just plain rude.

So I chowed down on the salad and waited for what I really needed. Less than ten minutes later sirens neared, and I wondered what was up. Since my life change and hanging out with cops, I've been acutely attuned to the sound of sirens.

Then Sam charged to the table and I knew what was up. He sat, picked up my glass of water and guzzled the entire thing, reminding me too well of how he had downed the tequila the other day. Down, girl.

"Thanks. I'm fuckin' starved." He motioned the waiter over. "Give me whatever she's having." The waiter nodded and headed to the kitchen. Sam peered at me. "Your eyes look okay, so what's the deal?"

"I needed flesh." Then I looked up at him, the inference clear. Of course, he sat there with a self-satisfied amusement on his face, and I had the good grace to blush. Slightly. Over the past week, I'd certainly had enough of *his* flesh, but it wasn't the right kind to sustain me for a ritual. I gave him a look. "You know what

I mean. Gearing up for tonight. Needed the extra load of protein and stuff."

I said *stuff* because the women at the table next to us were getting a little too curious. Though I have to agree, Sam makes a stunning table companion with his dark looks and commanding presence, they needed to mind their own business. It wasn't jealousy that crawled onto my back. Really. I'm certain it was just irritation at the disturbance. With a dark blue, nearly black blazer thrown on over those impeccable shoulders to cover his gun, he did indeed make fine eye candy.

But this was business. Totally business. I gave the women at the table a glare, and they looked away. Some people *were* susceptible to my glares, and that made me feel better.

"Do you practice that?"

"I do. Keeps the masses at bay, and I have fewer questions to answer." I chowed down a few bites, then told him about tonight. "Liz is going to have Dover and his lawyer at my office at nine. The wife should be ready by then."

"Sounds like a typical procedure. Why are you indulging in an extra dose of protein?" He speared a delightful-looking piece of flesh and smeared it in the steak sauce.

"Tonight's gonna be a giant energy suck, I can feel it already." I shrugged. "After the weekend, then the fire and that dark thing in the yard, I've got a bad feeling. I just want to make sure I've got enough juice to make it happen." I sighed. "It feels like there's one thing after another bombarding me and taking up a whole lot of my attention and energy. Makes me wonder if it's on purpose. If The Dark is going to make serious trouble for me. For us."

He glanced at one of his palms. His were healed, as were mine, but I knew he was thinking about when we had shared the blood for the Ramirez case. "I can help out again if you need it."

"I might. The last one kind of freaked me out." I wondered now about what the dark thing had said about my fears. If anyone died because of me or was injured because of me, I didn't know what I'd do. That was my greatest fear, and I think it knew it. Looking at Sam now, I knew I had to protect him if I could, but he certainly wasn't going to like it. He's the ex-military army Ranger cop who's decided to be the protector of the universe.

"Yeah, but you dealt with it, handled it, and everything worked out okay. Have you heard from that family?" The confidence coming off him was stunning. He truly believed in me and my abilities.

"Yeah. Once. Everything's cool with them. The boy's back in school, and has no memory of the event." I shook my head, amazed at the ability of children to bounce back from situations that would cripple an adult. I looked at the remaining food on my plate. It wasn't that my appetite went, but the reason I do what I do is because there are so many selfish people in the world. That hits me between the eyes now and then.

"You did a good thing, Dani. If the family paid you tenfold, it wouldn't have been enough. They have their child back, and that's more precious than you can imagine." His voice cracked. Family was very important to him. He'd lost his at some point and had never recovered. The intensity of him nearly glowed.

"I know. Believe me, I know." But I didn't know why *he* thought that. "What's that about?"

"Nothing." He clenched his jaw, and a flash of rage I'd never felt from him roared between us. Something was up with him, and I tried to reach out mentally to see what it was. I was either not good enough, or he blocked me from reading him. Again. His jaw worked for a second. "Just...you're not the only one with a past."

I dropped my gaze from his. That was the most he'd ever given me. Someday he'd tell me, or he wouldn't. Whatever it was, was obviously still painful and raw. Pushing wouldn't make that go away, so for now, I remained silent. Another time and another place.

"I know."

Chapter 11

"Who said there could be cameras here?" I nearly screeched. I hate that sound in my voice. It means I'm expending too much energy on things out of my control.

Liz pulled me aside. "This was my idea. If the judge can see the ritual and the results you get, she might sort out the cop-killer case."

"Dammit, you should have told me." I hate surprises. I mean really hated them. It's all about control, I know. "I need to be ready for stuff like this."

"Simmer down, Dani. All you're going to do is your usual thing. There is simply one extra person with a camera."

"And a light system to rival Isotopes stadium." That's our resident minor league baseball team. Popcorn and beer anyone?

"It's not that bad." She gave an exasperated sigh. "If the lighting isn't right, we won't have the best images for the judge."

I could see her point. I just didn't like it. "Okay, but if he gets in my way, I'm not going to be held responsible for anything that happens to him."

"Agreed."

Sam approached after Liz returned to the camera guy.

"I know you're not okay with this, but try to settle yourself, focus on what's in front of you."

"You're in front of me." It was a small attempt at a joke, and Sam did smile.

"The case, babe, the case." A quick surge of emotional energy pulsed from him to me.

"Okay. Okay." I closed my eyes and took a deep breath. There are times when I feel silly doing the things I do in front of others. It's kind of like having an orgasm with an audience. I was just waiting for the judges to flash scorecards.

So I stood with Sam shielding me while I prepared myself, which I knew was his intention. Ever the protector. He had such strength and I wanted to know where it had come from. But not now.

My ritual items had already been prepared and were lying on a red silk scarf beside the recently thawed corpse of Edna Dover. Liz, the camera guy, Stan, Mr. Dover and Vernon waited in a corner of the room. All were silent and anticipation hung heavy in the room. The only thing not ready at the moment was me.

So I focused on the crystal amulet hanging around

my neck and took in three or four deep breaths. My eyes opened halfway and I gazed at, but didn't focus upon, Sam's chest. The power in me simmered and then sparked through my veins. It permeated every molecule in my body and electrified my blood. Although my blood was already a living organism within me, now it became almost sentient.

Noise in the room fell silent, or the bubble of protection I created around myself pushed everything except the necessary elements away. After a nod from me, Sam moved away. I was ready.

Generally, I wear jeans, boots, a T-shirt and a blazer. For tonight I had felt a need for a ritual outfit more congruous with ceremony. So I had chosen a red kimono-style silk jacket. The pants were drawstring, made of silk that whispered across my skin. I was also barefoot, needing to connect as much as possible with the earth, though we were in the basement of the building in the cryo lab. It was close enough.

Reaching out, I pulled the drape back from Edna's face and tried not to react. Her face was a mess, so I wasn't sure how she was going to answer any questions. I walked a circle around the gurney and focused my energy, my concentration, on Edna's body and pulled my power from deep inside. I began to glow. Power drawn down from the universe, enhanced by my amulet, blended with the strange mix already inside me and fed by my connection to Sam. My body was the conduit through which the souls passed, but for now, I simply needed information from Edna.

"Peacemakers of the universe, hear me now. Help me

free the soul of Edna Dover. Tonight, spirits of those beyond, we gather to right the wrong done to this being. Hear me now, and let it be." A blood sacrifice is always required to open the portal between the worlds, but this night, it didn't need to be a big one. The dagger that had been given to me at the time of my recovery lay on the red silk and I took it, drew it across my forearm. A line of red immediately appeared. Shaking my arm, I flicked the blood onto Edna's body. "Take my blood offering and awaken, child of the universe."

I held my hands over Edna's body, let them hover about six inches or so away from her chilly skin, covered by a sheet for modesty. The first sign I had of some success was a twitch beneath the sheet.

"Edna Dover, spirit of the universe, I command you to rise and speak. Your eternal future and that of your mate requires this action." If you don't use the proper language and instruction, the dead simply don't know what to do.

I had to admit, it was creepy. The corpse sat on the edge of the gurney, and the sheet fell away to puddle at her hips, revealing her body that was entirely too thin to have been healthy in her life. She had been wasting away, as Dover had said. It took a few seconds, maybe half a minute, for her to blink her one good eye and focus on me.

"Are we speaking to the spirit of Edna Dover?" I always had to make sure, just in case some mischievous spirit had somehow made it through to jerk me around. Under the influence of the ritual, they could not lie.

"Yes."

"Edna Dover, you are required to speak only the truth."

"About what?" She tilted her head, focusing intently on me.

"That's my Edna," Harry Dover said from the other side of the room.

Edna sat up straight and took in a gasping breath. She had seen Harry.

"Your husband is accused of murdering you. We can return you to a state of physical being should you wish, but the spirit known as Harold Dover will be sent to the nebula and be no more on this plane." I know it's a lot to ask of a newly undead to process that, but on some level they understand.

"N-o-o-o-o!" she roared. Yes, she actually roared, because my hair blew back from my face. With that response, I was guessing she required no further explanation. "It's *not* true."

"Your mate has been convicted of a heinous crime on this plane. The choice is yours whether to return to a physical state, or to return in the nebula."

"We promised." The *s* came out like a hissing sound because the soft palate of her mouth was missing, but I understood her. At a deeper level, I understood what she meant, but had to clarify for the others and the damned camera.

"You promised to take care of each other and protect each other? Is that correct?"

Edna nodded.

"You do not believe that Harold committed an act of violence against you, but saved you by terminating your physical body so your spirit could go to the place beyond where it yearned to go?"

She hesitated, and her attention wavered.

"Is that correct, spirit of Edna Dover?"

"Yes-s-s-s."

"Do you wish to remain on this plane and return to your previous state?"

"N-o-o-o. Send. Me. Home."

Turning to the others, I tried to focus on them and not the brilliant lights searing my eyeballs. "Seems she's pretty clear about not wanting to come back." With that, I had fulfilled my part of the bargain, to ask and allow her to make her own decision.

"I told you," Harry said. It wasn't said with a smug attitude, but with the conviction of one who was certain at the depth of his soul.

"I know, Harry, but there is still the law on this plane to consider. You have two options, stay and live your days in jail, or go with her now." Although I'd never made that offer to anyone else, the words just came out of my mouth as if I'd channeled one of the othersiders. Hmm. Maybe that was part of my recent upgrade. I knew I could do it, I knew I could release him with a minimum of fanfare.

Harry glanced from me to her and tears filled his eyes. "I can go with her now?" Liz clasped her hands over her face, her eyes wide, and the cameraman's eyes widened, as well. Dover's lawyer stood stone-faced, and I couldn't decide if he was frozen with fear or he had messed his shorts. I turned back, expecting to see the corpse ready to attack.

Instead, what I saw nearly broke me.

Edna's corpse leaned forward, her arthritic and gnarled hands stretched out to Harry. She wept, and silent sobs convulsed the cadaver. "Let's…go…home."

Harold staggered forward, still shackled, and he reached out to her as much as the restraints allowed him to. "Don't worry, darling. I'll take care of you. I promised."

Those words brought tears to my eyes, and I glanced at Sam. These people, spirits, were so at odds to the relationship that I had had with my ex-husband, and I wondered what would happen between Sam and me. Could we find something even close to the commitment they had made? Harold was so dedicated to her that he even killed for her. Would Sam do that for me? The men of Dover's generation were dying by the thousands every day. They'd been through wars and depressions and knew what suffering was. Things that we who were born past the 1960s had little experience with. If we had hardships, they were usually of our own making. Sam stood strong and his presence reassured me. If there was a man I could count on, it was him. But I didn't know if I could give back to him what he needed.

These two had suffered and survived together. Who was I to keep them apart now? I focused deep again and clasped my crystal. I don't know why. Maybe I was hoping it would give me answers or could somehow connect me to the other-siders who had more knowledge than I did. I pushed aside my feelings, my emotions about my own life that had fallen into a deep, dark chasm long ago. What was important was the right now in front of me. This was the right thing to do. I knew it and they knew it. Make it so and let it be.

"I will return the spirit of Edna Dover as is her wish. Does the spirit of Harold Dover wish to return to the nebula now?"

"Send me home." He spoke to me, but his focus remained on Edna. There was nothing except love glowing from him. This man had done what he believed was in the best interest of another. Though the act on this plane was wrong, the intention was pure.

"Be at peace. Together you will return to the nebula." I picked up my dagger again. The feel was cool against my skin for a second, then it heated against my palm.

Edna returned to a prone position and closed her eye. The guards released Harold, who climbed onto the gurney beside her. I didn't want to pick him off the floor after he was dead. I wasn't in the mood for a herniated disc.

"Miss Wright?" he asked.

"Yes?" I approached and looked down on him as I had looked down at many patients in the past.

"Thank you for this. You don't know how much I appreciate it."

"It's my pleasure, Harold."

"Don't ever stop. We need this." I knew he meant more than just Edna and him. The balance of the universe had to be restored or humanity faced destruction. With dark forces like those I'd encountered running interference, my job was going to get harder. Other resurrectionists had died trying to balance the good against the evil. I couldn't give up, ever.

His eyes were bright with emotion and something else, maybe gratitude, but that certainly couldn't describe what I felt from him. There was something I couldn't interpret unless I touched him. "You are the only one who saw my plight for what it was. Thank you." Reaching out, he clasped my hand and kissed the back of it.

In that second I knew what he had been hiding from me at the jail.

He was dying. He was full of cancer. That's why he'd acted when he had, before he didn't have the strength. Sympathy nearly gushed out of me, but I choked it back. If I lost control now, I might not be able to go on with the ritual. My heart ached for the choice he felt he didn't have.

"Be at peace. I'll see you again, spirit of Harold Dover." I believed that. We souls had spent eternity roaming back and forth from this plane to others. There was an infinity to explore out there.

"Let nothing stop you." After that, he removed his glasses, folded them, and tucked them into the pocket of his shirt and relaxed. "I'm ready."

"Spirits of those beyond, open the doorway for these friends who wish to return to you." I sliced the dagger across my palm and shook the blood over both Edna and Harry. The droplets hit each of them. I held one hand toward them and one hand toward the roof. The portal inside me opened, and I closed my eyes in order to view the other-siders better.

"Our friends are welcome to return."

"Hear me now and let it be." I spoke the words that

would encourage the spirits to move through me and seal the portal until the next time. I didn't have to tell them what to do. They knew. This was their home, and they gravitated toward it as small orbs of purple-opalescent colors that evolved and shifted and changed.

They were visible to the naked eye as they rose from their bodies, then shot to the ceiling. That's when things went truly wrong.

Darkness exploded and blanketed the doorway just as the souls entered. In a flash of light, it was all gone. All I saw was the other-sider and my crystal glowing like a freakin' strobe light.

"What the hell was that?" I focused on the other-sider.

"The Dark has taken them." There's never any emotion from the other-siders. I'm not certain if they're capable of emotions as humans know it, but there was distress or something coming from the being.

"Why would it take them? I thought it just wanted to mess with me." I sensed it was related to The Dark being in my yard, but I didn't want to believe it. This was so out there, I didn't want to be a part of it, but like Harold, I was feeling I had little choice.

"The Dark. It has taken the spirits. They are the eternal stars of the universe and The Dark is taking them."

"And you didn't feel a need to tell me about this? Why would it do that?" My head was about to explode from the unanswered questions boiling in it. I was hyperventilating and stars appeared in my vision. If I didn't calm down I was gonna barf or pass out. Either was unappealing in front of witnesses.

"We had hoped it would return to the nebula as it should have, but it is growing more powerful. With each capture of eternal stars it grows more powerful." The being glowed gloriously bright, but it didn't seem to affect my vision. "Danielle Wright, spirit friend, you must help us." Its vibration hummed at a higher level, and the hairs on my arms stood out.

"I thought I was already doing that by restoring the *balance*." I wasn't out here knitting booties.

"Your efforts have not gone unnoticed."

"Well, thanks for *that* vote of confidence." Sarcasm was my deal, not theirs.

"Your inner strength and power grows daily. So does your confidence."

"I'm not here for a self-esteem boost. I'm here to help, because I *need* to help." Whatever was in me wouldn't let me walk away, but I was not sacrificing anyone for their cause. The innocent spirit of my child was enough. No more.

"We are aware."

"Then help me. I don't know how to help if this entity is more powerful than the other-siders." If it was, we were so cosmically toasted.

"We have sent you assistance."

"Yeah, Burton's incredibly helpful." I refrained from snorting. That wouldn't earn me any eternal brownie points.

"You are not alone. Look to your allies, and your source will be revealed."

Give me a break. Why does every question have to be answered with another friggin' riddle? You'd think after so many thousand millennia these beings would communicate better. I know, I know. I've read the parables about struggle, and I *hate* every one of them. No one said life was going to be easy, but does it have to be so damned hard sometimes?

With that bomb dropped on my head, the portal snapped shut and the ritual ended. The light of my crystal faded to its usual color, and all energy fell out of me in a long, tired sigh. My eyes closed and darkness seemed to swallow my brain. Sam caught me. As off balance as I was at that moment, if I had tried to walk under my own power, I would have landed on my face. How nice for the camera.

"You okay?" Sam held one hand on my shoulder, the other at my waist, pressing my weight against him.

I blinked a few times and nodded, trying to clear my head. "Do you believe that?"

"Believe what?"

"What just happened, what the other-sider said." Hadn't he been listening?

"Dani, we didn't hear anything. There was a big flash of light, and everything was quiet for a second, then you fainted."

"I. Did. Not." As if. He, of all people, should know better.

"You did. You were going over backward." He squeezed my shoulder and a surge of comfort pulsed into me. "Your eyes rolled back."

Ew. Definitely a neurological sign of loss of consciousness, though. "Didn't you hear what it said about The Dark?"

"It all happened in about half a second." He nodded to the others, who watched us, then leaned closer to my ear. "I heard it in my head, but to the others, nothing happened."

"Got it." I pulled away from him. I took a deep breath and braced myself to face the others. But first, I checked on the bodies of the Dovers. Edna was still a mess. Harold, however, was a different story. When some people died, depending on their physical condition and disease processes at work, they turned various colors after death. By the time I saw most people, they were either a waxy yellow with a hint of green, or purple. Harry looked as if he had simply gone to sleep and quit breathing.

I respected Harry for his choice. I wondered if I would have made the same one. "That's it then. I'll do the pronouncement for Harold."

"You can't do that, Dani. It's a conflict of interest. Or it appears to be anyway." Liz moved forward and motioned the cameraman to come with her.

Huh? Since when? "I'm a deputy medical examiner, certified by the state of New Mexico to attend deaths and make the pronouncements. I do it all the time." Then I looked at Vernon, who had a smug look on his face. Now what? Something else was up, and if I did the pronouncement of death, then I was not going to like it. Call it gut instinct, or whatever, but I didn't want to make this guy's day, so I listened to Liz. She didn't even have to argue with me this time. "Okay. I'll call the medical examiner, and they can take it from here." I looked at the rat-face lawyer, wanting to sneer back at him, but at the moment I didn't know what I would be sneering about, so I resisted. "What's your problem?" All I needed was an excuse, and I'd smack him. However, I did put down the blade in case the urge to use it overwhelmed me.

"Be in my office tomorrow morning at ten." Apparently, Dover's death meant nothing to him, because he was rocking back and forth from the balls to heels of his feet. At least some part of him had balls.

"Why?" I didn't want to be anywhere except my own bed at ten. We were nearing 3 a.m. now, and I was beat.

"For the reading of the will."

"Whose will, and why would I need to be there?" I was more confused than ever. Someone take pity on me and just answer a question in a straightforward manner, pretty please?

"Dover's. He left everything to you."

Why don't people ever do what you ask them to? That's all I want, just stick to the rules and everything will be fine. Take Harold Dover for instance. All I wanted was the fee I usually charged, to cover expenses, my time and expertise, with a little left over for a pedicure and a laser hair removal. I'm getting tired of shaving my legs.

Unfortunately, I was sitting in his lawyer's office. Sam and Liz were with me. Sam was supposed to keep me from assaulting the guy, and Liz was keeping me from doing something stupid, such as giving it all back. Both of those options would have been quite satisfying for a moment or two, but in the long run, bad for business.

I still wanted to call him Vermin, because with those small dark eyes that watched everything, he looked quite ratlike. I knew if I turned my back on him for a second, he'd pull a hunk of baby Swiss out of his desk and start nibbling. "The estate is roughly worth three million dollars," Vernon said without preamble.

"Three mill…?" I was stunned. "What am I going to do with all that?" I turned to Liz, cool as ever. Sure. It wasn't happening to her. Sam's brows twitched once. He knew better than to wise-crack me at the moment. Good man.

"We're going to set up an endowment. This is going to make headlines everywhere, Dani, and there may be others out there who might also like to contribute to your work." Liz adjusted her skirt that had ridden up. Vernon's eyes lingered a little too long on her. Rat bastard. "This doesn't benefit you personally, just the business."

"Thank the stars for that! What the hell would I do with that kind of money anyway?" I know, you think that's totally stupid, but truly, too much money has ruined many lives of people who weren't prepared for it.

"We'll set up a meeting with an investment guy I know. Don't worry."

"Thanks, Liz." I stood. Meeting over.

"Keep in touch, Miss Wright," Vernon said and handed me a business card. I took it, making sure I didn't touch his fingers. Who knew what kind of vibes I'd get from that guy? *Ick*.

We left the office and opened the door to pure chaos. Someone had alerted the media about our meeting. We were assaulted on all sides by camera flashes, people shouting at us and others throwing insults. "Come on, Dani, give us a minute," one of the reporters called out.

"Hi, Mike." I paused on the steps, and Sam nearly ran me down, but managed to keep us from embarrassing ourselves in front of the cameras. He stood behind me until he caught his balance. He was so close that I felt his gun pressing into my butt. At least I think it was his gun.

"We hear you're a wealthy woman now, Miss Wright. Will you now perform resurrections without the support of the state?"

"Now, where'd you hear that? I'll be continuing on as usual."

"You know my sources are protected. Is there any truth to it?"

"I'll continue to perform resurrections as long as the requests fall within current guidelines." Deep breath in and long breath out. I'd talked to the press just a few days ago. I could do it again without having a coronary.

"We'll keep you posted. Right now we're on our way to another appointment," Liz said. Sam took each of us under his arms and escorted us away from the gawkers and press. Trying to go down the stairs together was awkward, but after a few seconds, we arrived at his truck, and he released us.

"Jeez. Of all the—"

Three shots popped and a window on Sam's truck shattered. It was the middle of the damned day! Glass grazed my cheek. Getting out of bed so early had been a righteous mistake. I dropped and rolled under the truck, not caring if I was hit by a car on the street, but I was not about to be shot in the back by a coward. Whoever it was. With my right hand I pulled the gun and scraped the back of my hand on the pavement.

"Sam! Liz!"

"Stay under the truck," he said. From where I was, I could see him crouched by the front tire.

"Where's Liz?"

"She's with me," Sam said. She didn't reply, so I was certain he'd shushed her. Then I realized something else was wrong as the crowd scattered. The gunman was getting closer. Surely someone had called 911 by now. I focused on the guy who was trying to kill us. This was taking protest a little too far. I rolled again, coming out from under the truck at the tailgate.

"Come out, come out, wherever you are." A man with a singsongy voice called to us and every hair on my body stood out. There was something so sinister of the intent in opposition to the sweet voice, it gave me more creeps than I already had. I didn't recognize the voice and wasn't about to stick my head out to try to ID him.

Then I heard what I never wanted to hear again. The sound of someone trying to breathe through blood in their lungs. Someone was hit, bad. I didn't know who it was. I might be able to help if I could get out from under the damned tires, but the gunman was getting closer.

Footsteps approached, then hesitated. I got a look at a pair of scuffed loafers. And jeans. Not helpful. "Where are you, my little lamb chop?" Who the hell was lamb chop? It wasn't me, and it certainly wasn't Sam.

Liz.

No! This wasn't going to happen. I wouldn't, I couldn't let a spirit die because of my work. Dammit, I should have listened to the warning from The Dark, but how was I supposed to do that and live with myself? I crawled toward the passenger side of the truck and was able to scoot around the right rear tire, then duckwalk toward the front. I heard him moving around the front. Sam was gonna put a bullet in his brain the second he made the corner. If this asshole had hurt Liz, I wanted him alive so I could pound him into the ground myself.

The raspy breathing sounds grew louder as I approached the front of the truck. My stomach clenched, but I pushed it down.

"There you are, darling," he said. "I've missed you."

I came around the front. "Stop." The halt-or-I'll-shoot thing doesn't work for me.

Liz sat, legs sprawled out in front of her by the back tire. She looked like a rag doll that had fallen over and lost a shoe.

"Go ahead, shoot me," the guy said and raised his gun toward Liz. Before I could even think of blinking, a cannon went off behind me, and the guy dropped.

Sam surged forward, and kicked the guy's pistol out of reach. "Dani, you okay?"

"Yeah." I rushed to Liz, knowing that Sam was going to handle the dude on the ground. "Liz!" I tried to sit her upright again, but she was unconscious. "No, no, no, no, no." I tried to shake her. "Liz, wake up." Desperation clawed at my insides.

I holstered my gun and shot into E.R.-nurse mode. Once an E.R. nurse, always an E.R. nurse. First, I had to see how injured she was. Maybe it was just fright or a good scare, and she had simply fainted. As she turned from a sickly pale to a ghastly gray, I knew she was dying. Her head was okay, nothing in the neck, but blood pooled between her legs and puddled beneath my boots. I ripped open her shirt, heedless of her modesty. As soon as I clasped the fabric, I knew she was bleeding out. The blouse squished in my fingers. When I tore it apart, bloody splatters flew in all directions.

There was a hole, right over her left chest wall. It didn't look like much, but some bullet wounds don't. It was about the size of a dime with jagged edges. It gushed like a raging river. Her aorta or another major vessel was gone. My breath came in short gasps, almost matching her dying breaths.

I clenched my teeth together and tried not to scream. If I started, I'd never stop. "Liz. Stay with me, girl, stay with me." I pressed the palm of my hand to her wound, and that was a mistake. Her pain became mine, but how the hell else could I stop the flow of her life onto the pavement? The only thing I had was my hand.

Sam hovered close to me. "Help's coming. How is she?"

"Dying." From the tone of his voice a second ago, he already knew what I was going to say.

"If anyone can save her, it's you." He placed his hand on my shoulder and squeezed. He tried to push energy to me, but the emotion of it would undo me, so I pushed it back. Dammit! This had to be more influence of The Dark. It was fucking ruining my life, and I wasn't going to let it. Nothing was going to stop me from bringing Liz back. Nothing. Not even an unseen foe from the beyond. Somehow, I would find a way to defeat it, starting with resurrecting Liz.

My lips trembled and tears filled my eyes, dripping down to mingle with the flood of blood. I was so not a tough chick at the moment. "Liz, I'm going to save you. I'm going to bring you back. Don't worry." I whispered what I hoped were soothing words to her that I knew she would hear on some level.

My worst fears were coming true, and The Dark was winning.

She died in my arms.

Chapter 12

For the rest of the day, I was in a numb fog. I felt as if I was walking through chest-deep water. Of course, we had to give statements to the police. Several other people were injured, but only Liz had been killed. I didn't know whether to be thankful or outrageously pissed. The gunman was her damned ex-husband, Jerry. He'd never been this aggressive before, so I wondered if The Dark was somehow manipulating him, egging him on. Thankfully, Sam hadn't killed him, so there was a chance for resurrection and life-swap. Having known Liz as I did, she would have wanted the resurrection. Dying like this was not in her makeup, especially not at Jerry's hands. She'd worked too hard to get away from him and would never have wanted him to win.

When I was certain nothing more could be done for

Liz, I removed my hand from her chest, and held her, leaning against Sam's truck. I vowed to bring her back to life as well as the justice she deserved. Every victim like Liz deserved justice. The violated part inside me screamed for it for every woman, child or man who had been murdered. Every cell in my body vibrated at a new frequency, fueled by the atrocity playing out in front of me.

One paramedic crew looked after Jerry and whisked him away, lights flashing, sirens blaring to the hospital. Yeah. His life was gonna get saved. Until I took it from him.

Sam approached. I stood and dropped the blanket. I didn't even look at him, just started walking. "Get me out of here."

"Gladly."

We walked side by side away from the scene and caught a cab back to my truck, parked at the police station. I didn't want to go inside, to see the sympathy and feel the grief hanging around the office.

"Move over," Sam said and shoved me across the seat from the driver's side to the passenger side.

"This is my truck, dammit."

"Yeah, and I'm driving it." He held his hand out, and I reluctantly slapped the keys into it. If anyone else had said that, I'd have stuck my fist up his nose. But it was Sam, and I trusted him with my life, my firearms, my body and now, apparently, my truck. In silence we drove to my place.

"Everything's gone to hell, hasn't it?" I mumbled aloud as he pulled into my driveway. Crime scene tape was an obnoxious yellow color. Now, it fluttered brightly in front of my door. The insurance adjuster had been there and made his assessment, but I still probably ought to find a hotel. First, I needed a shower.

"Pack a bag. Enough for a few days."

"Why?"

"We're getting out of town. I'm on forced leave for a few days, and you need to rest after today." He turned off the truck, and we went inside. It didn't take long to shower and pack a bag. I had my weapons in one already, and I stuffed a bunch of crap I probably didn't need into another.

"Where?" I didn't much care.

"Zuni Mountains. My uncle has a place out there we can use."

Two and a half hours passed as we drove west on Interstate 40 in silence. Just west of Albuquerque there's a whole lot of nothing. The road cuts right through red rock canyons, then an Indian reservation, Laguna Pueblo. After that it's just miles of high desert until you reach the small town of Grants. It had been a boomtown at one time for uranium mining. Now, the old miners were glowing in the dark. They're dying of cancers related to uranium exposure, thanks to our government. When will we ever learn?

We headed south on a two-lane road that began to climb from around sixty-five hundred feet up over the Continental Divide to over seven thousand feet. Made my ears pop. Then down past the blown-out cauldron of an ancient volcano. The edge of it was still visible as we moved around the curves of the road that seemed to hug the land and move with it, instead of plowing through it like the highway.

Past El Morro National Monument we turned again, and by then the sky had turned a dusky shade, somewhere between purple and lavender with peach swiped over top. Sort of like melting ice cream, instead of sorbet this time, but without the calories.

Eventually, just as darkness draped its inky cloak over us, we pulled into the driveway of a modest adobe house. I stood in the doorway, not quite sure what to do with myself, so I shoved my hands into the pockets of my blazer and discovered my cell phone. It hadn't gone off in hours. I pulled it out to check for messages. None and no service out here either. There was a goddess.

Sam busied himself bringing firewood in, and he built a fire in the kiva in the corner of the living room. A kiva is an adobe fireplace built into a corner of the house, with an oval mouth where the wood burns. Cedar, mesquite and juniper are mostly what are found around here. "Tell me what you need. Wanna get drunk? It's too dark to go shoot anything now, but we can in the morning." The man knows me too well. Maybe that blood-exchange thingie hadn't been a good idea after all.

Anger and the need for revenge burned inside me and needed an outlet or it would feed on me. I felt as if The Dark was now influencing me. By causing my friend to be killed, it stimulated the harsher side of me. By putting horrific cases like Roberto in front of me, it tried to shake my confidence and my resolve. Now that I realized this, I was more determined than ever. With

Sam as my partner, we could be invincible. Slowly, I raised my eyes to his and found a tiny measure of energy pulsing to life. "I need to hit something."

"Why am I not surprised?" He removed his jacket and gun, tugged off his boots and socks, and scooted the coffee table out of the way.

"What are you doing?"

"A little sparring might improve your mood."

"My mood is fine." I clenched my teeth together, trying not to make that sour face my grandmother does when she doesn't want to take her medicine.

"Doesn't look like it to me." He poked me in the shoulder.

"Fine." I tore off my jacket and tossed it on top of his while he circled me. The man was sneaky, and he had military training, so I watched him closely as I shed the shoulder holster and the knife sheath on my left arm. And the derringer tucked somewhere you don't want to know about. The boots were last, because they were the hardest to get rid of. I bent over and pulled them off, tossed them and my socks beside the couch. "Is your uncle going to mind if we wreck his house?"

"We aren't going to wreck it. We're just going to burn off a little energy." He crowded me, arms at his sides. "Hit me."

"No." I couldn't just smack him. That wasn't fair. Backing up, I tried to get away from him, but he kept pushing me.

"Come on, Dani. I can take it." He bumped me again and knocked me back a few feet, but I recovered quickly. "Show me what you got, baby."

He'd already seen what I got, but that was a whole different kind of sport.

"Get away from me, you Neanderthal." I twisted to the side, but he anticipated and blocked me. Probably learned that shit in the military. And I thought I was gonna spar with *him?* I was out of my mind.

"What are you afraid of, *chica?*"

"Not you." I ground my teeth together. He was not going to get to me. I could hold my ground. I didn't care what kind of training he had. I had been dead and survived.

"Think you can't handle me? Think I'm too much for you? Without your gun you're nothing, and you know it."

He was trying to piss me off. Though I knew this intellectually, emotionally was something else. The fire in me burned brighter.

"Fine." I came at him, but he was quick, and I wasn't trying very hard. We'd never sparred together, so neither of us knew what the other was capable of. I had my suspicions that Sam was going to take me in more ways than one, given the height and weight difference. But I was pissed. At the universe, The Dark, the othersiders, but mostly at myself for not saving Liz. Anger can be very motivating. Or it can work against you. I was betting that it was going to do things for me. Anger boiled somewhere deep inside me like the ruptured volcano we had passed. I just hadn't blown yet.

"Come on, baby, I can take what you got, whatever it is." He bounced lightly on his feet, but kept his hands loose in front of him, and I looked for an opening. "You're such a girl."

That did it.

No one, not even Sam, called me a girl and got away with it. I went at him, kicking, jabbing, anything, but he pushed me easily away with a patronizing smile plastered on his face. Dammit, he was having fun, enjoying it too much.

"That all you got?" He came after me and had the unfair advantage of long arms and legs. With my height I almost held my own, but he had a reach I couldn't defend against. Each time I attacked he pushed me off. When he attacked I lost ground, and I sensed he was holding back.

Dammit. I was *such* a girl. Unable to penetrate his defenses, I groaned, and punched out from pure frustration.

I hit him right in the nose. He recoiled and bent over, grabbing his face. My anger vanished. Shit. I hadn't really meant to hurt him. If I broke that beautiful nose of his, I was gonna pay a plastic surgeon to put it back.

"Oh! Sam, I'm sorry. Are you okay?" I put my hand on his shoulder. I was such an idiot sometimes and let my emotions get the better of me. "Let me see."

Slowly he turned, then straightened. There wasn't a mark on him. "I'll show you mine if you show me yours." Before I knew it, he had me on my back on the floor.

I gasped, outraged. "You *cheat!*" Squirming, I struggled to free myself from his grip, but he only held me tighter. I hadn't known he was that strong, or I would have never engaged him in a spar. "Get off me."

"No." He took my hands and shoved them over my head. Just like that. So much for self-defense classes. I want my money back.

"Get off me. I'm not kidding." I was so not kidding, but I was so stuck.

"Make me."

Oh, I *hate* when people say that. I always feel compelled to try. Just as I was back in grade school getting into fights with boys on the playground. I grew up with boys, and the only way I knew how to communicate with them was by giving them a good wallop. That usually got their attention. Now, struggling, I gave everything I had left to Sam, but he didn't freakin' budge. Oaf.

"Give up?" he asked and trapped my legs with his.

"Never." I never give up. It's what had kept me alive. Never mind *want,* I'm going to *demand* my money back for those self-defense classes. They obviously had taught me nothing.

Renewed struggling on my part simply resulted in a massive erection on his part. This was not going as I had planned, so it was time to change tactics. "Sam." For a second I stilled to catch my breath. My heart was racing, and I wasn't sure if it was from the struggle or something else looming inside me.

"All you have to say is 'surrender.'" He grinned, knowing that word was so not in my vocab.

"Never." Struggling again was useless, but I tried anyway. All I succeeded in doing was grinding my crotch into his and making him grin wider. "I hate you!" Chest working too hard, I gasped for air and glared at him. I would not say the word. "I am *not* a girl."

He gave a low chuckle and allowed his gaze to trot down over my chest and back up over my face. "You certainly are not a girl. You're all woman. Every last inch of you."

The light in his eyes turned from playful to wanting. I allowed my gaze to drift down to his mouth, which had moved closer to mine. His nearness was intoxicating. Who needed tequila when Sam was around? I took a deep breath that left me in an unexpected, erratic rush. I was *so* not doing the emotional scene. I wasn't, I wasn't, I wasn't. It just wasn't me, but tears pricked my eyes and overflowed down into my ears anyway.

"Let it go, babe. Just let it go." His gentle voice unlocked the dam of frustrated emotions inside me.

"I can't," I said, my lower lip wobbling anyway. "I don't cry." As the emotions of the day overwhelmed me, I did indeed cry. Sobs choked out of me, and I made sounds I had never made before.

Liz was dead. Two eternal stars had been captured. Was The Dark behind Robbie Ramirez, too? The Dark wanted to force me to stop my work, but I couldn't. If I didn't give in, was Sam next?

Sam released my hands and legs and simply held me as I cried. Rolling over, I pressed my face to the cool tile floor and let it go.

Curled against my back, Sam held me loosely in his arms. Spanish words of comfort flowed out of him and soothed me, as did the gentleness of his touch. So many times in the past week I'd needed him, and he'd helped me, but other than satisfying his sexual needs, had I really extended myself to help him the way he helped me now? He had hurts that burned him deeply. Could I ease his pain? I didn't know.

Thankfully, it was mostly dark, except for the light from the kiva. I turned and sat. Sam sat, too. With only the firelight for illumination, I was glad it hid my messy face. I tried to brush the remaining tears away, but new ones simply replaced them. Without a word, Sam gathered me against his chest, and I let him. I was sort of sitting on the floor between his legs, leaning into his chest, and his arms curved around me. He soothed me, and rocked me, and for once, I didn't argue. I trusted him more than any man I'd ever known, and more than my libido was falling for him. Allowing him to hold me felt really good. No one had held me when I returned from the dead, and this embrace was an indulgence I rarely made.

"Better?"

"No." The headache behind my eyes was throbbing already, as if someone had stuck a screwdriver through my left eye. Raising my hand to his cheek, I turned his face to mine. The soft sound of his voice created a hum in my blood that had nothing to do with soothing. "Thanks." I gave him a soft kiss he accepted, and my blood warmed. I guess it was the contact of my palm with his skin that did it. For a moment I'd forgotten about guarding my palms against the contact. It could have been the emotional outburst, but whatever it was, I needed it. I needed Sam.

Sam cupped the left side of my face with his right hand. "Things are different between us since we shared the blood." He stroked his thumb over my lower lip, and I tasted salt on my tongue.

"I noticed." There was no denying that. Even when he wasn't inside me, he was inside me.

"I feel you in me, in my mind, sometimes. Faint, but you're there." He brushed my hair back from my face with his fingers, then tucked the mass behind my ear. It was such a sweet gesture, and the tears nearly returned.

I could only nod, as the experience had been the same with me. "I need you now. Can you feel that?" Clutching his shirt in my fist, I pulled him toward me.

"Yeah. I feel it. I need you, too. Like I've never needed anyone." He lowered his head and kissed me. Eagerly, I parted my lips for him, the taste of him. The silken glide of his tongue against mine turned the emotion of the day into the rapture of the night.

Soft and slow, he kissed me, seduced me with this mouth, and lowered me to the floor. My trembling fingers tugged at his shirt, and he pulled back long enough to whip the garment off. His gentle hands eased the hem of my shirt up and off, then worked the front-hook clasp of my bra. I love front-hook bras for this very reason. Whoever invented them ought to get a Pulitzer. Tenderness drove every movement, and he sucked my nipples. There's a little-known neurological highway that runs between a woman's nipples and her clitoris. Sam must have been aware of this secret, because he used it so well. He'd obviously paid attention in anatomy class.

Some women have been known to orgasm from nipple stimulation alone, and I was well on my way.

The rest of our clothing fell away as we undressed each other, touching, teasing, relearning the shape and feel of each other. He was a sight to behold as I lay back, and he moved over me. The firelight illuminated his face, but left shadows of mystery. I wanted his weight on me, I wanted his sweat dripping on me, I wanted him buried deep inside me. I needed it. I needed him. Now.

I parted my legs and reached for his erection, guiding him to my center. He was hot and hard in my hand, and I stroked my thumb over the peak of him. He was ready and so was I. Sam eased into me. Parting my feminine flesh, he joined with me at last, and I sighed as he filled me, filling parts of me I hadn't known were empty.

"Surrender," I sighed into his mouth. The fire that had just raged within me now burned slow and white hot. He kissed me again, and there were no more words between us. I tightened my legs around him, pulling him deep. The fire flared brighter inside me, flashed to a critical point. The fire in the kiva sparked, and then I did. The quick wave of pleasure took me, caught me by surprise, and I gave in to it. It crested and crashed, dragging me under with it. My cries were smothered beneath Sam's mouth, and soon his cries mingled with mine. Together we came, pulsing to a rhythm shared by the ancients that only deepened with the night.

"You didn't let me finish." Sam raised his head.

"I beg your pardon." I wiggled my hips. "I believe you finished quite nicely."

"Not what I meant." He remained joined with me,

but eased some of his weight up with his hands. "When I said I could hear you in my mind sometimes."

"Oh, that. How silly of me." A flaming orgasm just makes me giddy. So sue me.

Now, he eased back and settled beside me. "Like when you opened the portal at the Dover ritual and I heard the other-sider speak to you."

I sat up, reluctantly coming back to the real world, and curled my feet under me. Being naked in front of Sam was no longer so frightening. And it was still quite dark, so my scars were mostly hidden.

"The others were there and nobody else saw or heard anything." He shrugged. "But I did."

"Do you know what this means?" Reaching out, I stroked my hand down one strong shoulder and over his arm. Little sparks flashed from him to me, but they were only pulses of good feelings.

"No, do you?"

"Hell, no. But I'm hoping that together we can learn more about what's going on. You have cop instincts I just don't have, and I have an unfortunate learning experience that you don't. Together we might be able to pool our power and take back the eternal stars." Oh, this was exciting stuff! The Dovers might not be done for just yet.

Sam paused for a second, looked away from me, then back. "About that unfortunate learning experience. You told me about how you died." He stroked a hand down my back and rested it on my hip, as if he liked the feel of my skin beneath his. "Do you think it would help for me to know all of the details?"

That was a change of topic I hadn't expected, and I swallowed down the anxiety that immediately tried to surge up my throat. It was my turn to hesitate. I looked at him, considering. "You ask me to share my secrets, but I don't know any of yours."

He pulled back. "Nothing about me will help save the Dovers."

"How do you know? This universal imbalance didn't just start with me. It's been going on since time began probably."

"I've probably done more to harm than balance the scales," he said and looked away. He was withdrawing. I felt it inside me, and I reached out to him.

"Don't leave me, Sam. Don't leave." Panic flared, but I shoved it down. "We're together for a reason. I know it."

"I'm not going anywhere," he said, but his jaw was still clenched, eyes guarded.

"If I've overstepped my boundaries, I'm sorry." I shoved a hand through my hair, wanting to push him a little. "There's so much about you I don't know. We're off balance, and I'm beginning to realize there needs to be balance in any relationship."

"Ask me whatever you want, but it won't help." He clenched his jaw and a muscle twitched in it. Although he hated that I was asking, he would answer me, tell me the truth of him. For now, that was enough.

"Will you tell me about your pain someday? I know you have it. I feel it inside me sometimes, but you always push it back."

The look in his eyes pulled me in. There was pain

there and also relief. Sharing a story takes the sting out of some things.

"Yes."

I've shared more with this man than any other. He knows me better than anyone, knows me as well as I allow anyone to know me. There are some secrets that are mine alone to keep, but he knows me.

This moment, this request from him, although not couched in those terms, was about trust. Did I trust him with my past, with what could get me killed? I did, but did he trust me?

He did. I know he did, but some pain is too deep to ever recover from.

We sat entwined in each other, still naked, but warmed by the fire. So I told him everything. The kidnapping, having my child cut out of me, his death, my death, and then meeting with the other-sider who healed me.

"You know pretty much the rest. Survived, hospitalization and recovery, then focused on weapons training, martial arts and opening the business." I shrugged. Some of it seemed too long ago. "It made me a completely different person than I had been." There was no shame in any of it. No apology for who I had been or who I am now.

Sam cupped my face in his hands and made me look up him. He was so intense, so serious, and I was surprised at the ferocity of him. A flash of memory that I knew wasn't mine surfaced. Firefight in a jungle. Bombs screeching overhead. The weight of another slung over my shoulder. More death than one could imagine. For a second I was sucked into the noise and assaulted by the smells, then Sam's voice brought me out of it. "I will never, *ever* call you a girl again."

"If you do, I'll bust your ass. No one calls me a girl and gets away with it." I gave him a playful slug in the chest as the memory faded. Protecting my hands against touching him again, I kept a loose fist. Not that I'd have hurt him anyway. He's such a rock.

"You have my apology."

"Apology not necessary, but accepted." I stood and stretched. Sitting on a tile floor for too long makes my bones ache.

"Oh!" Turning, I stared at him a second. Something just occurred to me. "Do you remember when I stayed with you the night of the fire? We woke up dreaming early in the morning."

"Yeah. What about it?" He stood and stretched too. So he wasn't impervious to physical exertion or hard tiles either. Good to know.

"You said you heard something, and I thought I had too. I didn't tell you." I grabbed my jeans and stuck them on. "I had an auditory hallucination when I was in the steam room at the karate studio."

"A hallucination? Was there something funky in the steam?" He pulled his clothing on. "Incense gone bad or something?"

"No, weirdo. I guess I fell asleep. A voice woke me up, saying 'it's in the yard.' Any idea what that could mean, supersleuth?" Now that I was dressed, I was feeling a little more snarky and back to my usual charming self. Maybe a good cry and smokin' sex helped my disposition, though I could have lived without the crying part.

"None."

He opened the front door.

"Are we leaving?" I was confused. We'd just gotten there.

"No. Just going outside for a minute."

O-*kay*. Pausing for a second, I pondered whether to follow or give him some space. Eh, I voted going outside. Danger was my middle name, and I kick personal boundaries in the teeth.

Two steps out into the driveway my breath lodged in my throat, and I halted. The nubs on my legs stood out. Sam stood there casually looking up at the sky. However, the spectacular view overhead stunned me stupid.

"Oh, wow." I stood there with my mouth hanging open. "That's the most amazing thing I've ever seen."

"Thank you."

I nearly choked and tried not to snort. "Not you. The sky, you egomaniac."

"Oh." He walked closer to me and admired the view, as well. "I'd almost forgotten how close the stars are out here."

"Do you think the other-sider was right? That the stars are being taken by The Dark? I mean, if you believe the stars are souls that come and go." How can you tell if there are fewer stars up there?

"I don't know what I believe about that, but having heard the other-sider tell you about The Dark, I'm inclined to believe it."

My grief over the journals and Liz extended to him.

"I'm sorry I got you into this." So many people had been hurt or killed because of my work. Had I gotten careless, or too cavalier, or had the world taken on a more sinister tone?

"If I hadn't wanted to share my blood with you, I wouldn't have. It's not your fault, Dani. None of this is. I was raised by a resurrectionist. I know the score. I chose to help you, and I would choose to again." He put his arm around my shoulders, and the gesture was a comfort.

"Thank you." The sky drew my attention again as a series of stars dropped from the inky sky and plummeted toward us. I almost reached out to catch them. "I wonder if those are the souls coming back."

"If we choose to believe the other-siders, you could be right. If we choose to only believe science or religion, you're wrong, and we're witnessing a meteor shower." After a pause, he continued. "Maybe we can help them."

"I hope so." Leaning against Sam, I watched as more stars fell. A sense of peace came over me for a moment, as if I were in the right place at the right time, and I knew my purpose here. For once, all felt right with me.

And then it was over.

Chapter 13

A spectacular light glowed behind us, and we turned. Why was I not surprised to see an other-sider there? "Hello." Freaking out when they arrived was just a waste of energy, so I stopped doing that. Then two more appeared, and I reconsidered.

"We greet you, Danielle." This was a little different, seeing them out here and no Burton in sight. "Your suppositions are correct. What you view are the souls of our brethren returning to your plane. They also chose, as did Samuel, before coming to this plane." Their focus moved away from me, to him.

Though I didn't hear a voice aloud, I felt it vibrating inside my mind, communicating to us. Sam was definitely in on this conversation. "How can we help you?"

"Balance is being destroyed by The Dark. It has chosen to steal the souls returning to the nebula. If it is not stopped, the universe will go dark."

Uh-oh. That didn't sound good for any of us. "How are we going to stop that from happening? That's way out of our league." We were so small compared with what they were talking about.

"Continue the work you do, and we will help."

"You can help me by sending someone to help me." That sounded odd, but they knew what I meant.

"The soul beside you was sent to you. Do you not find him helpful?"

For a nanosecond I pictured us in a naked clinch. Now I *know* that wasn't what they meant, but yeah, I found him *helpful*. "Thank you." Humility in front of eternal beings could only score me some brownie points, right?

"The blood inside him carries that of another like you."

"Yeah, we figured that out already." Thanks, *abuela*.

"More blood sacrifice may be required to fulfill your mission."

"No. Absolutely not." I was not sacrificing Sam to further the cause. "I will never sacrifice Sam or any of my friends again. Why can't you…people, or whatever you are, bloody well just answer a question when I ask?" I shoved my hand through my hair. "What does, 'it's in the yard' mean? Someone from the other side spoke to us, trying to give us information. I know they did, but we can't figure it out by ourselves."

"Do you not wish to learn?" No judgments, just a simple question. They were so unemotional.

"Not right now, I don't." Frustration doesn't even begin to explain it. I'm out here trying to learn my craft. There is no resurrectionist library to reference. I'm almost alone. Even as much as Sam helps me, he isn't a resurrectionist.

"Your crystal is a guide. It is not simply decorative."

"I gathered that when it nearly blinded me."

"Dani," Sam said through clenched teeth and nudged me. I'd forgotten he'd never seen them before and was probably freaked out.

"Sorry." So much for humility. For me, it's fleeting, just like my charm. I took a deep breath and let it out slowly.

"The wisdom you seek is there between you." One of them held out an appendage that couldn't rightly be called a hand or arm, but something dangled from it. "The choice has always been yours, Samuel. Take this amulet and wear it. It will join your soul with Danielle's when you choose to make it so."

Without hesitation, Sam took the amulet from the other-sider. He's such a man, so responsible, so good. So wasted on me. He placed the pendant around his neck, but nothing happened. That was a relief. It was just a crystal shaped like a helix, kind of a double corkscrew made of quartz. Just like mine.

"It's not doing anything." He looked from the pendant to the other-sider.

"When you choose it, it will bond you. For now, it is dormant." Now that just explained everything, didn't it?

The other-siders eased back from us, and I sensed they were about to go.

"We can't do this." Someone had to tell them, so it might as well be me. "We just can't do what you ask of us. It's too much. Why can't you do it on your own? I'm plenty busy with the first mission you gave me." I thought about Liz, and my heart cramped.

"We are aware of your dedication to Elizabeth. If our efforts had been fruitful, we would not wish to enlist your assistance."

"If you can't figure out how to stop it, how the hell do you think I'm going to? And how do we retrieve the Dover souls from The Dark?" I'm not that smart.

"Our council of old souls is meeting to assist in their recovery, but those questions do not have answers at this time."

"Figures."

I felt a shift in the energy coming off them. It wasn't a good feeling, either. "You can't give up. If you've taught me anything since my return, you've taught me that."

"That sentiment is one of benefit to you."

"But not to you? How can you say that?" I was about to tear my hair out over this.

"The future is not set, and we have hope, but The Dark is a strong force."

"You are stronger." Of that I was certain. I refused to think otherwise, or I'd never succeed at any of this.

"The struggle is not over. The future is not set."

Sam raised the amulet, then let it drop against his chest. "Thank you for this."

"We feel your sentiment is genuine, Samuel, and we will gift you now."

Another uh-oh. When I had been gifted by them, I became a resurrectionist. What did they have in mind for Sam? RoboCop?

"Do not worry, young star." It spoke to me. "Do not fear for this one. All is well. Samuel will be able to hear you now when you call to him. The communication between you must flow both ways to be balanced."

Whatever was flowing between us was already powerful, but I'd take better communication any day. Then, in a snap, they vanished like falling stars in reverse, and the night returned to its previous state of tranquility.

"Wow." Reaching out to Sam, I held his amulet in my fingers. It was cool, nothing special right now.

"I'm just glad I didn't have to be eviscerated to get mine," he said and looked wide-eyed at me. Mr. Innocence, my ass.

Unable to stop it, a laughing snort found its way out of me and a coyote yipped in reply. "You're such a dork sometimes. You have no idea how lucky you are." No freakin' idea.

After admiring the night and its glory for a while longer, we went into the house and slept until the sun could be ignored no more. We spent the remainder of the day brainstorming what to do about Liz and Jerry. Sam made some calls to get an update on his condition. He'd live.

Long enough for me to kill him.

Who says there's no job satisfaction anymore? This case will give me tons, and I won't even charge Liz for it. After the endowment from Dover, I can afford a gratis now and then. Though she charges me for her legal services, this is different. I want her back. I need her back. She's part of the team that's going to bring justice to the cops and their families, to the people who need the service Sam and I provide. She gives voice to the people whom no one can hear. They need it and it's part of the paradigm that will bring balance to the universe. We need the good to counter the evil. That has been going on since time began and can't end now because The Dark has its panties in a twist.

After two days away from Albuquerque, I wanted to get back. We made the trip a lot livelier than we were coming out. The respite was good for both of us.

Sam had to face an internal investigation about the shooting, and I had to get an order to resurrect Liz. Although Jerry wasn't in charge of her estate, I wasn't sure if her parents were, but they would be the logical choice. While discussing other people's deaths, we'd talked about the end of our lives in general terms. After a few conversations and knowing the way she felt about Jerry, I was absolutely certain she'd want the resurrection.

"Want me to drop you off at the station?" I asked Sam. On the way back, I drove. How very modern of him.

"Sure. I have to see when I can get my truck out of impound. There's at least one window to get replaced."

I touched my cheek, but the small wound had healed. "Keep me posted." I pulled up to the curb, and he got out, but left his gym bag on the floor. Appearances. If anyone saw us, he didn't want them to think we'd been together all weekend. Appearances make a difference in how the men treat me, and what they think of Sam.

If they think Sam is banging me, their respect for him will go down the toilet.

We were back to being professionals once more. Without a word, he walked up the stairs to the P.D., and I didn't stick around to watch him go inside.

I had a spontaneous appointment with a certain rat-face lawyer who was going to help me, whether he liked it or not.

My truck requires a full-size space, so I had to park it down the street a few blocks from Vernon's office. As I approached the curb where it had all gone down a few days ago, I shivered, then clenched my teeth and looked away. But I could see in my peripheral vision that the blood had been cleaned up and the curb was in its usual state.

The farther I walked, the faster and more determined I became. I charged up the stairs to Vernon's office. If he hadn't alerted the press, Liz would still be alive.

Who knocked when they were in the mood I was in? I barged straight past the receptionist.

"Hi, Vernon." He was alone, and stood. Panic made the whites of his eyes show, and he began to sweat. Good.

"Now, Miss Wright. What are you doing here?" He held his hands out as if to ward off an evil spirit. In the mood I was in, I wasn't far from it.

"I've come to collect, Vernon."

"What, the inheritance? It'll be locked up in probate for a while I'm afraid." He dropped his hands and rubbed them on his slacks. I could smell his sweat. Must be one of my enhanced traits.

Making myself at home, I strode to the small refrigerator, grabbed a soda and sat in the plush chair across from him. "That's not why I'm here."

Suspicion appeared in his eyes, but also keen curiosity. He knew I was up to something, but had no idea what. "Then enlighten me. Why are you here?"

"I want Liz back, and you're going to help me."

He gave me that patronizing look that men who thought they were superior acquired, and I knew he was going to say something totally stupid and condescending. So I was ready for it.

"Liz is dead."

See? I knew it was going to be stupid. "I know, you idiot, she died in front of me." I wasn't going to tell him that she died while I held her and felt her spirit slip away while I sobbed in the middle of the street. Deliberately, I set my soda on his desk. An unblemished mahogany desk and not a coaster in sight. Too bad. "If you hadn't alerted the press to our meeting, none of this would have happened." At least I was pretty sure of that. The Dark's powers were growing, that was more obvious every day. I believed that it could influence people into doing things they normally wouldn't, but with a little encouragement from the dark side, who knew what it was capable of? "You're going to help make it right."

"What? I am not." A frown just pinched up his rat face even more.

"Shall I call Mike and ask who sent the press a tip? You know he loves to chat over coffee. It was you or someone in your office, I know." I whipped out my cell phone for added drama. That made him pause a second, and I knew I had him. "I want a court order to resurrect her, and send Jerry to the 'yard."

"I can't do that." The man's eyes nearly popped.

"You're gonna."

"How? It's not my area of practice."

"I don't care. You're going to help me set this to rights."

"Jerry is guilty, has admitted it, so there's little to argue about." At least that confession made things somewhat easier to bear, but I worried about how The Dark was influencing this situation and how pervasive it could be.

"No court battle?" he asked.

"No. Just the life-swap."

"No judge is going to agree to that so soon." He shrugged. "At least no clean one."

"I'm sure you can find one that will." I shifted my position so my blazer drifted away from my body and the gun was clearly visible in my shoulder holster. His gaze went exactly where I wanted it to. That is, after he had a good look at my chest. I knew the second his gaze shifted from my breasts to my gun. No threats were exchanged. I didn't have to threaten him. He looked at me again, and swallowed. Carefully. New respect emerged in his gaze, and he nodded. I wouldn't hurt him to get what I wanted, but he didn't know that.

"I'll see what I can do." The tone of his voice dropped, and I knew I had him for sure.

"Do that." I stood and picked up the soda, then dropped a business card on the desk. "You've got twenty-four hours to make this happen." That was ridiculous, even I knew that, but he didn't know that I knew that.

"There's no way—"

"Find a way." I left and took the stairs down. Elevators are death traps, and I don't need that today.

The medical investigator's office is located behind University Hospital between the law school and the heart of the University of New Mexico. The hospital itself is massive. It's a regional trauma center with a burn unit, and now it boasts a world-class cancer treatment center. The ME's office is a low, nondescript building, but it's a very busy nondescript building.

After signing in and asking to speak to Dr. Allen Goodman, the physician who runs the place, I paced the waiting room. Eagerness pulsed through me. Three days usually have to pass before authorization for release of the body is obtained, so I had plenty of time to get Liz's body to my cryo storage bunker. We'd spent two in the Zuni Mountains, so we were good. It was Monday, early afternoon.

"Hey, Dani. How can I help you?" Dr. Goodman arrived and ushered me out of the locked waiting area. Everything's locked, every entry, every hallway and closet. Even the bathrooms required a code to get into them. Made me wonder if you needed one to get out.

"I've come about Liz. Elizabeth Watkins."

"Oh, yes. Sorry about her. A terrible shame." He shook his head and clucked his tongue.

It wasn't a shame, it was a freaking *crime*. But I nodded and played the grieved friend, which was what I was, even though I had other intentions.

"I didn't do her autopsy, but let's get her paperwork and see what's going on with her." Dr. Goodman carries a load of administrative duties as well as performs autopsies. All of the names are recorded in various places, but the easiest way to find one is by looking at the dry-erase board behind the clerk's desk.

Dr. Goodman made that curious *hmm* sound all physicians learn somewhere. He squinted at the board from behind wire-rimmed glasses, then flipped through the first few sheets on the clipboard.

"What is it?" I was getting a sneaking suspicion I wasn't going to like something.

"She's gone. Been released to the funeral home. For cremation."

"What?" I grabbed him by the lapel of his lab coat. I had to, or I was going to keel over. "No. Look again." If she's been cremated already, there will be no bringing her back. There's no way that Sam and I, even with our power pooled, could overcome that kind of challenge.

"Dani, I'm sorry." He put down the clipboard and patted my hand. "Mortuary picked her up two hours ago."

"What? Which mortuary?" I was freaking out. Had her parents lost their minds? Or were they so grief stricken they weren't thinking right?

"Autopsy was done on Saturday and the body released to her family this morning. Dani, I'm sorry." His eyes were wide and his brows raised. He looked a little scared.

"When's the cremation?" If it wasn't too late, maybe I could get to her family and convince them I could help.

Liz obviously hadn't communicated her final wishes to them. Probably because she never dreamed Jerry would kill her. If I couldn't get to them, Vernon would have to get a court order to stop it. What would that be? A stay of cremation? I didn't know, but I had to get out of there fast.

"Cremations are done at night, and it's Streamline Services down on Fourth Street."

"Thanks, Doc." I tossed him my visitor's badge and dashed out the loading dock entrance, pulling my phone out of my pocket at the same time. I raced around the building to my truck. Think, think, think, dammit.

Though I drove through sixteen red lights, the chase was futile. I got nowhere with the mortuary. The watch-dog secretary at the front wouldn't give me anything. So much for professional courtesy. I send them business all the time, but could they give me one shred of help? No.

Against company policy to give out information. If you're not family we can't help you, don'tcha know?

Sarcasm was just oozing out of me. I hate it when I have to be nice to get information out of people, when reaching over the desk and choking it out of them would be so much simpler and more satisfying. Of course, the bulletproof glass the woman sat behind had been an issue.

Jerry.

He'd know the information I wanted. Jumping back into the truck, I headed back through the same sixteen lights to University Hospital. This had been my hospital once. I knew all of the stairwells, the shortcuts, the staff entrances and the back ways around it.

Until construction had screwed everything up. Dammit. I was going to have to go in there like a civilian. I stopped at security for a visitor's pass. They were new guys and didn't recognize me as a former staff person, so I made sure my blazer covered my gun. I have a carry permit, but security guys get overly excited when they see a visitor carrying weapons. Don't need that today.

I asked for Jerry, but he wasn't listed. Sam had put two bullets in him three days ago. Unless he died of fright, he was still here. There was a DNI status that VIPs could be admitted under. So could wastes of human flesh, for their own protection. Do Not Identify. No information about them was to be made public, not even that they were in the hospital.

"Since I'm here, I might as well eat. Where's the cafeteria?" I accepted the visitor's badge and clipped it to the chain on my crystal.

"Nice piece," the guy with Roy on his name tag said. "Guy was in here a bit ago with one just like it."

"This is a one of a kind. No one has one like it." Idiot.

"You got ripped off, lady, 'cause there was a guy wearing one just like it." He snorted, obviously thinking I was the idiot. We'd see about that. "Take the elevator down one flight, then follow the yellow brick road to the cafeteria."

Sometimes I just can't help myself, and one day it's going to get me into trouble. I widened my eyes and gasped. "Like, OMG, you have a Yellow Brick Road, just like in the *Wizard of Oz?*" I flipped my hair back and gave a brilliant smile to ol' Roy. "Are there, like, flying monkeys, too? That's *s-o-o-o-o-o-o* unsanitary."

"Uh, no. There are just yellow tiles *painted* on the floor. Just follow them, and you'll get there." He frowned and considered my mental capacity. "I think."

I nodded and blinked a few times, as if I were having difficulty processing that information. "O-o-h. I get it." I turned and walked away, leaving Roy more confused than ever. Some men are just meant to be tortured.

Shoving through the door to the stairwell beside the elevator, I paused. Had Sam been here? He'd know how to find Jerry. I paused on the landing below and pulled out my phone to call him. No bars. No cell phone service inside the hospital. Too many electronic gizmos in one place interferes with cell service. Was I actually going to have to do it the old-fashioned way and find a landline to call him on? OMG indeed. If he were still in the hospital, he wouldn't get the call anyway. Dammit.

Then something the other-siders had said jolted my brain. They had said our communication abilities were enhanced now. So, could I just make a *cerebral call* to Sam? Oh, this was just too weird, but I had to try. Time was running out.

So, did I just think of him or actually say his name in my head? *Sam? Sam, are you here?*

I waited a few seconds, but there was no returning call in my mind. I was such an idiot for believing in this. At least I was an idiot alone in the stairwell.

Just as I reached for the door to the first floor to let myself out, it opened.

Sam stood there.

"I know it's a relatively small city, but how is it even remotely possible that you're standing there?"

"You called me, didn't you?" He stood to the side to let me through.

"There's no cell service in the hospital." See what he had to say about that as I led the way toward the cafeteria.

"In my mind. I heard you in my head, Dani."

He said it as if it was something I did every day. I shook my head. Wow. Maybe balancing things was going to be possible, if this was any evidence. Maybe Sam and I together had something special that could defeat The Dark, or at least put its panties in a twist. We needed those damned journals though to prove it. "What I mean is, doesn't this even seem remotely freaky to you?"

"Yes, it's extremely freaky to me. I keep wondering if I'm going to wake up from a head injury or something."

Stopping in the hallway that was flooded with staff coming and going, I pulled him to the side. I gave him the details about the pending cremation.

"Do you know where Jerry is? What floor, what unit?" There are so many different types of units for different types of patients scattered throughout the hospital, we'd never be able to track him down.

"He's on the pediatric ward."

"Peds? What the hell is he doing there?"

"Who's going to look for an adult prisoner with guards in the children's ward?"

"Who, indeed?" Not even I had thought of that one. I patted him on the arm. "Glad you have connections. Let's go."

"Dani, you just can't go barging in there." I ignored the amusement on his face.

"Watch me."

Or not.

I charged toward the elevators, away from the pediatric unit, steam fuming from every orifice, and Sam standing silently beside me. The energy coming off him was so I-told-you-so, he didn't have to speak it. By now, he knows better.

The guard outside Jerry's door was like a Hispanic version of Mr. Clean. Big, bad, bald. There had been no getting past him with or without credentials. Rather than getting myself arrested and becoming totally useless, I left.

"Now what?" Sam asked.

"I'm going to have to steal a body, and you're going to help me."

"I can't believe this." He shook his head. The doors to the elevator swooshed open. Sam and I squeezed out as others squeezed in. There is no courtesy at the doors of elevators. "I've done a lot of unsavory things in my life, but never something like this." I'd have to ask about that unsavory stuff later.

"It's the only way to save Liz." Desperation made me ask, and I felt the resistance of him in the confined space as well as within my brain.

"Surely there's another way."

"If there is, I don't know it. I need you with me on this. I can't do it without you." Needed as I never needed before.

"I know, but we've got to figure out a way around this."

"You're my liaison. You're supposed to help me."

"Not by breaking the law."

"Dammit, Sam. Are you saying you won't help me?" The breath huffing in and out of my chest turned painful. I felt as if I'd been shot in the chest, too. As Sam's anger flared, so did mine. I felt the waves of pain coming off him. The painful waves of a memory flitted at the edge of my mind. A memory that wasn't mine.

"I made a promise, and I don't break my promises." He clenched his jaw. The stare he gave me almost made me want to cringe. He'd never looked at me like that before, let alone refused to help me. I wondered if The Dark was now influencing him.

Flashes of a jungle scene moved like a scratched film in my mind. The weight of another body across my shoulders tried to push me to my knees, but the weight of a promise was stronger and kept me moving. One foot after another I trudged with the weight of a friend on my shoulders. I had to save him. I had promised.

Though a firefight surrounded us with little chance of anyone surviving, I rushed through, my breath wheezing in and out. *I promised. I promised.* The mantra rang in my mind, drowning out the danger around me. After what seemed like an eternity, I made it safely to the bunker and collapsed under the weight of my friend.

I had kept my promise.

Then I snapped back to the present and some of the steam went out of me. This was Sam's secret, Sam's memory, and part of what burned inside him.

Chapter 14

I touched him on the chest over his heart, unable to put into words the effect his memory had on me. Now was not the time anyway for softer emotions, and I refocused on the task at hand.

"Well, I'm out of ideas. If you have any I'd love to hear them." Furious, frustrated and hungry, we left the hospital. We had to find a place for me to eat or I was going to turn into a psychopathic monster.

Sam walked with me to my truck, and we headed toward a diner, conveniently enough, in the general direction of the mortuary.

"Did you get your truck back?" I asked after I had mowed through about half my steak and three glasses of water. I was on overload and needed more energy than I ever had before. Or at least that's what it seemed like. Something was building. Something was coming to a head, and we were going to be in the middle of it. Maybe we were already in the middle of it and didn't know it. I just hoped we all came out of it alive.

"Yeah."

"When's your review?" There was no question of if, but when he could get back to work. If anyone found out he helped me steal a body, it wasn't going to go well.

"Tomorrow, noon."

"Good. That should buy me enough time to figure out what to do. Vernon should have the court order by then, and we should have Liz back by Friday night. Cool." I was hopeful, if not delusional, that this was all going to work out the way I wanted it to.

"There's a lot of *shoulds* in there." Sam's eyes were guarded as he watched me. He had a burger and ate more slowly than me.

"Don't bother me with details. By now you ought to know what my life is like, right?"

"I should." He shook his head, but I didn't know whether in disbelief at me, or that he was going to help me despite his claim to the contrary. "Do you have any idea how you're going to do this?"

"There's one last thing we have to check first before we commit any felonies. Where are Liz's effects?"

"Probably still at the station, unless her family picked them up." Now that was something I hadn't thought of.

"If I could just talk to her parents, maybe I can convince them to stop the cremation. I'm certain she'd want the resurrection, but I don't know if she's ever talked to her parents about it." I was certain that when Liz divorced, she'd returned her powers of attorney to her parents. There was no way she'd leave things in Jerry's incapable hands.

"I can get you in to look at her possessions. Her phone is probably there with the numbers plugged right in it."

I nearly threw myself across the table at him. "Sam. If you can get me in there, I'll kiss your feet."

He laughed and his eyes glowed hot for a second. "You don't have to go that far down, but I'll get you in." He pointed to my plate. "Finish up. Change of shift is the best time to do it."

"Forget it." I stood, tossed some money on the table. "Dinner's on me tonight. Let's go."

We arrived at the station just before 6 p.m. Change of shift is when mistakes are made, no matter what industry you're talking about. People either try to pass things on to the next shift because they want to go home, or get pissed because they catch whatever it is and have to actually go to work the second they're on duty. Not just cops and clerks, but nurses as well. Change of shift is also when most patients are found dead in their beds.

"Hey, Martinez," Sam said, greeting the cop at the desk. They spoke for a moment in Spanish, then he introduced me. I was polite and subservient, just the way I had been raised, but had long since overcome. Sometimes playing a cultural ace helps. It might be wrong, but I would do just about anything to get hold of Liz's phone.

As I said before, my life's in my phone and so was hers. After a short search, Martinez brought out the small bag of items that belonged to Liz: her jewelry, her purse and a notebook. I could see through the clear, zippered bag that there was no phone, and I wanted to cry.

"Thank you, Sergeant Martinez." Holding Liz's belongings, especially her stupid purse, renewed my grief, like stirring a pot of dust that nearly choked me with its dry taste on my tongue. I opened her purse and nearly fainted. There it was.

"So, I heard you just had a baby, right?" Sam said to Martinez, who broke out from ear to ear in one of the proudest new-daddy smiles I've ever seen.

"Yeah. He's two months old." Already the man was reaching for his wallet. "Wanna see some pictures?"

"Sure." Sam nodded and turned his back to me. "Bring 'em out and let me see that boy."

I knew he was giving me an opportunity, and I stuck the phone into my pocket. After looking through the remainder of Liz's purse, I realized there was nothing else helpful in there. I did see her driver's license, and it didn't indicate organ donation. Thank the stars. If her organs had been harvested already, there wouldn't be any way of returning her to a living state. Time was not our friend, and with each passing second she was wasting away and turning to dust. I had to get her to the cryo room as soon as possible and just hoped to hell that The Dark was having a nap.

After zipping the bag, I pushed it back across the desk. "Thank you, Sergeant Martinez. I appreciate your help." I hesitated a second, not certain what made me want to ask. "Can I see the pictures, too?"

"Oh, yeah. Sorry. I get so excited sometimes, my

manners walk off without me." He turned the picture in his hand toward me. It was him in civilian clothing, his wife, who looked beautiful, and the baby, who was only a few weeks old, so chubby his eyes were nearly lost in his round little face.

"He's adorable." Seeing pictures of babies shouldn't make me uncomfortable or make me wish for one of my own. Sometimes it does, but now I was just happy for him.

"Thanks. I think he looks like me now." Martinez grinned again and scrunched his eyes up.

I had to laugh. "He sure does."

"I'm sorry about your friend," he said and returned the pictures to his wallet, then picked up the bag with Liz's items in it. He scrawled in the ledger, signing the items back in.

I dropped my head. Sam turned, putting his arm around my shoulders, and brought me up against his side. I knew it was for show, for Martinez's benefit that I was a grieving friend, but Sam's touch comforted me more than he knew and probably more than I was willing to admit.

Once we were at the truck, I turned on the phone, or tried to, as the battery was dead. There was only enough juice to flash that there was no juice. Fortunately, I had a universal charger and it fit. One thing had gone right, but in the grand scheme of things, it meant little.

Flipping through the numbers, I came to the emergency information, but it was my number. I didn't know whether to be pleased or disturbed.

"Did you find it?"

"No." Frowning, I kept scrolling to the Ms. Mom and Dad. There it was. "Got it!" I pushed Dial and waited for someone to pick up.

"Wait. Hang up."

"No. I've got to talk to them." Was he nuts?

"Listen. How freaked would you be if someone called you from your dead daughter's phone?"

I hung up. "Shit. I hadn't thought about that." A shiver crawled over me. "You're right."

I opened my phone and dialed the number that was in Liz's phone. Waiting, waiting, waiting, no answer. "Dammit." Voice mail. "What does the universe have against me today?" Nothing had gone right, and I felt the influence of The Dark bearing down on me with every incident that had prevented me from taking possession of Liz's body.

"Do I even want to try to answer that?"

"No." I tried the number again and got voice mail again. This time I left an urgent message.

"Wouldn't her parents want her to be resurrected?"

"They aren't in my camp of supports, from what Liz has said. Although they'd want their daughter back, they wouldn't necessarily want her this way." I leaned my forehead against the steering wheel. "It's weird. We can't wait on them."

Although Albuquerque is a city spread across a large land mass, you can get to many places pretty quickly. Most of the city is set up in a grid pattern with few one-way streets, the exception being right downtown. You can also drive forty-five miles to get from one side of the city to the other. It's a long way over the river and through the desert. Fortunately, for the moment, we were near where I wanted to be. Fourth Street. There were some savagely good restaurants down in this part of town. My thoughts weren't on food for a change, but on kidnapping. Or more correctly, body snatching.

I pulled up to the front door of the mortuary facing Fourth Street. It's a small business area. Car lots, burger joints and a most excellent rubber stamp store. Everyone's gotta have a hobby, right?

Sam got out, closed the door and joined me on the sidewalk. I was as close to a nervous breakdown as I'd been in years. Later. I didn't have time for it.

"Do you have a plan?" He tugged on the front door, but it was locked.

"No." Disbelief and denial warred within me. I grabbed the door with both hands and shook, but it didn't budge. "If you want to go, you can." I had to release him from helping me. It just wasn't fair to ask him to do something that violated his beliefs, even if it was for Liz and for me.

"You could have told me that sooner. Now I have to walk home."

I nodded and closed my eyes. I wanted to scream, to cry, to bash my head against the wall, but none of it would help and would only give me a righteous headache.

The light touch of a breeze lifted my hair, and I tucked it behind my ear. In seconds, a raging, black whirlwind developed between Sam and me, and we dove in opposite directions. Generally, dust devils and whirlwinds are harmless and far away, but this one landed right on top of us, as if sentient. It was strong enough to suck the fillings out of my teeth. I pressed myself into a doorway, and Sam dashed to the truck. "Hold on to something!" Screeching over the vortex wasn't helpful, so I screeched in my mind. Rocks, dust and pieces of debris pelted me, and I turned my face into the corner. I hoped Sam was faring better.

What I hadn't realized when I stepped into the arched doorway was that I had trapped myself with no escape.

The whirlwind pressed in on me. Air filled with dirt and the stench of death consumed the space around me, creating a vacuum that made it impossible to breathe. My body was flattened against the hard adobe surface. Gasping, I tried to suck in a breath, but the wind forced my lungs nearly flat. Struggling against the wall, I tried to draw a breath and felt my reserve of air being forced out.

"You are no foe to *me*." An oily, dark voice reverberated around me.

The Dark.

I'd let myself be vulnerable, and it had taken full advantage of my lapse. If I died tonight, it was due to my own stupidity, my own arrogant belief that I could defeat this entity on my own. It could obviously suck the life out of me anytime it wanted to, but apparently taunting me was more fun. Moving my hands up to cup my mouth and nose was impossible, and I couldn't breathe. Spots of black appeared in my mind, and any remaining energy was fading. The only person who could possibly help was Sam. With his strength, I was stronger. With his nearness, I would survive.

Sam. Sam. Sam.

Thinking of his name and the power we shared together was all I could manage. He was close, and I felt him getting closer, but the wind kept him from pressing forward. Guns were of no help. Only by our personal power would we defeat this entity. I didn't need any journals to tell me that.

Then the pressure against me vanished. I fell backward as I sucked in a big lungful of dirty air. Then Sam's arms were around me, helping me to the ground as I coughed and gagged and gasped for air.

"Dani! Are you okay?" The urgency, the concern and the outright fear in Sam's voice penetrated my fog.

"Friggin'…Dark again." Turning, I let him help me sit again, and my lungs finally felt as if they were going to inflate. "What happened?" At least no monkeys this time.

"All I could see was a damned black shadow holding you in the doorway." Sam yanked me into his arms. He shook and trembled. He was as freaked out as I was. "Oh, my God."

"It's okay. It's okay."

"I can't lose you, too." He squeezed me tighter, and I heard him in my mind. *I won't lose you, too.*

"How did you get through it?" That was a miracle.

"I don't know. I grabbed the amulet in my hand, charged toward the doorway, and it vanished."

Standing with his help, I steadied myself and he wiped some of the grit from my face. "Wow. That was something I never expected."

"Me, either." Although he released me, I still felt the

vibration of him from a foot away. He glanced down and then stooped, picking something up from the pile of dirt in the corner.

"What's that?" It looked like a book had blown in with the debris.

"It's one of *abuela's* journals." He gave me a look of utter shock tinged with hope. "I'll be damned. Look at this."

Taking the leather-bound volume, I could see it was singed and burned all around the edges, but the leather had resisted the heat of the fire. Another good reason to use natural leather products. "It *is* one of her journals, but why?"

"Maybe The Dark thought it would flaunt its power over us, but something obviously went wrong."

"Obviously." I snorted. "We're more powerful together. When we pool our energies, something happens. It knows this and is defenseless against it." I held up the journal. "Your *abuela* knew it, too. There's something in here, or it wouldn't have kept this one." I opened it and looked at the foreign words lining the pages. "We have to figure this out, Sam. We have to use the information she left for us. It's her legacy, and it shouldn't be forgotten."

"It won't be." The tone of his voice dropped and the emotion surging off him brought tears to my eyes. My warrior, so strong, so true in his convictions, was going to help me defeat this entity.

I clutched the journal to my chest and looked at Sam, the emotion of the day almost overwhelming me. "We're a force to be reckoned with. I know it."

He planted a hard kiss on my mouth. "So does The Dark."

The lighting in this area was crap, but I opened the journal anyway. The lights from the truck were still on, so I held the journal into the beam. Thumbing through the first ruined pages, I stopped at a place where the words were still legible, but again, in Spanish. "Help me out. Can you see anything off the bat?"

Sam leaned over my shoulder, trying to read, then he took the book from me. Frowning, he read, shook his head, but said nothing.

"Well?" Patient, I am not.

"It's something, but makes no sense. Like it's in code or something. Just talking again about daily tasks, but in a very weird way. Like using things as weapons or defenses. *Put grape jelly in the windows to protect from external threats.* Now that makes no sense."

"Grape jelly?" Did she have an allergy to strawberry? "That is weird." I knew I wasn't going to figure it out tonight. I put my hand over Sam's and he looked up, the frown still in place and surges of frustration wafting off him like the blaze of a blowtorch.

"It'll take more time than we have right now to figure it out."

He nodded and a muscle in his jaw twitched.

I took another deep breath, determined to get back to the quest that had brought us here, though deciphering the book was high on my priority list. "We've got to get to the mortuary. We've been delayed long enough." Although less than twenty minutes had passed, it felt like a lifetime. The way Sam charged into The Dark humbled me more than I cared to admit. I owed him so much.

"I won't ask you to jeopardize your job any more than you have, but I need help to save Liz." There was only one person who could do that, and I had no way of contacting him.

Reaching to my chest, I clutched the amulet in my fingers and squeezed. The other-siders had said it was not merely decorative, and Sam just proved it. I shut my eyes and pictured Burton. *Burton, I need your help. It's an emergency.* I said the words in my head, not seriously believing he would show up, but after the communication with Sam, who knew? I opened my eyes. There was no preemptive skateboard sound preceding Burton's arrival, and we were alone on the street.

I closed my eyes again and took a deep breath. I had a death grip on the amulet. *Burton! Get your ass down here!* I screeched inside, digging deep within myself to a place that I rarely had to go. This was for Liz, not me.

"Jeez, *chica*," Burton said. "I heard you the first time."

I jumped. He stood behind me holding his skateboard and rubbing one ear.

"Burton," I breathed, scarcely able to believe he was there.

"You called. I came. Where's the fire, dude?"

"Inside, right now. They're going to cremate Liz, and we have to get her back." I let the *dude* comment slide, this time.

"I guess there really is a fire." His eyes popped wide. All I did was blink, and we were inside the locked mortuary. I don't want to know how we got there. I was just glad we were. "I don't even know where to look."

"This way." Burton moved in his lanky, long-legged lope to a door I hadn't seen. He spoke a word I didn't understand, and the door opened without setting off any alarms. Curious.

Burton leaned against a counter and pointed to the middle locker on the far right row. "There."

"Thank you, Burton. I'll never be able to repay you for this. If we get out of here without getting arrested, I'll do something for you. I don't know what, but I will." I handed my keys to Sam. "Will you bring the truck around?"

He took the keys, but paused. "Are you asking me to assist you in committing a felony?"

"Uh, no. Not technically. All I'm asking you to do is move my truck." I hated to ask, but I did anyway. "These are dire circumstances."

"I know. If you're letting me drive your truck twice in a week, things are definitely out of control." With a sigh, he left the room via the loading dock. I didn't know if asking him to help would bring us closer together or drive us apart.

My heart was racing, was beating away, and I didn't know if it was from relief at having arrived in time, anticipation of getting caught or the thrill of getting away with it. "Can you fix the paperwork trail, the computer entries and all that?"

"Already done."

"But how?" He hadn't moved from the counter.

"The mind is a powerful tool if you use it right." He

grinned and looked like such a kid again that I could only shake my head.

"You're gonna have to sign me up for that class."

Trembling, I opened the door to the drawer where her body was kept and pulled back the sheet to look at her. Just in case. But this was her body, so lifeless, so pale and empty. By the end of the week I hoped to have her back to her usual state of consciousness, filled with life and energy. For now, we had to get her out of here.

Burton and I eased her onto a stretcher. I closed the door and turned around, expecting to see someone calling the cops, but we remained alone. He pushed the gurney to the dock entrance, and I opened the doors. My truck sat there. Sam stood beside it. The lump in my throat I'd tried to choke down for days tried to crawl up at the sight of him. I owed this man so much.

We eased Liz's body, still in a bag, into the bed of my truck and shut the tailgate. I took a step back and cursed. It looked exactly as if I had a body in the back of my truck. We weren't going to make it without being seen by either a cop or some nosy person who just *had* to call 911.

"Don't worry, *chica*. No one will see you." He sort of waved a hand toward the truck and for a second it glowed. A shield had been placed over the truck as well as Sam and me. To others, we were invisible.

"Thank you again, Burton. Remind me to buy you a gift certificate to the skate shop."

He tossed his board onto the sidewalk and jumped onto it. With a wave, he disappeared into the night.

Despite my hands reshaping themselves into claws

on the steering wheel, gray hairs sprouting and new wrinkles appearing between my eyebrows from glaring at all the people who decided they needed to be in front of me, we made it to the lab without incident.

The second we closed the door to the cryo tube, my hands shook. Then for some reason the ligaments in my knees melted away. What had once been my cast-iron stomach now quivered as if I'd had a hefty dose of Mexican jumping beans. Or maybe I had parasites. I drank the water.

It was only when my lungs began to burn and holes appeared in my vision that I knew I was in trouble. I opened my mouth, but nothing came out. Trying to catch Sam's attention before I hit the floor was apparently also impossible. I was in a dreamscape, all the colors and shapes melted together, and whatever consciousness I had left me in a rush. The last thing I remember was an overwhelming need to sleep, so I closed my eyes, not caring that I was vertical and sleeping upright wasn't in my skill set.

A vision of Sam racing toward me, his blazer flapping, was the last image I recall before the neurons in my brain went on strike.

Someone had stuck a screwdriver through my left eye and drove it straight into my brain. Unable to open my eyes, I raised my hand to remove the screwdriver. I didn't care if I lost an eye. I had to remove that spear from my head.

Hmm. Curious. I patted my face. No screwdriver. I extended my senses outward and discovered I was lying down and there was a cool washcloth on my forehead. Moving, attempting to sit up, renewed the screwdriver pain, and I groaned.

"Dani. Thank God." There was movement, and I recognized Sam's voice. "Are you okay?"

"I don't know." I fluttered my eyelids, trying to see. "The light." It pierced my brain.

Sam dimmed the light, and I could open my eyes. I was on the couch in my office. "What happened?"

"You fainted." He knelt beside me again.

"Quit saying that. I did not." I was made of sterner stuff than most people. Fainting is not what I do. I might check out for a while, but I do *not* faint.

"Well, you did this time." The muscle in his jaw twitched. The man was more upset than he let on, and I tried to comfort him in my mind, but he pushed me away, more irritated than he wanted to admit.

"Maybe it was something else." I wanted it to be anything else. Low blood sugar, high blood pressure, electrolyte imbalance, nail fungus. Anything.

"When was the last time you ate?" I could hear the recrimination in his voice and was sorry I had put it there.

"With you. Whenever that was. I had a busy day. What time is it?"

"Almost midnight."

Shit. "Uh, about ten hours ago, maybe more."

"Dammit, Dani. You know better. You need to feed whatever it is inside you, or you're going to faint again." A tremor shot through him and into me.

"I told you, I don't faint." I sat up and fought against

the tide of vertigo that wanted to send me horizontal and make a liar out of me.

He said something nasty under his breath, but I heard it in my mind. "Let's go."

"Go? Where?"

"To get you a bloody steak." He stood and assisted me to my feet.

"But Liz—"

"Isn't going anywhere. She's safe and secure. Let me see to you, Dani. For once, let me take care of you."

Something in his voice made me look up. We stopped in the doorway of the office and stood there for a moment. Time ceased to move forward, or at least it slowed down for a few seconds. He'd been scared. That's why he was angry. Men like Sam don't do scared. They break things instead of admitting they suffer a weakness. I was apparently Sam's weakness. I just hope he hadn't broken anything while I was out.

Chapter 15

After we ate, Sam took me home. We hadn't spoken much during dinner. I was too ravenous to make polite conversation and rather than saying something stupid, I remained silent. Shocking, I know.

Doing the cop thing, Sam stalked around my house checking doors, windows, closets and behind furniture. At the moment I was glad for his company and for his guard-dog attitude. I was too hosed to do any of it myself, though I followed the same routine every time I'd been away from home. Being murdered will do that do a person.

Sam removed my jacket from my shoulders, took off my shoulder holster and checked my gun. After that, he squatted at my feet and tugged off my boots. "Come on." He took me by the hand.

I must have been tired, because I didn't protest any of this. If I were feeling myself, I'd be tossing him out of my house and yelling at him for being bossy again. Strangely enough, I was glad he was there. If left to my own devices, I might have simply stood in the living room and not remembered what to do.

We entered my bedroom, and he left me for a moment. The sound of the taps running drew my attention, and I realized he was fixing a bath. I looked down at my soiled clothing, the grit that filled every crevice, and wrinkled my nose. I was a mess and should be hosed off in the yard. Seconds later, the fragrance of my body wash filled the room. I love lavender. Stimulates the mind and refreshes the soul. If there was a heaven, that's what it would smell like.

He removed his blazer, but kept the shoulder rig on. Reaching out, he gripped the hem of my shirt and tugged it over my head. Next was the bra, the jeans, socks and finally the panties. I stood naked in front of him, but there wasn't a spec of desire in his eyes. Apparently, I'd lost my touch or he was still pissed.

Silently, he led me to the bathroom and put me into the tub.

The second my feet hit the water, I wanted to melt away, to give up my bones, flesh and skin to become one with the bubbles. I groaned out loud, closed my eyes and sank beneath the water as far as I could go and still breathe.

Sam chuckled, and I opened my eyes far enough to watch him. "Good?" He closed the toilet lid and sat on it.

"Exquisite." I dragged in a long, beautiful breath and sighed it out, settling down into the decadent luxury of the perfectly hot water. In a few minutes Sam moved, but I didn't open my eyes to see what he was doing.

The scent of him, spicy and masculine, alerted me to his nearness. Speaking would have broken the spell of the moment as I opened my eyes. His sleeves were rolled up, and he was kneeling beside the tub, a washcloth in his hand, and I immediately guessed his intention. Am I sharp, or what?

Dunking the cloth beneath the water, he soaked it, then took the bottle of body wash and squeezed entirely too much onto the cloth, then set the bottle aside. Beginning at one hand he scrubbed with a gentle touch, worked his way up to my neck, then down to the other arm, beneath each breast, down my abdomen, which was blessedly covered by bubbles, and then the rest. After he finished with the top portion, I leaned forward and let him scrub my back. There's nothing that feels as good, or almost nothing, as having the skin and muscles tended to by someone else.

Nothing in his touch, his gaze or his demeanor told me he was after anything more. I think this was just his way of coming down off his fear. "Sam?"

Silently, he looked at me and there was tension around his mouth, between his eyes and in the stiff way he held himself. I wish I'd noticed this earlier, but earlier I was just recovering from a light coma.

"Will you tell me about it? About your grandmother and what happened to your family?" Though he blocked the majority of those memories from me, I felt the pain of them now and then. At times such as now when his emotions were raw, I could sense the pain he'd kept to himself for way too long.

I swallowed down the nameless emotion wanting to rise up from my gut to choke me. This man had saved my life more than once, and I'd saved his a time or two. Now, we were connected by much more than shared job interests. The least I could do was help him with grief he had run from most his life. He needed this, and I wanted to help. I needed to help.

"No. It's the past, and I want it to stay there."

"You know as well as I do that the past never stays where it belongs." A maelstrom of emotion sparked off him and nearly electrocuted me in the tub. I jumped at the ferocity of his pain. "Tell me. It will help."

"I can't," he whispered. The tone of his voice dropped with the pain he couldn't speak. Sadness and grief poured off him. The strong muscles in his throat worked as he swallowed down the pain.

"Will you show it to me, then? Let me see it?" He knew I could do it, could read his memories. He just had to open himself in order for me to see them. If he shared them this way, it would ease his pain. "Please, just show me?"

"Dani—"

"You once told me you'd keep my secrets. Won't you trust me with yours?"

Without a word, he closed his eyes and leaned toward me. This proud man of mine was lost. He didn't know how to put the pain behind him. He could only push it away when it threatened to consume him. After all the things we'd been through, all the passion and the pain we'd shared, we were closer than ever, but this one thing kept him from reaching out fully to me. I needed him more than he could possibly know, and I wanted him to be free.

After shaking most of the water off, I gently placed the heel of one hand on his forehead and let my fingers drop over the top of his head. The story unfolded as if Sam were telling it to me out loud.

Gunshots shattered the night and panic burned in my chest. Hysterical screams, babies crying and dark voices mixed together. Leaving the safety of the bedroom wasn't the smartest move, even at age twelve I knew that, but someone had to do something.

My mother screamed in terror, and her cry was cut off. I opened the door only a crack, but it was enough to see the bodies of my parents on the living room floor. A dark figure stood over my father, cursing his name, cursing his family, cursing his blood. "Now you know what it is to bleed," the man said.

I must have made a noise, because the next thing I knew I was on the floor with a gun in my face. A stranger held me down and shoved a pistol in my mouth.

"Stop it! We're not killing no kid." Another voice spoke from the shadows. One of my sisters woke and began to cry. Then another one cried out. If even one of them got up, they'd all die.

"Let's go. The job is done." The man sitting on me was dragged away by his companion.

Panicked and hysterical, I crawled to my father, who lay gasping on the floor. One look at my mother, and I

*knew she was dead. Those beautiful eyes of hers would
never again sparkle with laughter. My sisters would
never be held by her again. Tears fell down my face and
a pain raged in my chest. Pain shot through my head
as I leaned over my father.*

*"Papa? Papa!" I shook him and wanted him to wake
up.*

*"Sammy?" My father's voice was a whisper, and I
collapsed beside him.*

*"I'm here, Papa." My voice sounded small, like a
little child's. I wanted him to stand and make it all go
away, to tell me to wake up from this nightmare I was in.*

*"Protect the girls." He took in a gasping breath as
he tried to give me the message most important to him.
"You're the only one who can take care of them," he
said, and I vowed then that nothing would happen to
the people I loved.*

*"I'll get help. I'll get help!" Tears blinded me, and
I couldn't see the numbers on the phone. "I'm calling."
Gasps choked out of my body and I couldn't breathe.
I couldn't think.*

*"You're the only one," he said in a rush. Reaching
out, he clasped my arm. "Sammy. My little man. Protect them. Always." Papa's hand fell away. I knew he
was dead. I ran to the neighbor's house for help. Help
came. But it was too late.*

Sam shuddered as he came out of the vision. This
explained so much about him, and why it was such a
painful story to tell, why his heart broke every time he
made a promise.

Tears filled my eyes and rushed down my face. I

broke the contact with Sam's forehead, and I fell out of his memory. "Why?"

"One or both of them witnessed something, a robbery or another serious crime, and could identify the perpetrators. That's all I can figure, because they were good people." Sam sat back on his heels. "Back then they didn't have any protection as witnesses." He reached out to stroke my face, the pain in his eyes almost tangible. The energy coming off him was black and heavy, and I wanted to console him, but there was nothing that would take away this pain. "That's when *abuela* came from Mexico to take care of us."

"I'm so sorry." There were no words to tell him how deeply I felt his pain. Nothing, not even time, would heal those wounds. Time only softened the point of the dagger.

"I know." He wrung the washcloth out and hung it over the edge of the tub. Reaching behind him, he dragged a towel from the metal rack and stood, holding it out.

"There was nothing you could have done to save them."

"Who knows." He shrugged again and looked away. He blamed himself, but I now understood why he took the protection thing to such a degree. The only thing he could do was take care of his sisters. It was a vow he'd never broken and had expanded to include me in the circle of those he protected. I couldn't blame him. He wasn't just being bossy. By not protecting me, he was breaking a vow that made him part of who he was.

"Thank you for sharing that with me." I touched his

cheek, and the ache dulled to a throb. "I know it hurts, but you aren't to blame, and you kept your promise."

"Let's get you out of there." Conversation was over for now. This was as much as he could give me, and I accepted it. I stood and accepted his ministrations to dry me, put on a nightshirt and put me into bed.

"Go to sleep now." He tucked me in, and I let him, but reached out and took his hand.

"Stay. Please."

After a moment's hesitation he removed his boots and lay down beside me. Turning toward him seemed natural, and the heavy sigh he emitted made me think that some of his pain had eased. I hoped so. I didn't want him to hurt so much. My eyes closed and I drifted away, powerless to do anything else. My body had betrayed me despite my will. Guess I was still human after all. Sometimes I wondered.

When I woke, ten damned hours later, I sat straight up in the bed, blinked a few times and did the only thing I could do. Ran straight to the bathroom and peed like a racehorse. A woman's bladder was not made for long-term storage.

The smell of freshly brewing coffee drew me downstairs like an addict to the opium dens of long ago. Frankly, I think caffeine's a better deal and a hell of a lot less expensive. You don't have to hide your caffeine addiction either, because all the other addicts were right there with you cheering you on. Coffee, anyone? I felt as if I was drifting on a cloud of caffeine, drawn in by its lure and promise of immediate satisfaction. Yeah.

Sam stood in the kitchen, looking all rumpled and sexy. Barefoot, he looked as if he'd just pulled his jeans on, halfheartedly zipped them, forgot about the button, tossed on his button-down shirt and left it. My mouth was kind of like his shirt. Hanging open.

Weak as I was, that was not the first thing I needed to see after a ten-hour coma.

"How are you?"

"Starved, caffeine withdrawn, stupefied by you standing there and about as grumpy as a cat in heat." I turned with my cup and glared at him.

"Back to normal then?"

I nodded and couldn't prevent the grin from hitting me. "Pretty much."

"Glad to have you back, babe." He laughed and raised his mug in salute. I clinked my mug with his and sipped. Okay, rest was over. I was back, and we were a team again. Time to get moving.

"We got a body to resurrect and a life-swap to perform."

The paperwork was in order. Vernon, the little rat bastard, had done it. Now I knew he was afraid of me. I felt a laugh, similar to my evil ringtone, making its way up out of me, but I resisted. Gloating could wait until later. Oh, by the gods, this was going to be a good day. I could feel it in every tingling little neuron throughout my body.

Sam had gone off to do what he had to do for a while. Yesterday had been the last of his three days of administrative leave, and today who knew what was going to happen. For now, I was on my own, and that's the way I usually like it, though I did feel a bit as if I was missing something. Last night had changed things between us. Seriously. We hadn't exchanged any bodily fluids, but I felt closer to Sam than I ever had.

Ten seconds later, the day seemed to explode with activity. Noon came and went before I had a chance to lift my head and go get food. If I didn't eat, there would be no ritual tonight, and Liz would have to wait another day. I raced to the nearest carnivore café and got what I needed. Minimal fanfare sometimes is all that's required to get the job done. Kind of like why women buy vibrators. No muss, no fuss, gets the job done and you don't have to compliment man or machine.

"Vernon," I said into the phone. Scooting aside the petrified hunk of wood, I shut my office door. "We'll do the resurrection at midnight. Have Jerry here by eleven-thirty. We'll take him to the 'yard after I bring Liz back."

"I'll make the arrangements." Something in his tone made me suspicious. He normally wasn't so agreeable.

"What's going on, Vernon? There'd better not be a single screwup in this."

"I don't anticipate any, Miss Wright."

I frowned, suspicious. "Then what's wrong? You don't sound like your usual self." That was polite, wasn't it? I left out the smarmy part.

"Let's just say I'm having a deep philosophical issue at the moment and leave it at that. I'll see you tonight."

"Fine." Anticipation hummed through me, so I didn't

care what kind of philosophical issue he had going on as long as he got the deed done.

Two o'clock. Ten whole hours to fill. Dammit.

My phone rang. "Wright."

"It's Sam."

"Hey."

"I need your help."

"Sure. What kind?" Anything for this man.

"Come to Elena's and bring a shovel." The line went dead.

Cripes. Couldn't anyone just say goodbye anymore? I turned off the phone, then got a shock to my system. Hot damn! We were going to look for the missing journals. I didn't know whether that was a sense from Sam or just brilliant deduction on my part.

I arrived, shovel in hand, to find Sam walking around with a metal detector. Watching a man hard at work had always been an endless source of entertainment for me. I don't know why. Doesn't matter the type of work, from digging ditches, to neuro surgery, when a man is in his element and focused on what he is doing, I'm fascinated. Maybe that just means I'm easily entertained.

"Whatcha doin'?" As if I couldn't see.

"Fishing, what do you think?"

Uh-oh. The frown between his eyes gave away his frustration level, and I got a weird vibe from him. He'd obviously been at it awhile before he called me. "Catching anything?"

"A pile of change. A bunch of old toy cars, some of which were probably mine. A few nails, odds and ends like that."

"Did you think you'd find the journals with that thing?"

"Yes." His mouth tightened for a moment, and he kept his eyes on his work. He'd become nearly as obsessed as I had, though we now had one journal to work from that had the seeds of useful information in it. "She had to have put them in something to protect them from the weather, time, someone finding them. I remembered seeing her out here at night, but she always said she was checking food she was fermenting."

"Oh, gross." Don't get me started about fermented foods. "Do you know how long Clostridium botulinum spores live?" I didn't wait for him to answer because he didn't know what the hell I was talking about. "For-freaking-ever. You're probably going to find some pot of dead raccoon that's been there for twenty years and stinks to high heaven."

Sam shot me a glare. "I don't think so. I think she was hiding her journals so we couldn't find them."

"Smart woman. What kid would go near that smell?"

"Not us. That's for sure."

"Okay, think about her, how she would have secured the journals from you kids, animals and people who would use them against her, yet still be available for someone to use at a later date."

Sam stopped and considered that, though he didn't look at me. "She'd have had to have a box made that was metal, had it buried or buried it herself. She was tiny, but she was strong. And she'd have had to have convenient access to it."

"Was there anything that used to be here that isn't

anymore? A chicken coop, a barn." I searched my mind for anything. "Old cars, old furniture, a workshop of some kind. A spring house, a root cellar, a bomb shelter."

"Bomb shelter?" At that I got the first inkling of a shift in mood from him.

"I'm reaching here, just trying to think of things." Brainstorming ain't perfect.

Sam shook his head. "I can't think of anything. She didn't like a lot of mess around, said it made us look poor. We were, but she said we didn't have to look it."

I laughed. "I think I would have liked her."

Finally, he raised his head and looked directly at me. "Together, you two would have been unstoppable."

"Kind of like you and me, now, huh?" A lump formed in my throat, and I swallowed it back down where it belonged. "How did she die?"

"Breast cancer. About five years ago." He began to pace with the detector again.

"I'm sorry, Sam."

"It's the way the world works. I'm just glad she didn't suffer."

"Yeah. Me, too." There are definitely worse things than dying, and suffering was one of them. "Maybe one day I'll see her eternal star."

Sam gave a nod.

"How old is this house?" I asked as something occurred to me. We were near the Rio Grandé River, where many homes had irrigation rights. Channels were built alongside these properties and diverted river water for residents to use for farming. Not very long ago everyone in this area had farmed and raised animals. Some still did.

"Probably late 1800s. It's been updated over and over, so it doesn't look as old as it really is."

"I assume that it was hooked up to the city water at some time." Hmm. This was giving me ideas.

"Of course." Sam looked at me and grinned.

"A well," we said together.

Sam put the metal detector down and strode right to me. Without a word, he grabbed me by the shoulders and planted a hard kiss on my mouth. "You're the smartest woman I've ever known."

Not giving me time to bask in the glow of that, he released me and strode across the yard toward the far end of the property. It was long and narrow, rather than being a square the way many properties are these days. This place had once accommodated farmland and livestock away from the house, closer to the source of the water.

Not needing the shovel, I dropped it and ran after Sam. We were going to find the remaining journals, finally! I caught up to him. He stood with his hands on his hips looking totally disgusted. "Now what?"

"Sealed over. With cement." Now that we were more connected, his language was starting to resemble mine. Weeds and thorny things had grown up around the site, hiding it from the casual observer. Sam had found it only because he knew it was there.

"What?" Shocked, I stared dumbfounded at him. "Why?"

"Until now, I'd forgotten. When that baby girl fell

down an old well in Texas, Grandma freaked out." He cursed. "Of course, we were always playing on top of it, so she had the damned thing closed off."

Disappointment nearly broke me. "If her journals had been there, surely she moved them before sealing the well." I'd been so sure we'd find them, I'd never considered anything else. "Well. Hell. Couldn't she have had it closed off with a lid that opened?"

"What would be the point of sealing off something you could open?" he asked with a raised brow.

"I don't know." Raking a hand through my hair, I sighed, more bummed than I wanted to admit. Though I had started out believing today was going to be great, now it was going down the tubes.

"That would have been a good hiding place." The afternoon had begun to wane. Shadows grew behind trees and overhead in the great cottonwood trees I was sure Sam had climbed as a kid. I gave a shiver, remembering the skeletal monkeys, and my attention rose upward.

The remnants of an old tree house filled the crook of one tree. Wooden steps that had once been nailed securely into the tree now hung precariously. There was a flat platform that had served as the base, and two of the four sides were still intact. There was no roof, but what kid needed a roof when you were in a tree house? "That yours?"

"What?"

I pointed up. "The tree house."

He paused and a nostalgic look covered his face. "Yeah. That was mine. With so many girls around, I needed a place to call my own."

"Your very first bachelor pad. Doesn't look like anyone's used it for years."

"Elena's kids are hooked on computer games and crap like that. The simple things are entirely beyond their comprehension. Unless it's hooked to a computer screen, they don't get it." He had a curious expression on his face, as if seeing the thing triggered memories. "I had a lot of good times up there."

"I'll bet you did." I could almost imagine him playing army up there.

"Had my first kiss up there." With a grin, he hooked his thumbs in the waistband of his jeans.

"How old were you?" Intrigued, I wanted more information. I knew so little about his life before we met. He was a man of mystery and secrets, and I wanted to know all of them.

"Ten, I think. Bernice Alvarez." He snorted a laugh. "She was the only one who could climb trees well enough to get up there. I added the steps later."

"Show me. I think I can climb as well as Bernice Alvarez." I removed my blazer and hung it over a low branch.

"Dani, this thing is so old, I don't think it's safe anymore."

"Come on. Where's your sense of adventure?" I leaped up, caught a branch and pulled myself up. Chin-ups were in my workout regime, but I hated them and struggled to bring myself upright. Sam gave me a lift into the tree. I think he just wanted to handle my ass.

"Okay, but if you get up there, just don't hit me."

"Why would I hit you? This time, I mean." I could think of a lot of reasons, but not at the moment.

"After I kissed Bernice, she slugged me one. I fell out of the tree and broke my arm." That made me laugh, and I nearly lost my grip. I finally caught my feet on a branch and heaved myself up to the base. It was too small for me to fit into so I leaned over and looked into the space.

The laugh stopped.

Sitting in front of me, hidden right out in the open, was a small metal foot locker, about the size of two loaves of bread and twice as high.

"What's wrong?" He caught the change in me right away.

"I think I found the journals."

Chapter 16

"What do you see?"

"A metal box. Beat to hell, but intact." I tried to balance myself on a branch that would support me and reach in at the same time. Finally, I was able to grab one of the handles on the side of the box. As I dragged it toward me, it scraped and bumped and then hung up on the nearly rotted floor of the tree house. I almost had it. Reaching out, I scooted it closer to me, and I grabbed the handle more securely. Tremors shot through me as I touched it.

"It's heavy. Can you reach up for it?"

"Yeah." Sam stood beneath me, and I pulled the box over my lap, then gripped a branch with one hand and handed him the box with the other.

And the branch snapped.

I didn't have time to scream or even take a breath. One second I was on the branch ten feet up, the next second I was on the ground, on top of Sam, on top of the box, on top of a pile of toothpicks that used to be a branch.

Sam grunted, and I rolled off him with a groan. "Are you okay?"

"Yeah." His breath wheezed in and out of his lungs. He crawled to his hands and knees, trying to catch his breath.

In the meantime, I eyed the box that had popped open. "Keep breathing, Sam. Just keep breathing." Eventually, the paralysis of the diaphragm causing the suffocating feeling resolves. It's only a few seconds; it just feels like an eternity.

Pushing aside the mangled and rusted lid, I nearly screamed. "It's them. It has to be." Trembling, I pulled one of the leather-bound journals from the splinters. I was trembling from excitement, and my gaze flashed to Sam.

He'd turned over and was sitting on the ground now. At least his coloring had returned to normal. "Let's see." He held out a hand for one, and I gave it to him, knowing he was still going to have to translate.

Oh, please, please, please, let it be them, I muttered. *Abuela, I need your help.* Clasping my hands together, it was as close to a prayer as I could get.

Sam cracked open the book and began to read. In seconds, he grinned. "It's them. This is what we need. I'm sure of it."

Launching myself at him, we fell over and landed in a pile in the dirt. "Oh, thank you, Sam!"

"You're the one who found them." He looked up at me from his prone position.

What I felt coming off him unnerved me. There was tenderness and respect, but there was a need, an ache that I hadn't expected, and I looked deeply into his eyes, as if I could see into his mind and his heart. I no longer needed my hands in full contact with him to read him. Something in my heart cramped, and I wished for things that could never be between us. I was falling for him in ways that would only hurt us both.

He was a protector and that was great. He was also dedicated to family, and that was something I could never give him. Having had my uterus severely damaged in my attack, I was told by doctors I would never carry another baby. Too much scar tissue. Although it disappointed me, I thought it had been a good thing at the time. Until now. Until I fell in love with Sam. He was so about family and connections that not having children would pain him forever. He should be bouncing babies on his knee someday, pacing the floor with a sleeping child on his shoulder and loving a woman who would complete him. I couldn't do any of that, and I wouldn't stop him from finding that happiness with someone else. I loved him too much to stand in his way.

"I don't want anyone else, Dani." His voice was a whisper, and a shock wave echoed through me.

"How could you…"

"I know, Dani. I know." He pulled me down to him and opened his mouth over mine. Resisting occurred to me, but I'd become less interested in pushing away things I wanted. Someday soon, I'd no longer be able to have Sam as a lover. I could feel our time together coming to a close. We'd still be partners in the professional sense, but we couldn't be intimate the way we were now. This was only a respite. At least that's what I tried to convince myself. I parted my lips to the searching quest of his tongue. I wanted to milk every bit of pleasure out of our arrangement while we could. Once it ended, we'd never be able to go back.

I raised my head and looked at him, as if he had the answers to questions I didn't even know how to ask.

"Come inside with me." The yearning in him matched that bubbling up within me.

"Sam—"

"Don't pull away from me. Not now." He pressed a hard kiss to my mouth. "Not yet. I'm not ready."

I didn't know what that meant, but he'd never asked me for anything. Could I deny a request I stood to benefit from? I wasn't very self-sacrificing. He heard the answer in my mind and rolled me over, pressing me into the ground. There was desperation now rising up between us.

He stood and helped me to my feet, then picked up the journals. Urgency filled every footstep as we entered the house. He set the box down, locked the door behind us and reached for me. Though his mouth was the driving force setting the pace, his touch was gentle, reverent, and I settled into the feel of him.

"I need you." And I did. How I could admit that and walk away from him, I didn't know. But for now, I needed him, and I wanted to fulfill the need burning within him.

He eased my jeans open and dragged them down. Pressing kisses to my breasts, my abdomen, my hips, Sam worshipped my body and I began to quake inside. The heat of his mouth seared my core, and my knees nearly buckled. Thankfully, I was leaning up against the wall. A whimper of need left me as the searing texture of his tongue touched my flesh. Cupping my bottom, he tipped me into his mouth and pleasured me. In seconds I was ready to explode. With my hands holding his head, I could only hold on as he took me to the edge and flung me over it. Spasms of intense pleasure erupted, and in that moment I knew I loved Sam beyond all else.

I knew I couldn't, that I shouldn't, but I did. Here was a man who deserved so much more than I could give him. For now, I could give him the pleasure of sharing my body. I urged him up to me, and with trembling fingers I released his erection into my eager hands. I needed him to know the pleasure he'd given me.

He pulled my right leg up around his hip and eased into my flesh. The groan of pleasure echoed in my mind. This was what I could give him. In my mind, I spoke. *Take me, Sam. Take me the way you want to. Don't hold back.*

Withdrawing from me, he spun me around and pressed me down onto the table, leaned over me, his breath hot in my ear. "This is what I want."

Arching my back, I wasn't going to protest as he eased the length of his shaft inside me. He filled me in a way that stirred new sensations. Though I'd just had an orgasm, when he reached in front of me to touch my flesh, I knew I was going to have another one. My body no longer seemed to be something that I controlled, but something I had given over to Sam's hands. He moved in and out of me, drawing out every bit of pleasure for us both. Faster and harder, each movement brought us closer to the brink. Any second now, we were gonna blow.

Gasping for breath, I clutched the sides of the table and held on while Sam did what he had to do. When his fingers dug hard into my hips I knew he was close, and for some reason I opened myself up more fully to him mentally, allowing myself to feel him, feel his pleasure and the sudden release. His orgasm became mine, and together we scorched the air around us. Then he collapsed over me and pressed me into the table. Unintelligible Spanish words flowed out of him. I didn't know exactly what he said, but I was sure the content had to do with being sexually fulfilled in that moment, and it made me smile. I was so there, too.

After we had our senses together again, I covered my face with my hand. "Your *abuela* would be ashamed of us. We find the journals then fornicate like a couple of teenagers."

"She'd have laughed her ass off."

"Really?" I was relieved, but surprised. People of her generation were a lot more conservative than me.

"She was no prude. How could she be and still be a resurrectionist?"

"Really?" That made me feel a lot better and more connected to Sam than ever.

Thunder rumbled outside, and I looked out the window. Black, ominous clouds threatened to rain down on us like nothing we'd ever seen. As Sam joined me at the window, I knew this night was far from over. We had a job to do, and it wasn't going to be easy. Bringing Liz back was only the first step of many that would be required to push back The Dark, if only temporarily.

"What do you think that's all about?"

"The balance. We're doing something right The Dark doesn't like. It's trying to scare us. Like the monkeys and the whirlwind." The Dark had it in for me, for us. I looked at the way the trees trembled, nearly bent in half by the breeze. That had been me once. Trembling at the slightest ill wind, but not anymore. I was stronger with Sam by my side.

"The next time it might not play so nice."

"Nice? The whirlwind nearly sucked the life from me."

"I know. That's why we need to get at these right away. I'll take them to my place and start interpreting before the resurrection tonight."

"Okay. Let's get out of here before the monkeys come back."

Finally, the hour arrived. Liz was ready, I was ready, and so was Sam. Over the past few weeks he'd turned into my go-to guy in so many ways. I was depending on him more than I ever had, which made me wonder about that teeny little blood exchange of ours. Would I be able to manage without him, or were we more connected than ever? Was it even possible for me to let go of him?

The buzzer to the outside door rang and the guards ushered in more guards with Jerry in tow. Vernon was with them and hung back just a little. The look in his eyes wasn't as amused as it had been the last time we were in this room. Must be the philosophical issue he'd mentioned. Maybe he was finally coming around to our side.

"Bring him over here." I motioned to a spot close enough to Liz's body, but far enough away from me that his toxic energy didn't touch me.

Tonight, again, I'd made a change in my attire. For whatever reason, I felt the ceremony demanded it. I wore a red silk robe. With Liz's death, something inside me had changed. Maybe I was having my own philosophical issue.

Barefoot, I moved to Liz. I moved slowly, reverently. Made me look ethereal, I guess, because Jerry's eyes widened when I eased past him, and he turned a sick shade of green. I pulled the sheet back from Liz's face. She was perfect and beautiful, just as she'd been in life.

I raised one hand to the ceiling and placed one hand over Liz's forehead and began the ceremony. There was no reason to delay.

"Hear me now, guardian spirits of the west. We implore you to return this child, wrongly taken, back from the light. We seek your guidance and knowledge, to right the wrong done here. Return the spirit Elizabeth Watkins and restore the balance." I cleared my throat as overwhelming emotion began to claw its way up my throat, and I let the tears flow. It was right. "In her place, we send the fallen star, Jerry, who ended her life. Hear me now, and let it be."

I never knew quite how the other-siders would arrive. Sometimes they just appeared. Other times there was a great gust of wind inside the room, and other times a sprinkle of what looked like glitter, but was probably stardust. Tonight, the stardust appeared in an arc from the corner of the room, widening into a stream of glittering lights. Out of the light stepped an other-sider, then two more. Lately, they seemed to come in threes. More power, I guess.

"Thank you, friends. We are honored by your presence. Elizabeth was brutally and wrongly murdered. Her killer stands before us, and will be given over to make amends for his crime against her and against humanity."

"We have heard the honor in your cry for help. We, too, wish to restore the balance."

With those words, I picked up the sacred dagger. It vibrated in my hand. Off duty it was quiet, but during a ceremony it vibrated with life, almost sentient. I sliced it across my left forearm, perpendicular to the bones. Accidentally hitting a vessel and bleeding to death right now would ruin my day. A red line appeared as soon as I slid the blade over my skin. Holding my arm over Liz's chest, I allowed my blood to drip onto her.

The atmosphere in the room changed. The heaviness lightened, somehow came alive. No one moved, no one spoke.

Sam's presence behind me was a comfort. Closing my eyes, I drew on the strength and energy he was sending my direction. I drew on the strength of a promise. I, too, had made a promise to Liz to return her, and my conviction now was as strong as Sam's. Maybe it was the new connection between us, or just the friendship we'd developed, but whatever it was, I needed it right now.

"Spirit known as Elizabeth Watkins, return now to this plane. We seek to right the wrong done to you." I took a deep breath as I felt her presence returning from the nebula. The energy of the room sizzled with her presence, and the other-siders glowed brighter. Tears overflowed my eyes, and I let them fall. Sometimes being tough just takes too much energy.

Reanimating a corpse is no easy task. Reanimating one that is your friend is monumental.

The signs are subtle at first. The coloring comes back into the face, neck, and upper body. I suppose it's like the cardiovascular system shutting down at death, only in reverse. Some people return with a huge gasping breath, sucking in oxygen as if they'd never get another breath. Others simply open their eyes and take in breaths as usual, as if they're awakening from a deep sleep.

Liz was the gasping kind. She took in that deep, deep breath full of oxygen, awakening her cells and setting them on fire again. She opened her eyes, blinked several times, looked around the room and finally focused her vision.

She was royally pissed.

Liz was a smart woman, and she knew exactly what had happened, why she was in her current state of undress, covered by only a sheet, and in a room full of men, one of whom was her ex-husband sporting shackles. Yeah. She put it together more quickly than your average undead. A woman scorned *and* a woman murdered is not someone you want to have focused on you.

"You," she hissed, looking at Jerry. *Looking* was probably the wrong word. Shooting poisoned spears that would explode with flesh-eating bacteria would be a better description of what her eyes looked like.

It was quite amusing.

Now that the bulk of the drama was over, I settled in for a good show. Unfortunately, I didn't have any popcorn. She tried to sit up, but couldn't quite manage it, so I helped her to swing her legs over the edge of the gurney and balance while keeping her covered. "Easy, Liz. You don't have your legs under you just yet."

"I'm going to have more than that under me in a few minutes." Hopping down, she draped the white sheet around her like a toga, then grabbed the dagger from the table. "I'm going to have two hundred pounds of asshole under me." She charged forward, but I grabbed her by the waist and held her back. As entertaining as it would have been to watch her carve Jerry into bite-size pieces, I couldn't let her. I'd just rectified one disaster. I didn't want it undone thirty seconds later.

"Hi, Liz." Jerry stood there, his eyes glittering, from what I wasn't certain. They certainly weren't unshed tears of joy clinging to his eyeballs. He was probably scared shitless. I was just glad I didn't have to wash his shorts after this.

"Hi, yourself, you prick. What did you do to me?"

Trembling with rage, she marched forward as if she were the queen of England, and I let her go. Minus the dagger.

"I had a bad moment." He shrugged, as if that explained it. "Got drunk, followed you and put a bullet in your back."

The gasp she drew nearly sucked the hair off my arms. I swear, I could feel the vacuum of it, and the air in the room shifted directions. "How could you?"

Jerry's gaze shifted to Sam. "I was actually hoping you'd kill me." The disappointment in his expression was clear.

Sam simply grinned and looked at me. "I know better."

Good man. Well trained. I should keep him around.

"Coward," Liz said. Her right hand curled into a fist, and she coldcocked Jerry in the nose. His head snapped back and blood spurted from both nostrils. He screamed like a girl and dropped to his knees, then fell over and hit his nose again. Shackles. Oopsie.

Way to go, Liz. She did *not* hit like a girl. Someone had taught her a few things about fighting dirty. Hmm. We'd have to chat later.

"Somebody help me," Jerry whined from the floor, but no one moved.

"Guys?" I drew their attention. "Help him into the van. We're going to the 'yard in a few." My security guys hauled Jerry to his feet, and Liz went after him again, but Sam grabbed her this time. She was much stronger now with the power of righteous indignation

firing to life inside. Didn't need extra powers to understand that.

The other-siders drew my attention by speaking into
my mind. "We are complete." They disappeared in a
fraction of a second, and I turned back to Liz.

"I've got some clothing for you. If you want to go to
the 'yard with us, that's fine. Otherwise, I'll have one
of the guys take you home."

"Are you kidding? I'm seeing this through so I can
spit on his dead carcass."

Okay, then, decision made. I handed her a bag with
loose clothing in it and a pair of slip-on shoes. Her
autopsy scars would begin to heal as soon as Jerry's
soul departed, but until then, they would hurt like hell.
"You can change in the locker room." I led her out and
watched as Sam, not my security, hauled Jerry to his
feet. Now that was interesting. Maybe he was taking
special interest in this one since he had taken Jerry
down. Or he felt what I felt, and needed to extract a
little vengeance of his own.

I was okay with either one.

Liz changed, and I assisted her. We'd never been real
girlie-pals, but now, it didn't matter. I was a nurse, so
naked bodies didn't bother me, and I'd seen just about
every kind of scar there was, hosting a multitude of
my own. When Liz turned away from me to drop the
sheet, I knew she was freaked about the Y incision in
her body. It extended from both collarbones, met over
her sternum and extended down past her navel.

"It will heal and fade. Please don't be ashamed in
front of me." I wanted to reach out and hug her, to give

her some of the strength that I had needed when I'd re-turned.

"It's hideous." She hung her head, and I heard the tears in her voice. "I know you say it will heal, but what if it doesn't?"

"There are some wonderful plastic surgeons in town whom I can refer you to if necessary." Excluding my ex-husband. Not referring a dead dog to his practice.

A sob ripped out of her, and she collapsed onto the wooden bench beside her. She turned away from me, and I felt waves of shame rolling off her. The shame in this wasn't hers to bear.

"You are not to blame in any of this." I sat beside her, wanting to reach out to her, wanting to comfort my friend. Absolution wasn't my job, but I wanted to as-sure her nothing she had done had brought about this incident. She knew I had scars, too, but she didn't know how extensive mine were. "It's not your fault."

"I married the bastard in the first place. I knew I shouldn't have, but sometimes you start believing the garbage people feed you." Tears dribbled down her nose and landed on her hands.

"I know. I know." Now, I eased her back against me and held her in my arms for a moment, making full contact with my palms on her shoulders. The contact seemed to soothe her, and her tears faded. For some reason, it soothed me, too. "You're stronger than you know right now."

"Thanks." She pulled the sheet up and wiped her eyes with it.

"Let me show you something." There was no shame

in me. No fear, no guilt. Some things just were. I finally understood that. Standing, I parted my robe, and revealed my abdomen, which was scattered with lines and scars in all directions. Some were surgical scars from the multitude of repairs I'd undergone, some were the result of having my baby cut from my belly. None was pretty. They would never fade completely.

"Oh, Dani." Her tearful eyes looked directly at me for the first time since we'd entered the locker room. "I had no idea." Her gaze dropped to my abdomen again, and she reached out to touch me. We'd never had such an intimate moment before, but two women who are scarred inside and out overcome many barriers when they connect.

"We have a lot more in common now than we used to."

"Yeah. Kind of sisters in suffrage." She dropped her hand, and I closed the robe. "What an exclusive club to belong to."

I laughed. "Maybe we need a secret handshake or something."

"Yeah." With a deep breath and a long sigh out, she collected herself, pulling herself together. She was going to be okay.

"Let's get the hell out of here and finish it. I need a drink." Did I ever.

"Amen to that, sister. Amen to that." She slipped her feet into the sandals, and we returned to the lab.

Chapter 17

The ride to the 'yard seemed longer than usual. Liz and I rode with Sam in his truck, giving me a shiver of remembrance when I realized the last time we were all together in it was the day Liz had been killed. Weird, freaky and full circle. Isn't that how life works sometimes? If you don't laugh at the weird stuff, you'll end up in the loony bin ripping the wings off of flies.

Closing my eyes, I allowed my energy to percolate, to brew, to grow and re-create itself. My part in this energy show wasn't over yet. I still had to put Jerry in the ground.

Fear, especially the mortal kind, does strange things to people. It turns the wicked suddenly moral and the nonbelievers righteous. It turned Jerry an odd shade of green. Chartreuse, I'd say.

Without preamble, I began the ritual. "Now, I finish it." With the sacred dagger vibrating in my right hand, I raised both arms skyward. I called on different spirits to complete the ceremony and take the spirit of Jerry away. We weren't playing nice anymore. "Angels of death, come to me now as we turn over the soul of this criminal."

As each resurrection is different, so is each life-swap. The sound of an ancient, rusted door screeching open flowed over the 'yard and through me. Shivers broke out on my flesh, and I tried hard to control them as whatever-it-was ruffled my robe. Instinctively, we all react the same as the stench of rotting flesh touches us. I knew it was here not to take us away, so I relaxed as the spirit of whatever-it-was whooshed past us.

A black robe, tattered at every edge, covered the thing that glided across the desert toward us. Jerry began to hyperventilate. "No. No. I. Didn't. Mean. It."

"We offer you this soul to pay for the crimes it has committed on this plane."

The being, death, whatever-you-wanted-to-call-it, bypassed Jerry, and stopped in front of me. O-*kay,* this was new. It had never engaged with me before, just taken the murderer with its appendage and moved off. *Fetid* was the only way to describe the smell coming off it. As a nurse and a resurrectionist, I've smelled my share of vile things. Try an anaerobic organism in close quarters some time.

This odoriferous creature put them all to shame, and I resisted the urge to pinch my nose shut. Breathing through my mouth didn't help. Just added a nasty taste to the stench. I *so* needed a mint.

"Yes?" I didn't quite know how to address a being from the underworld.

"Spirit known as Danielle Wright. You restore the balance."

I guess that was as much of an acknowledgment or thank-you as I was going to get from this good ol' boy. "As do your kind." Honestly, I didn't now if there were others like it, or what, but somehow, there had to be.

"The Dark will be defeated. By your convictions it will be defeated."

Shocked at that tidbit of information, I blinked several times as the soul taker remained in front of me, but what the hell did it mean? I alone had to defeat The Dark? Was I seriously the only freakin' person in the universe who could do it?

"Tell me how. I need information, help that's stronger than me." I was ready to scream at so many cryptic messages from the universe.

"None is stronger than you. Join forces with your allies to strengthen your power. Allow the power to join you. The underworld also wishes for your success."

"Seriously?"

"There is none more powerful than what you are tonight."

The stench was too much, and I took a step back. The creature took that as a sign our conversation was over, as it moved off in Jerry's direction. I had to complete the ritual before I freaked out and forgot how. I raised the dagger of vengeance, prepared to slice my arm again. "Blood seals the pact between us and closes the portal between the worlds."

"Wait!" Liz cried.

Oh, gods. "You're not having second thoughts, are you?" I paused with the blade just inches from my skin. Now *I* was starting to hyperventilate.

"Oh, no." She stepped forward and held her arm toward the dagger. "This one is mine. I want to be the one who sends him to hell."

Now, I no longer believe in hell in the traditional sense, but as another realm where souls exist. If she chose to believe in it as hell, that was fine with me. "I accept your gift of blood." Before she could change her mind, I sliced her arm.

One quick stroke of the dagger opened a small wound in her arm. She jumped and gave a surprised gasp. I spoke the words, she spilled the blood. We were true sisters in vengeance.

"Take this spirit with you now and leave this plane. Hear me now and let it be." The words sealed Jerry's fate.

The dark being moved toward Jerry, who now cried like the coward he was. I had no feeling for him. He'd sealed his fate.

I simply sealed the portal.

The dark being oozed across the ground. Rather than stopping, it mowed him over, encompassing Jerry's physical body into the gelatinous goo that it was. Jerry fell over, screaming as the life force was sucked out of him, gurgled, then his voice fell silent, his body twitching, jiggling, slowing, as his brain died without the soul to operate it. Though he had appeared somewhat green upon our arrival, he now was so pale his body appeared devoid of blood. Maybe it was. Who knew. Maybe the thing that had come for him had sucked it from the body for a midnight snack.

"Balance has been restored. Hear me now and let it be." Those words ended the ritual and sealed it permanently. The spirit known as Jerry would never return to this plane. The thought occurred to me at this moment that it might now be possible to resolve the psyche-patient-cop-killer case now. If the underworld was willing to work with me and obviously approved of what I was doing, this case might take a turn for the better. Sometime it had to end, if only to ease the misery of their families.

Turning away from the sight of Jerry's body, I let the men do their thing with it. The lawyers and guards from the prison ambled off talking about getting a drink on the way back. I'm sure they needed it. I ushered Liz back to Sam's truck, and we headed to her house. She had given me a spare set of keys, and I used them now. Hers were still in the P.D.

It was kind of freaky, I have to admit, walking into her house. It felt as if it had been in mourning, too. All of her plants were dead. Except the succulents and cacti that required little attention and were their usual thorny selves.

But it was the energy, or lack of it, that struck me the most as we entered the two-story condo. It was a person's presence that made a house a home. Now that

Liz had returned to it, it was filling up again, breathing life into itself and sighing that it was now complete.

The first thing Liz did was go to the kitchen and pull out a bottle of tequila and three glasses and pour us each a shot.

"What, no lime?" Sarcasm is just a side benefit I don't charge my clients for.

"Sorry, chick. I've been dead for a week and didn't have time to shop." She smiled at me. "But I do have salt." She reached into the cupboard and got down the margarita salt. We licked our hands, dabbed salt on them and raised our glasses, clinking them together.

"Welcome back." I blinked away tears that wanted to erupt. I looked at Sam, who held my gaze and gave a nod. He was as emotional as I was, but controlled it better.

"Thanks for bringing me back." The look in her eyes was heartfelt and serious and something I couldn't stand for very long without making a smart-ass comment. Not wanting to spoil the moment, I licked the salt and the others followed suit. Tossing back the most excellent tequila I'd ever had on an empty stomach may not have been the wisest move, but was better than Liz's decision to partake, since she'd had no sustenance for a week. I saw stars when I swallowed, and I swear fire blazed out my nostrils.

"Holy mother of god, that's good." I needed a bottle of that for myself. I sucked in a breath and clutched the counter. I looked at Sam, and he simply wiped the back of his hand across his mouth, his eyes locked on me. I knew he was remembering the last time we'd had tequila in a kitchen and the aftermath of it.

Gulp.

Liz slammed her glass on the counter, and I jumped. "I need a damned shower."

That made me smile. I really was going to have to work on a gift bag. "Go ahead. I suspect you'll sleep for twelve hours after that. Don't expect to be back to your old self in a snap. Take a shower, get something to eat, and I'll call you tomorrow evening." It was approaching 4 a.m. now, and we all needed some sleep. "We'll get out of here."

I hugged her, and she clung to me for a few seconds.

"Dani, thank you. I'll never be able to repay you for this." She pulled back and sniffed.

"Will you be okay tonight, or do you want me to stay?"

"I'll be fine since Jerry's gone for good." She gave a nervous laugh. "I might actually be able to sleep in peace now."

I was happy to give her that. "Rest up. You're going to need it."

Sam and I left her alone and got into the truck. For a few seconds, I relaxed my head back against the seat and closed my eyes. I could feel Sam's attention on me and turned my head toward him, but kept my eyes closed. "What a weird night."

"That's one way to put it." His voice was very close to me and searching for that place inside me where we connected. I knew he wanted me. There was a new intensity about him I hadn't felt before. Something I almost recognized and needed from him. My heart was aching for him. All I had to do was reach out.

I opened my eyes and his face was inches from mine. Raising my hand, I cupped his face. "Take me home."

He did.

"I'll walk you up."

Fatigue overwhelmed me, and all I could do was nod. He would have whether or not I agreed, so it was easier than disagreeing and trying to be the tough girl. He knew better anyway.

After his prowl around the house, he was satisfied. "Do you want me to stay?" He stood just a few feet from me. The night was almost gone.

"I need a shower before I can think of anything else."

"Go ahead. I'll wait."

After a hot shower and scrubbing every inch of me, I left my hair damp and combed straight back from my head. I wrapped a light robe around me. Barefoot, I followed the smell of coffee to the kitchen and found Sam at the table. He'd removed his blazer and gun, rolled up the sleeves of his shirt to the elbows and leaned back in a chair. I was glad he was comfortable enough in my kitchen to make his sexy self at home. I bit my lip. Seeing him like this was getting too good to walk away from. I had to end it between us for his sake. I couldn't be what he needed.

Reaching down into a place I hated to go, I searched for the conviction that the soul eater had spoken of. My conviction was going to get me through these next few moments. It was the *only* thing that was going to get me through.

Getting closer to him, I felt that hum between us vibrate faster, and my conviction began to wane.

"Find everything okay?" I stopped in front of him, letting the fragrance of my soap and shampoo flow over him. I knew it did, because the light in his eyes changed.

"Almost."

What, was I out of sugar?

He tugged on the belt of the robe and eased it free. The act of opening the robe, of sliding the fabric against itself, freed something that had been tied up in me. I don't know what it was, but I knew at this moment another level of feminine power opened up inside me.

The knot popped free and the sides of the robe parted, yet remained on my shoulders. He eased the robe open and bared my body to him. The quick brush of his hands against the skin of my abdomen sent a sharp pang of desire through me. This is what I wanted. This is what I needed and would never be able to have again. For this moment only, I would allow myself to savor one last moment with Sam.

The skin is the largest organ of the body and is filled with a gazillion nerve endings. It feels everything and transmits those sensations to our brains for interpretation. At the moment, I was interpreting lust.

"Beautiful," he whispered. "You're just beautiful."

At that moment, I felt it. Tingles and surges of moisture flooded my body as Sam reached for me. My amulet hung from its chain between my breasts. Seconds ago, it had been only as warm as my skin, but now it glowed hotter as Sam's breath blew across my skin. When he leaned forward, his amulet swung free and glowed amber. This was the first time I'd noticed it change color.

He opened his mouth and took one nipple inside, teasing it, tugging, as his hands clasped the curve of my waist and drew me closer to him.

Resting my fisted hands on his shoulders, I allowed him complete access to me. What woman in her right mind was going to push a man like Sam away? As he worked at my other breast, I worked at his shirt and pushed it off. I wanted to see his skin, to feel that large expanse beneath my hands. He shrugged out of the shirt and parted his thighs to bring me closer. The amulets pulsed brighter.

He always seemed to shake me up, and I wanted to do some shaking of my own. Leaning back in the chair, he gave me access to what I wanted. Breathing no longer seemed important, but I did it anyway. My heart raced, fluttering wildly in my chest as I drew down the zipper and opened his jeans.

Now that I had what I wanted, I looked into Sam's eyes. I'm certain the need, the want, the desire I saw there was reflected in my own eyes. I could never hide my emotions and didn't see any reason to now.

"More."

Sam raised his hips up, and I dragged his jeans down to his knees. Then I reached for his mouth and parted my lips over his. Tongues and teeth and hands ranged everywhere. Sam eased me onto his lap and I straddled his legs, hooking my heels on the back of the chair. His cock was positioned so that when my flesh parted, it rubbed against the right place. I was so wet, so ready for him one last time.

With his expert hands, he clasped my bottom and pulled me tighter against him. The feel of his rigid shaft nearly had me gasping for air. Nothing was as important or as perfect as his touch, his fire, his erection. Clutching my hands to his shoulders, I urged him on. Moans and groans and little cries of pleasure burst out of me. Every nerve ending in my body was on fire. Every place Sam touched was imprinted with the feel of him, the taste of his mouth against mine, the scent of him locked in my brain. Rocking my hips back and forth against him, I nearly exploded, but I held back, wanting to take us as far as we could go. When his breathing became as restless as mine, I knew the time was right. I reached between us and straightened his erection, torturing him with my moist flesh. There is no anticipation like that of hot sex, and we were dripping with it.

His eyes glazed over, and his fingers dug into my hips. I took him inside me.

His amulet glowed supersonic. And so did mine.

Sam threw his head back, gritting his teeth against the tide of primal pleasure that washed over us. I felt the pleasure he was feeling inside me, the pressure, the heat, the wild animal of sex in him that wanted out.

"Dani." I heard his voice in my ears and in my mind. I was unable to resist the heat or the emotion joining us together. Devoid of thought now, I clutched him to me. I had no control and didn't want any. The prelude to an orgasm is kind of like tightening a spring. Each touch, each lick, each sensation winds that coil until it can no longer tolerate the pressure and it blows.

That's what happened between us. Each movement brought us closer together until we were reduced to one body, one mind, one flesh searching for the same release.

I bit my lower lip as my coil sprang open. Digging my fingers into his shoulders, I held on as spasms of carnal pleasure overwhelmed me. My legs trembled, and I curved forward, my head bowed as each pulse rocked through me. His fingers dug into my hips as I felt the orgasm rip through him. This time, I screamed, and Sam came apart in my arms.

The aftermath was nothing like I'd expected. After we recovered a bit and could speak rationally, I pulled back and looked at him. He was hot and sweaty and very satisfied looking.

"What happened with the amulets?"

He cupped my face and pressed his forehead to mine. *I love you, Dani.* I heard it in my mind.

"No." I tried to pull back, but he wouldn't let me, and I wasn't working that hard. They were words I wanted to hear, but couldn't let him say. "Sam, you can't."

"Yes. We're bound to each other. I love you, and I know you love me." He lifted his face skyward. "Hear me now and let it be."

I remembered the conversation in the mountains with the other-siders. *When Sam was ready, the amulet would speak.*

"They won't let you work with me if we're involved." Concerned, I searched his eyes, but found no uncertainty. The conviction with which he spoke shook me more than anything. "This has to end."

"I agree." He clenched his jaw and a muscle twitched there. This was the hardest thing I'd ever done, and my throat closed against the emotions I couldn't voice. I loved Sam, but I had to give him up. I loved him with my entire soul, and that's what scared me. I was so in charge, so in control of my life. Would loving Sam this much change who I was? Would I still be in charge of my life, or would every decision revolve around how it would affect Sam?

"I'm sorry." My voice cracked and my vision blurred. The place in my chest where my heart lived fractured. This just wasn't going to work, no matter how much I wanted it.

"I'm not."

"What?" It was a whisper in my mind.

"What stops is the pretense. What stops is not claiming you as mine." He cupped my face in his hands. "I love you more than my damned job."

"I won't let The Dark hurt you, Sam. It wants me and the worst thing it can do is hurt you." That was my ultimate fear, and The Dark knew it.

"It's my choice and I choose you, Dani. The Dark we'll deal with together." He took a deep breath. "I feel you inside me every day. If we're not together, I feel like something's missing, like I forgot my underwear. Something's just not right."

I snorted a laugh at that. "I kinda like you commando."

"Be serious. We are one, you and I. I love you, and I

know you love me." He pulled me against him, the intensity of him almost overwhelming. "You don't have to say the words because I feel everything inside you." There was truth in his eyes. A truth I couldn't hide from. Not any longer.

"Will I have no secrets from you?"

"I don't know. I only know we have to work it out because unless I'm with you, I'm only half what I used to be." He held the amulet up between us. It had dimmed to a light golden hue. "I won't go back to what I was before, only half-alive."

My amulet matched his and I knew there was no other choice for us. We were destined by the stars above. Maybe we had known each other in another life on the other side. Becoming earthbound could have erased the memory of that other life from us, and it's taken until now for us to find each other.

I hugged him tight. Control? Did I really need it that badly? Wasn't there enough room in my life to share with Sam? A smile began in my heart and expanded outward. I knew there was. I just had to let it be. "If anything happens to you—"

"Nothing will happen now. We two are one and the other-siders will protect us. The Dark will be defeated. The balance can't be righted in one lifetime, so we'll have a long, long time together."

That supersonic light I'd never gotten used to appeared behind me, and I flashed around. An other-sider hovered there, glowing unnaturally in the confines of the house, but for the first time I was able to look directly at its colors, all mixed into one.

Er, can anyone say *awkward?* We were still half-naked.

"You are indeed correct, Samuel. The other-siders will provide information and assistance, but the two of you, joined together as one spiritual being, will be able to defeat The Dark in time. It has gone into hiding now with this new development of your joining. It will refocus and return more powerful than ever."

"So how are we going to defeat it, if it's more powerful?"

"You will lead a group of beings like yourself, and together the power of you will win. The most important step is joining with Samuel and accepting his power as your own."

Sam and I looked at each other. Yes, I had to agree that with our powers joined, we were more than we had been as individuals.

Then, the other-sider disappeared. There was a reprieve now. I felt it in the universe and I felt it between Sam and me. We could connect as never before.

The glow that began in my amulet filled the inside of me. Now that Sam and I could be together, there was no reason to resist. I opened the door and fully allowed him inside my soul.

"Sam. I love you in a way I have never loved anyone." I accepted him for who he was, scars and all. He accepted me, with all my faults, all my scars, and loved me anyway. The best thing I could ever do for him was to let him love me the way he wanted to. I accept that now, too.

He pressed his forehead against mine, and I felt the truth in him. I was enough.

I would always be enough for him.

"You have to do one thing for me." He pressed a soft kiss to my mouth.

"Anything." Did that just come out of my mouth? Boy, I was easy. A flaming orgasm, and I'd agree to anything.

"Marry me." His voice had softened with the emotion of that request.

"What? We've been together for millennia, I'm certain. We don't need a ceremony." Who needed a ceremony when you were an eternal star? Seriously.

"For our earthbound families, we do. They don't remember the beyond, so for them." The passion and the love in his eyes was my undoing. I'd do anything for this man.

I was silent for a few seconds, digesting this. He was right. Doing things for others generally wasn't my gig, but this time he was right.

"You know I'm right."

I glared, but there wasn't much heat to it. "Are you going to do this the rest of our lives?" I hate mind readers. They think they're always right.

"Absolutely." He grinned and any resistance I thought I had melted away.

"Once in a while you've got to let me be right, okay?" I stroked his face, loving the feel of him, the texture of his skin, and I was no longer afraid of the sensations.

"I will."

Whatever he thought he was going to say got lost

somewhere as we raced up the stairs to my bedroom. The universe would just have to wait on us for now.

My work, my mission to restore balance, had only begun, and there was time. There were many roads still to be paved for me, for others like me, so that we could exist together beside others in the normal world. We had a job, a mission, to right the wrongs committed against man in this world. I owed the other-siders something for saving my life and sending me back, so I would carry on. I owed them for putting Sam in my path and making him strong enough to resist my efforts to push him away, too. I've learned to reach out to those around me rather than trying to protect everyone on my own. I can't do that, but together we can be stronger than we ever were individually.

Though the weight of the world sometimes rested on my shoulders, with Sam, anything was possible. I had felt the power of him, the impressive personal strength he carried, and with us together The Dark would be defeated. We had pushed it back as surely as his *abuela* had years ago. With new information in the journals, with Liz reborn to our cause and with the power humming within all of us, we would win. The future wasn't set. Not even the other-siders could predict the outcome, so there was hope. There was always hope.

For now we would train, draw strength from each other and build a life together that nothing, not even forces from beyond, could destroy.

* * * * *

A sneaky peek at next month...

NOCTURNE™

AN EXHILARATING UNDERWORLD OF DARK DESIRES

My wish list for next month's titles...

In stores from 18th July 2014:

☐ Loyal Wolf – Linda O. Johnston

☐ Dark Wolf Returning – Rhyannon Byrd

In stores from 1st August 2014:

☐ Immortal Temptation – Denise Tompkins, Olivia Gates, Michele Hauf, Lisa Childs & Caridad Piñeiro

Includes 5 stories!

Available at WHSmith, Tesco, Asda, Eason, Amazon and Apple

Just can't wait?

Visit us Online

You can buy our books online a month before they hit the shops! **www.millsandboon.co.uk**

0714

Special Offers

very month we put together collections and
nger reads written by your favourite authors.

ere are some of next month's highlights—
nd don't miss our fabulous discount online!

On sale 18th July   On sale 18th July   On sale 18th July

Save 20%
on all Special Releases

Find out more at
www.millsandboon.co.uk/specialreleases

*Visit us
Online*

0814/ST/MB487

Join our *EXCLUSIVE* eBook club

FROM JUST £1.99 A MONTH!

Never miss a book again with our hassle-free eBook subscription.

★ Pick how many titles you want from each series with our flexible subscription

★ Your titles are delivered to your device on the first of every month

★ Zero risk, zero obligation!

There really is nothing standing in the way of you and your favourite books!

Start your eBook subscription today at www.millsandboon.co.uk/subscribe

EBOOK_SUBS

Discover more romance at

www.millsandboon.co.uk

- 💜 WIN great prizes in our exclusive competitions
- 💜 BUY new titles before they hit the shops
- 💜 BROWSE new books and REVIEW your favourites
- 💜 SAVE on new books with the Mills & Boon® Bookclub™
- 💜 DISCOVER new authors

PLUS, to chat about your favourite reads, get the latest news and find special offers:

- 📘 Find us on facebook.com/millsandboon
- 🐦 Follow us on twitter.com/millsandboonuk
- 💜 Sign up to our newsletter at millsandboon.co.uk

_WEB